Wait 'til You Hear What I Heard

JAN FREEMAN HIXSON

To Mary!
Enjoy!
Blessings
Jan Hixson

To order copies of this book, visit www.janhixson.com.

Published by Freeman Hixson Press LLC
Printed in the United States of America
Copyright © 2014 Jan Freeman Hixson

ISBN 978-0-615-97260-2

Cover Design by Moody Image

All Scripture quotations, unless otherwise noted, are taken from:
The King James Version (KJV)

This book is dedicated to the men in my life.

To my husband, Kenneth. Thank you for loving me unconditionally for thirty years.

To my sons, Bill and Joe. Being your mother is joy beyond description.

To Dr. Jere Mitchell for helping me find my way back to Jesus.

Welcome to Lake View, Texas
Home of the Lake View Lions
AA Texas State Football Champions
1967, 1968, 1969.

Football was serious business in east Texas. So serious, in fact, that the Rotary Club, the Kiwanis Club and the Booster Club all donated enough money to have a twenty-by-twenty-foot sign erected at the entrance to town in the fall of 1971, the year I began sixth grade. Not billboard size, of course. Lady Bird Johnson saw to it that Americans, even Texans, abided by the *Keep America Beautiful* law. I wasn't sure if it was a real law but residents wanted everyone who entered Lake View to realize that they had stepped foot in a Texas State Football Championship community and that we upheld the law, especially one promoted by a fellow Texan and former First Lady.

In keeping with the spirit, local merchants in town were encouraged to have three items in their store windows: an American flag (large or small), a Texas flag (preferably large), and a Lake View Lions poster. It didn't matter if it was The First National Bank on Main Street or Miss Mattie's House of Hair on the town square, there was an unwritten rule that these three items were a must.

So Daddy proudly displayed the trio in the bay window of his and Uncle Ed's sporting goods store. They had been in business together since 1946. Uncle Ed was quick to tell the story of how he and Daddy returned from WWII with no money and no car, only the clothes on their backs. However, with only a handful of items from the Army and Navy Surplus, they founded Lawson Brothers' Sporting Goods and never looked back. Every day after school, I rode my pink Schwinn, complete with white vinyl banana seat, to their store to see Daddy. Lawson Brothers' possessed one of the newer Coke machines on Bowie Square, Daddy possessed the only key to it, which, lucky for me, meant that every school day from 3-3:15, I possessed an icy cold, six and one-half ounce bottle of Coca Cola.

The Real Thing. The only drink that could teach the world to sing in perfect harmony.

Coke bottle in hand, I strolled around the store eyeing the new camouflage that Uncle Ed was unpacking.

"Looks like old man Peters got his deer stand built," Uncle Ed announced.

"Yep," replied Daddy, "when he came into that money last fall I wondered what he would buy with it."

"What money?"

"The money from that lawsuit he won when his boy got hit in the head by a backhoe bucket."

"Oh yeah. Well, it looks like he made good use of it. Betty told me this morning that Mrs. Peters wasn't too happy about it. Seems she had her heart set on carpeting the house, but the old man held his ground and got him a right fine deer stand." Uncle Ed's stubby cigar bobbed up and down in his mouth when he spoke.

My uncle knew all of the scuttlebutt in Bowie County because he was married to my aunt, Betty Lawson. Aunt Betty had a certain way of finding out everybody's business so she could pray for them. I had witnessed her dragging the details of one husband's nervous breakdown out of his poor, unsuspecting wife right in the middle of her flower shop, Betty's Bloomers. They were the kind of details you wouldn't tell your best friend, much less the local florist. Several "Bless your Hearts" and "Lordy, Lordies" later she would promise not to breathe a word of it to anyone but to take it to the Lord in prayer instead.

"You best be getting on home, Carol Ann. Your momma will be mad as a wet hen if she thinks you've been listening to the local gossip." Daddy winked at me.

"Yes, sir," I said as I started toward the door.

"Oh, that reminds me. The cigar box you wanted for school is in the office on my desk. You can take it on home if you like."

Mrs. Greene, my sixth grade teacher, required her students to keep their spelling words in a cigar box. Each week we printed twenty new words on index cards and added them to a growing stack of words. I loved spelling class and enjoyed sniffing the pungent magic marker I used to write what would surely become one outstanding vocabulary. I would use that vocabulary to get a high–powered job when I became a newswoman just like Mary Richards on the *Mary Tyler Moore Show*.

Twenty new words—most of them ending in "ent" and "ant"—awaited. I thanked Daddy for the cigar box, reluctantly returned the Coke bottle to the crate with the other empties and headed for home.

As I did, I pedaled toward our town's famous landmark: a bronze, larger–than–life statue of James Bowie. Armed with a Bowie knife in one hand and a gun in the other, the Texas hero stood watch over our small town. Just last year a group of teenage boys from Lone Tree thought it would be funny to put female lingerie on Mr. Bowie so they tied a lady's plus–sized, pink brassiere on James and wrapped a white feather boa around his neck. That prank caused more commotion than the time Lamar Webb turned a potbellied pig loose inside the packed Paramount movie theater during the screening of *Airport*.

Sheriff Whitehall caught the idiots and, as punishment, they had to pick up trash along Highway 59 for six weeks. The judge made them take turns wearing the pink brassiere while they worked. It was funny for all of us but terribly humiliating for them. A valuable lesson was taught that day: you can't put a pink brassiere on a Texas hero and get away with it.

Revenge: v. (ri-venj) the action of inflicting hurt or harm on someone for a wrong suffered at their hands

"Hurry up!" Nita Sue hollered. "You know Daddy hates it when we walk in late on Sunday night. Besides, I want to get a seat by Randy."

Yeah. Like Momma and Daddy were going to let their oldest daughter sit next to Brother Paul's son, Randy, during the evening worship service.

However, Nita Sue had other ideas. She scoped out the sanctuary for her true love. Meanwhile, Daddy and I parked ourselves on the third pew as usual and Momma practically ran to Fellowship Hall to put her tub of Spam salad in the refrigerator with all the other salads for tonight's church–wide fellowship. Baptists couldn't conduct a committee meeting or hold Sunday School without offering food—preferably casseroles—to everyone in attendance. That evening's menu consisted of salads, desserts, coffee and sweet tea.

That particular Sunday evening was The Lord's Supper. We observed the Lord's Supper four times a year at First Baptist, twice during the Sunday morning worship service and twice during the evening worship service. For some reason, unbeknownst to me, the Lord's Supper service was always longer than the other services.

I thought it was the perfect reason to shorten things up a bit. Pass the crackers, drink the grape juice and go home. In my mind, it should take less time than a regular service, shouldn't it?

But it seemed that Brother Paul and the deacons had other ideas.

We sang, prayed and he preached like always. Then he added the passing of the elements, a soloist, and finally an invitation. No wonder Baptists never got to see *The Wonderful World of Disney*. We didn't get home until 8:00 most Sunday nights. I'd be a grown woman before I got to see Tinker Bell light up Mr. Disney's castle.

I'd probably watch the yearly showing of *The Wizard of Oz* for the first time with my own children.

Settled in the pew, I turned my thoughts to the next day's geography test. I had studied part of that memorable afternoon. In fact, I skipped watching the Dallas Cowboys game altogether and invited my best friend, BJ Dodge, to come over. Coach Landry's Cowboys were playing some team no one cared about. If they had been playing the Redskins or the Steelers, then geography could have waited.

"Bolivia, Paraguay, Argentina, Chile." I listed the South American countries on my fingers as I whispered them to myself. "Brazil, Venezuela, adultery."

What? Did someone say *adultery*? I stared at the pulpit with six fingers frozen in place.

Standing in the pulpit was Mrs. Ruby Grimes. Why was she talking about adultery? She had been listed as the evening's soloist.

"...and so I ask y'all to pray for us. This has been a long row to hoe for both Raymond and me. For those of you who knew about his extramarital affairs all these years, I thank you for lifting us up in your prayers. For those of you who didn't know, well, I ask that you put us on your prayer list."

That being said, Mrs. Herron struck a chord on the piano and Mrs. Grimes began singing *Here at Thy Table, Lord*.

I was in shock. Had she just announced to everyone that Mr. Grimes had committed adultery? Could she do that in church? On a Sunday night? Mr. Grimes' pickup truck had an I LOVE MY WIFE sticker on the back bumper. Could a man ride around town with a bumper sticker like that and commit adultery? Evidently he could.

I looked over at Momma and Daddy to see if they had heard it, too. Yep. They heard it all right. Daddy was staring in disbelief, and Momma's mouth was hanging wide open. I slowly turned my head toward my older sister, Nita Sue, and saw that she, too, was dumbfounded. Maybe I was in the *Twilight Zone*. Wow! I'd never seen or heard anything like that in my eleven years of life. You could have heard a pin drop.

Two stanzas later, Mrs. Grimes descended the four steps and took her seat beside Mr. Grimes.

It was then time for two deacons to come forward to remove the white tablecloth from the Lord's Supper Table. Instead, they just sat there. Neither one of them moved. It was like that scene in *The Birds* when everyone is locked inside the café, staring at Tippi Hedren.

Brother Paul quickly tapped the two men on the shoulders and nudged them back to life. They hopped up from the front row and began the traditional folding of the cloth. Mr. Fontaine was so befuddled that he knocked the lid off the stack of grape juice trays. It hit the red carpet and rolled under the first pew. He dove for it, but it got away and came to rest at the feet of the couple seated on the second pew: Mr. and Mrs. Grimes.

Hey, this was better than watching *Disney* any time!

Brother Paul cleared his throat and began the usual Lord's Supper speech. He repeated the words that Jesus spoke to his disciples and held up the loaf of bread for all to see. Then the deacons passed the bread plates. As one came down our row, Daddy shot a stern look at Nita Sue and me.

There was no doubt in my mind that this was not the time to try and sneak one of those little crackers. The Lord's Supper was reserved for people who had walked the aisle during the invitation and been baptized. Neither of us had done that. In the Baptist church, the invitation was similar to altar calls in other churches, at least that's what I had been told. Nita Sue had threatened a quick trip down the aisle (numerous times) if it would get Mrs. Herron off the piano and Mrs. Pinkerton away from the organ. First Baptist was known for its lengthy invitations.

I leaned back in the pew and rehashed what had just taken place. Like a robot, I passed the grape juice tray to Momma. BJ would never believe this.

Softly and Tenderly drifted across the sanctuary. No one needed a hymnal for this song. It was the hymn of choice for Sunday night invitation singing.

I couldn't concentrate on the words because I was too busy replaying Mrs. Grimes' prayer request. I wondered if Mr. Grimes would come forward and repent. Surely a born–again Baptist couldn't be caught having an affair and not repent.

Four stanzas later, we exited the church with enough Spam salad to feed every Baptist in east Texas. No one said a word. No fellowshipping tonight. Husbands ushered their wives out of that church as fast as they could. Perhaps they were afraid of a chain reaction.

All I know is that we made it home in record time. I saw the preview for the next week's *Wonderful World of Disney* while I scarfed down two Spam salad sandwiches.

***

It didn't take long for news to travel around Lake View. Word had gotten around town about Mrs. Grimes' prayer request. BJ and I had discussed Mr. Grimes' violation of the seventh commandment over the telephone that evening. We knew that adultery meant you couldn't have more than one wife at a time, but we still weren't clear on how it all worked. I'd asked Momma about it at bedtime that night, but she told me that it wasn't something a girl my age should concern herself with. She reminded Nita Sue not to concern herself with it either in the form of gossiping about it to her friends at school. We agreed. Momma led us in a bedtime prayer for Mr. and Mrs. Grimes.

I wished we could have secret confessions every Sunday night so I could get home in time to watch some decent television shows. But I also knew that probably wasn't going to happen. Not anytime soon, anyway.

Texas Hair: n. (hay-yur) Hair that is tall enough to skim a ceiling fan on a humid day

The following Saturday, Mrs. Dodge drove BJ and me to the house where we would spend the afternoon babysitting her two cousins, Willis Ray and Chip Campbell. Mrs. Dodge and her sister–in–law were driving to Tyler to do some shopping.

We turned onto Olive Street and wound our way down the tree–lined streets in the older part of town. In its prime, this neighborhood had been home to some of the wealthiest railroad families in Lake View. Mrs. Campbell was one of their descendants.

The main streets of Lake View—Birch, Magnolia, Pine, Poplar and Sycamore—were named for trees, like every small town in America. Olive Street, where the Campbells lived, was paved in bricks. Not just any bricks, though. Legend had it that Mr. Feinstein, Mrs. Campbell's grandfather, brought the bricks with him when he moved from Kentucky to Lake View. He promptly paved the courtyard, barbecue pit and the street in front of his young bride's home. That young bride was Mrs. Campbell's grandmother.

Turning toward the backseat, Mrs. Dodge looked at us and said, "Girls, you can't leave these boys alone for one minute, you hear? Not *one minute*. Belinda Jean? Remember what happened last time you babysat?"

"Yes ma'am, I remember," BJ answered as she intentionally kicked my leg. Her well–worn green flip flop slipped off her foot.

"All right. Let's go inside."

"What happened last time?" I whispered to BJ.

"Shhh…I'll tell you later."

We were halfway up the Kentucky brick sidewalk when a six year old, towheaded boy dressed in a red bandana, black cowboy boots and red sheriff's hat, barreled out the front door, down the sidewalk, and into BJ.

"Hey, cousin! Lookee at what I got—a real BB gun!"

While BJ focused her attention on Sheriff No. 1, I spotted Sheriff No. 2 on the front porch wearing the same hat, boots, and bandana, but not a thing over his privates. If his appearance wasn't appalling enough, the boogers he was shoving in his mouth were.

"Mornin', Mrs. Dodge, Miss Belinda Jean. How you'uns today?" asked Beulah, the Campbell's maid. "And, who do we have here? Why, Miss Carol Ann, you growed a foot since I seen you last. We going have to put a rock on yo head." Beulah waddled down the porch steps to retrieve the hyper kid.

"Morning, Beulah," we answered simultaneously.

Looking up at me, Sheriff No. 1 screamed, "Hey you. What's your name again?"

"It's Carol Ann."

"Hey Carol Dan, want to see me shoot my new BB gun? Do ya? Do ya?"

Mexican jumping beans didn't have anything on this kid. He was either hyperactive or suffering from a serious sugar overload or maybe both. We followed the cowboys up the front steps and onto the massive porch.

"Lands sake, chile! Git inside dat house and put yo drawers on," Beulah said to the three year old. "You know Miss Ella don't want you runnin' in her fine yard half–naked. Now git inside befo' the neighbors see you!"

Beulah was right. I didn't want to look at it either.

"I'm fixin' to go to the Piggly Wiggly," Beulah explained, "and then on to the dry cleaners and the butcher shop. I'll be gone a while." She looked us up one side and down the other. "You two girls sure you can handle these here young uns?" Semi–confident in our babysitting skills, Beulah made her exit for the weekly shopping trip to Piggly Wiggly.

"You'll be good boys won't you?" Mrs. Dodge asked the two sheriffs. They stared at her.

At that moment, Mrs. Campbell emerged from her bedroom looking like Jackie Kennedy Onassis—except for the hair. She definitely wore Texas hair. As a matter–of–fact, she may have invented Texas hair.

Texas hair was serious business in Bowie County according to Miss Mattie, sole proprietor of Miss Mattie's House of Hair. She bought Dippity–do by the case. She said, the more Dippity–do, the stiffer the hair. The stiffer the hair, the bigger the tease. The bigger the tease, the bigger the hair. And voila: Texas hair.

Mrs. Campbell said, "You girls may watch television or listen to records if you like. If the wind is blowing, we can't get channel three, but we always get six and twelve. You may have to move the outside antennae a little bit. And listen," she said, "I don't let the boys watch *The Three Stooges* anymore. Willis Ray tried to hit Chip in the head with my skillet."

I couldn't imagine Willis Ray, boogers and all, trying to lift a ten pound, cast iron skillet high enough to hit brother over the head.

She lifted the couch cushions one by one—clearly looking for something. She found the clicker and said, "Sometimes this works, and sometimes it doesn't." Her well–manicured hand pushed two buttons. "If the buttons stick, jiggle those nickels together," she pointed to a crystal bowl full of nickels, "and the channels will change. I have no idea why that works, but it does. There's plenty of food and sweet tea in the refrigerator. Absolutely no sugar for the boys, understood?"

I politely nodded my head.

Sheriff No. 2 pulled on his mother's dress. "Willis Ray Campbell, *where* is your underwear?" Sheriff No. 2 shrugged his shoulders.

Mrs. Dodge jumped in. "Girls, why don't you take Willis Ray and Chip to their bedroom to play cowboys and Indians?" It was Mrs. Dodge's polite way of asking us to scram with the little guys so they could make their getaway.

"Yes, ma'am," BJ answered.

"Don't forget what we discussed in the car, ladies." Mrs. Dodge's head tipped down, and her eyebrows shot up. She stared long and hard at Belinda Jean Dodge.

"Don't worry, Mom. It's locked in." BJ tapped her left temple as she grinned.

Mrs. Campbell said, "Okay, now. Come give Mommy a goodbye kiss. I'll bring y'all a surprise from Tyler." One cheek kissed, one to go. Sheriff No. 2 was too busy digging out ear wax to kiss his mother. "Bye, boys."

"Don't worry about a thing. We're going to have lots of fun aren't we, boys?" I said this as if I were the expert in all babysitting matters. The truth was that I had never babysat a day in my life. I liked little kids, but all my free time was spent doing manual labor at Betty's Bloomers.

On hands and knees, we crawled down the hallway toward the boys' bedroom like real horses; Chip riding on BJ and Willis Ray walking beside me. No way was Sheriff No. 2 going to ride on my back—especially, naked.

"Whoa, horsey!" BJ said. "Hop off, Chip."

"Hey, BJ. Have you heard your mother talking about some big thing going on around town?" I asked.

BJ closed her eyes as Chip tried to lasso her neck. "No, I haven't heard anything. And, even if I had, I wouldn't tell you. You know how my parents are about spreading rumors."

"Yeah, I know. I just thought you might know something I didn't. Momma and Daddy were whispering the other night, but I got caught eavesdropping before I found out anything good."

"Were you using the stethoscope again?"

"Yeah. So?"

"You're awful," she said. For someone my age, BJ could be a bit too obedient.

"I'm not awful, just bored. Wouldn't it be cool if we had an axe murder or…" Both sheriffs stopped their sword fight and stared at me. "Or something?"

"Carol Ann," BJ whispered, "keep your voice down."

"Sorry." It was time to change the subject.

The sheriffs were sword fighting with their stick horses again. Sheriff No. 2 was holding on to something and it wasn't his cowboy hat.

"So, how about puttin' on some underwear there, sheriff?" I inquired in my best western voice. Willis Ray shook his head.

"Oh, come on now. You don't want to run around the house naked, do you?"

"I WANT TO TAKE A BATH!" he hollered.

"This kid has a set of lungs on him, doesn't he?"

"You're okay, Willis Ray. Come on." BJ tried to calm the little guy by walking him to his bathroom.

"NO! I WANT TO TAKE A REAL BATH IN MOMMY'S BATHTUB!" Willis Ray screamed.

"All right, Willis Ray," BJ said. "You can take a bath in your momma's bathtub."

"GIDDY–UP!" Willis Ray hollered as he rode his stick horse full speed.

"Make him stop screaming, will you?" I asked.

"Well, it's not that easy," she said to me as she sped after him.

"What do you mean, 'it's not that easy?'" I was making tracks now.

"Uh…well, you see, he only screams." We were hightailing it through the two–story colonial at breakneck speed.

"What do you mean 'he only screams'?"

"I mean, *he only screams*. What part of it don't you understand?" BJ's irritation with me was obvious.

"No one *only screams*, BJ. I mean, he has to talk in a regular voice sometime, doesn't he?"

She stopped, turned, and looked me square in the eyes and said, "I don't understand it, Carol Ann, but for some reason Willis Ray screams all the time. Okay? There's nothing I can do about it so why don't you just entertain Chip, and I'll be in charge of Willis Ray?" She paused for effect. "I'm sorry I didn't mention it to you, but I was afraid if I told you, you wouldn't help me babysit."

This situation was getting worse by the minute. I was spending my day with a BB–gun–toting, hyperactive kid and a screamer who didn't put on his underwear. I was under the impression that babysitting meant drinking Coke while watching the Dialing–for–Dollars afternoon movie.

"Oh, that's okay," I lied, "it'll be kind of fun to be around boys for a change."

"Thanks, Carol Ann. Please find Chip and see what he's doing."

At least she took the screamer, right? I would handle the kid on sugar overload for a few hours. After all, we were splitting the babysitting money.

Walking down a long hallway, I noticed what appeared to be fifty to sixty photographs hanging on the walls. These people had more photos in their hallway than we had in our entire house! I inspected a particular, gold–framed picture a little closer. One of the men looked just like LBJ. Was it?

Holy cow, Batman. Mr. and Mrs. Campbell knew President Lyndon Baines Johnson. In fact, they all stood side by side in tuxedos and evening gowns. The photo was autographed by LBJ and the other man, Senator Seth Nowlin, a United States Senator from Texas. Wow…these people were cooler than I had thought.

Next to that photograph was one of Mrs. Campbell riding on an enormous float, wearing a tiara. Was she a Tyler Rose Queen? I couldn't believe BJ never told me! I leaned in for a closer look. It was her all right and her hair was even bigger back then. I didn't think that was possible since it was already skimming the ceiling fan in the living room as it was.

Totally taken aback by this new discovery, I inspected the next photograph. It was Mrs. Campbell in another ball gown this time wearing a different tiara. In this photo her sash read: Miss Texas. Double wow! No way was this woman Miss Texas and a Tyler Rose Queen. I read the caption at the bottom of the photo: Miss Texas 1960. I was babysitting the offspring of a Tyler Rose Queen *and* a Miss Texas.

My mind suddenly returned to why I was there. Where was the precious cargo? I better get to work. Taking care of these two boys was of the utmost importance.

"Hey, BJ," I hollered, "I can't believe you didn't tell me that your aunt was a…" I stopped mid–sentence. *What were they doing in the bathroom?* I could hear Willis Ray screaming, "FIRE ONE, FIRE TWO." I stepped into the bathroom and saw BJ sitting on the side of the bathtub. She looked at me and shrugged her shoulders as if to say "whatever makes him happy." Willis Ray was still wearing his hat and bandana in the tub; however, his boots had escaped the baptism.

I leaned over only to discover Willis Ray pushing something white out of a tube into the water. As the white thing entered the water, it swelled up and propelled itself across the surface. A string glided behind it like the tail on a kite. It floated to the top and joined the others.

"What are all those white things?" I asked.

BJ rolled her eyes. "They're tampons, Dumb Dora."

"What are tampons?"

"Don't tell me you don't know what a tampon is."

"Noooo…" I thought it might be a submarine–like toy I missed out on, being a girl, and all.

"FIRE TWO! FIRE THREE!" he screamed.

"You mean you have a big sister and you don't know what tampons…" she was cut off by the sound of "Hey, Carol Dan, Cousin

BJ. Come see what I did! Come see what I did!" Chip was swinging that BB gun around like a majorette twirling a baton.

BJ's eyes grew as wide as moon pies. "Please tell me you've been watching him this whole time."

He added, "Y'all come on and see how many I shot!" His black cowboy boots sure were loud on Miss Texas' pink bathroom tiles.

"Uh oh," we said at the same time.

BJ grabbed Willis Ray out of the water. He was really screaming now. I ran after Chip and we all ran toward the backyard. Once outside, I stared in awe of what was staring back at me.

"Holy blackbird, Batman," I mumbled to no one in particular.

Six of the biggest blackbirds I'd ever seen were hanging side–by–side on Mrs. Campbell's clothesline—their wings held in place by twelve, wooden clothespins. Some of their heads were hanging to the side while the others rested on their chests. They reminded me a little bit of Mr. Burch snoozing during Brother Paul's lengthy sermons.

BJ and I stood there—staring. I couldn't think of anything to say.

"Hey, cousin. What do you think? Pretty good shooting, huh, Carol Dan?"

"Chip! How did you shoot this many blackbirds?" I asked.

"With my BB gun, silly girl." *Silly me, of course.*

"Mother is going to kill me!" BJ screamed. She was panic–stricken, and Willis Ray was dripping all over the imported Kentucky bricks. "She told us not to leave these two alone for a minute!"

Thunk. Blackbird No.5's right wing flapped in the breeze. Willis Ray had hurled a wad of tampons at the dead fowl.

"Oh my gosh. Oh my gosh!" Pandemonium set in. BJ was on the brink of losing it and *it* was my fault.

"Okay. Let's think for a minute," I said, "maybe it's not as bad as it looks. First things first. You take Willis Ray back inside, and I'll start cleaning up out here." I looked at the University of Texas clock on the patio. According to Bevo, we had plenty of time. "Go on, BJ."

She stared at the blackbirds.

"BJ!"

"Yeah, right, okay. I'll go back inside and start cleaning up the bathroom." BJ and her sack of joy maneuvered through the patio chairs. Then all of a sudden, I felt something smack the back of my head. I grabbed at my hair and pulled out a wet tampon by the string.

"Bye-bye Miss American Pie, Drove my Chevy to the levee but the levee was dry,
And good ole boys were drinking whiskey and rye,
Singing this'll be the day that I die. This'll be the day that I die."

Don McLean

BJ and I sang at the top of our lungs as we rode our bikes to the creek. It felt good to be free from the chaos of yesterday's babysitting job. Luckily, Beulah had returned home from Piggly Wiggly in time to help clean up the mess.

And what a mess it was.

Beulah dropped two sacks of groceries on to the patio when she saw the dangling blackbirds. Then she screamed when she realized that the eggs she had just bought were in one of the sacks.

"Oh Law! Have mercy! What on eart you two thinkin' lettin' them babies make a mess a dis house? And Miss Belinda Jean I know yo momma tol' you not to leave them chirren' alone fo one minit! Oh Law have mercy on my soul!"

Beulah waddled through the house yelling "Law" at everything, even the clean stuff. I didn't know who or what Law was, but man, she did. She yelled it over and over again. 'Law, look at dis here batroom!...Law, lookee here at dis clothesline! What in glory's name happen to dem blackbirds?' Halfway through her tirade, she grabbed a piece of patio furniture then clutched at her bosom while another blackbird tore loose from the clothespin.

"Beulah," I uttered, still reeling in disbelief myself, "it's my fault about the blackbirds. I was looking at the pictures in the hallway and that's when Chip shot all of those birds. I'm really, really sorry."

"Well, sorry ain't gonna bring dem blackbirds back to life, is it girl? You'uns git Mr. Tom's trashcan and unpin dem birds. No tellin' what kinda germs livin' on dem. 'An wash yo hands when you is done, hear?"

"Yes, ma'am," we said in unison. Willis Ray and Chip bawled their eyes out, their tears spilling on the Kentucky bricks. Beulah told them to "hush-up that cryin' and git in their room befo' she tanned they hides." BJ and I were more than happy to oblige Beulah even though it was kind of sad to watch the birds fall lifeless into the silver can.

"You gotta admit…he's a pretty good shot, don't you think?" My compliment wasn't heard with the same enthusiasm with which it was spoken.

"Yes, Carol Ann. He will probably grow up to be a sharpshooter for the FBI someday," she murmured, "and perhaps he'll thank the babysitter who started it all."

"Look, I know it's my fault, okay? I was trying to be positive, that's all."

BJ sighed. "I'm sorry. I didn't mean to snap at you, but Mother will probably ground me for life when she sees this mess."

"But she won't see it! Beulah will have this place cleaned up in no time." Just then, the last bird dropped right on top of the others.

Order was restored by the time Mrs. Dodge and Mrs. Campbell returned from Tyler, but only because Beulah stayed until Mr. Campbell came home. I remember thinking how well behaved the boys were when their father came home from work. All things considered, I rather enjoyed babysitting…

***

So there we were, on our bikes. Armed with two bottles of Coke and two packs of peanuts, we pedaled as fast as we could to Potter's Creek. Nestled among the bull pines of Lake View, Potter's Creek was our favorite spot. It flowed into Lake Lone Star which wasn't much of a lake, but it could be seen from the top of the only hill in our tiny town.

Lake View had been around for a hundred years. I knew this because last year was the town's centennial celebration. It was quite the party. Even dignitaries rolled into town for the month long activities, including the governor. When he stepped out of his limousine, my heart skipped a beat. I thought he was the most handsome man I'd ever laid eyes on. He reminded me of Davy Jones with his dark hair and white teeth—a man's man—that's what Daddy called him. And better yet, he was a Republican. Democrats were frowned upon at our house. The only strike against him was the fact that he was a Presbyterian and not a God–fearing Baptist.

Part of the centennial celebration had taken place at Potter's Creek. The centennial committee had devoted a lot of time cleaning up the trash that accumulated there. This pleased us because we were tired of kicking half–empty smelly Schlitz cans and Skoal tins away from the bank before we could sit down.

I pushed the kickstand down on my bicycle and plopped down by the creek. The sweet smell of honeysuckle filled the air.

"Are you going to enter the *Litter Bug* poster contest at school?" BJ asked me.

"I don't know, maybe. You?"

"I don't want to, but first prize is a gift certificate to Murphy's Five and Dime. I have my heart set on The Jackson 5's new album."

"I think I'll wait and enter the *Buckle Up for Safety* contest in May. The winner of that one gets a pass to the movies with free Coke and popcorn."

"What movie do you want to see?" BJ's face was aimed at the sun, but her eyes were open just enough to watch the ripples on the water.

"Whatever comes out next, I guess. I know what it won't be— *Valley of the Dolls*. Did I tell you what Nita Sue and Margaret did?"

"No, I don't think so."

"They told Momma that *Valley of the Dolls* was a movie about this doll maker in Switzerland, and how it had been nominated for a bunch of Academy Awards. She said it was a lot like the *Sound of Music*. Momma said it was just wonderful that good, wholesome movies were being made like *The Sound of Music*."

"Did she let them go?" BJ's head rested on her left shoulder as she asked the question.

"Oh yeah, they went all right," I said proudly, "and thought they had gotten away with it until one of the other mothers talked about it at Miss Mattie's House of Hair. Momma was sitting next to her at the shampoo bowl. She got so worked up that she stormed out of the beauty shop—wet hair and all—and headed straight home.

Nita Sue was grounded for two weeks. She couldn't talk on the phone or see Randy."

BJ thought this over before she asked, "Why is *Valley of the Dolls* so bad? What's it about?"

I rolled up the hem on my jeans and dangled both feet in the water. "I think it's about drugs. I overheard Momma and Aunt Betty talking about it. Momma said that it wasn't enough that all these love–ins and sit–ins were going on in California and up north, but now they were making it look glamorous on the movie screen."

BJ pondered this as she pulled a bottle opener from her jeans pocket. Motioning for me to hand over the Cokes, she popped the caps on both bottles. Fizz oozed down the sides, but not before I poured some Lance peanuts in my bottle. With my left arm holding up the weight of my body, I turned my Coke toward heaven and drank in The Real Thing.

"Do you ever think about doing drugs?" I asked between crunches.

"Nope. Dad's talked to us about how dangerous they are and about how you can get hooked if you ever try them." She sat up and shielded her eyes with her left hand. "You won't believe what happened at our house last night."

It must be good. BJ never sat up straight.

"What?"

"I'm not supposed to tell anyone this so you have to cross your heart that you won't tell."

I crossed my heart, hoped to die, pointed a pine needle at my eye and suppressed a burp.

She continued, "We were eating supper and Mom asked Dad how drug addicts got their needles. She had seen a group of hippies doing heroin or something on Huntley and Brinkley. Anyway, after he explained all that junk to her he gave us one of his lectures about the danger of experimenting with any drug, even cigarettes. And then Jack looked Dad right smack dab in the face and said he was going to try them as soon as he turned thirteen."

"Try what? The heroin or the cigarettes?"

"The cigarettes."

"Wow. What did your Daddy do?"

"First, Mom choked on her food. Dad jumped up and slapped her on the back a couple of times. When she finally stopped coughing Dad told Jack to get his butt in the study. Then it got real quiet. I've never heard Dad tell anyone to get their butt anywhere. He just doesn't talk like that."

"Then what?"

"Well, the rest of us sat at the table eating supper while Dad and Jack talked in his study." She paused. "I was so shocked at Daddy using the word "butt" that I didn't finish my dessert."

"What was it? Apple pie or peach cobbler?" This was an important piece of information because I was spending the night with BJ later that week. When the Dodges had apple pie one night they usually had fried pies a few days later. Bertie, the Dodge's maid, made the best fried pies in town.

"Apple pie. Anyway, Jack came out of the study in the middle of *Truth or Consequences*. He was as white as a sheet. Later, he told Bubba and me that Daddy showed him pictures of infected arms and lots of other gross stuff."

"Where did he get pictures like that?" I wanted to know in case I might like to look at them sometime.

"In his medical books. They're loaded with pictures of nasty–looking stuff." BJ was answering as if she, too, were a medical doctor.

"Like what?" *This was getting good.*

"Well, there's this one picture of a man's toenail growing out of his big toe and over his other four toes. It's all black and yellow with these red mole–looking things on the top of his feet."

"Yuck." *This might not be so good after all.*

"The page right before that shows a woman infected with worms. There's a worm you can get if you live in Africa and bathe in the creeks. You get bitten by a black fly and after it's sucked up your blood it lays its eggs on your skin."

I tasted those peanuts for a second time.

"Then the eggs turn into worms and they go all over your body—inside, of course."

Of course.

"If they die around your eyeballs, you can become blind for life." The word "life" was whispered for effect.

I could feel myself about to wretch. Perhaps this wasn't such a good idea. I might leave those medical pictures to Dr. Dodge and Jack.

As I pondered my own medical condition, BJ began pondering on Greg Brady in a *Teen Beat* magazine she brought from home. Momma didn't allow teen magazines in our house. She was of the opinion that they weren't wholesome.

"Anything good?" I asked.

"Nah, not really."

Pine needles floated past my feet as I tapped the top of the water with my toes. I was more than ready to change the subject so I asked, "Do your relatives ever come to town for football games?"

"Sometimes, why?"

"Momma planned our family reunion on a weekend when it's a home game. I hate it when all of her family comes to town. Our house is so small that I have to sleep on the couch or the floor. Plus, my Aunt Ada and Uncle Elmer treat me like I'm not part of the family."

"Why?"

"I guess because I'm adopted. If it doesn't bother me, I don't know why it should bother them."

"Do you ever think about your real parents? Where they are or why they gave you away?"

"I used to—when Momma and Daddy first told me. I imagined myself calling the adoption agency and asking for their name and telephone number. But Momma and Daddy don't know their names either. Besides, I don't feel adopted. I mean, I feel just like you or anybody else."

"I bet no one would guess that you're adopted unless you told them."

"Well, just remember, BJ, no one outside my family knows—only you."

BJ crossed her heart and hoped to die as a flashing, orange light appeared out of nowhere and grew larger as it headed toward us.

"Oh, great," I said. "Here comes Mr. Snodgrass."

Mr. Vernon Snodgrass stepped out of his city pickup and began walking toward BJ and me. He was the sole employee of the Lake View Parks Department and made sure everyone knew it. His gun dangled from a holster that looked an awful lot like the one Willis Ray was wearing yesterday.

The part in his hair was about an inch above his left ear. I'd bet a week's worth of lunch money that he had the longest comb over in town, maybe the state. And if that wasn't bad enough, he took some of the hair from the back of his head and combed it to the top and swirled it all together. Rumor had it he was the only man in town to use Dippity–do.

I didn't think so. I'd been up close and personal with Mr. Snodgrass and he smelled more like cod liver oil than Dippity–do. Whichever he used was beside the point. The man looked ridiculous.

"Well, well, well, what do we have here?" His overly starched, khaki colored LPD uniform looked more like a cardboard box than clothing.

"Hi, Mr. Snodgrass," we answered. The comb over was in its usual place and combed in its usual swirl.

"Them pop bottles belong to you?" he asked.

"Yes, sir."

"Technically, I could write you a ticket for littering. Am I right or am I right?" he asked. He didn't wait for our answer. "So, what's it going be? A ticket for littering or you gals going to clean up them soda pop bottles?"

"Well," I began, "we haven't finished drinking them yet. But when we do, we'll be sure to take them home with us. Daddy doesn't like to lose his deposit. We'll take the peanut wrappers, too. So technically we're not littering, yet."

He touched his gun. "Now, don't go smart mouthing me, Miss Lawson. I could slap you with a 10–15 quicker than you can say Gig 'em."

"Oh, I didn't mean any disrespect, Mr. Snodgrass."

"What's a 10–15?" BJ asked.

"For you information, a 10–15 is unlawful loitering in a state park," he said, "and this here is a state park. Am I right or am I right?"

"If you say so, Mr. Snodgrass," BJ answered, "but we're not loitering, we're littering."

I interrupted, "Mr. Snodgrass, can I ask you a question?"

"Yes ma'am. But make it quick. I got a lot of patrolling to do."

"Why do you carry a gun?" You would have thought I asked him why the sun comes up in the east every day.

"Why do I carry a gun? Did you say, 'Why do I carry a *gun*'?" His tongue slid across his front teeth and made a smacking sound. He did this three or four times before he answered.

"For your information, all parks department employees are licensed to carry a firearm. You never know who or what you might encounter in these parks. Am I right or am I right?"

What other employees? He was the only employee.

"Yes sir, I'm sure you're right. But do you ever use it? I mean, have you ever had to shoot anything?" I asked.

"Have I ever had to shoot anything?" He shook his greasy head. "Did you just say 'Have you ever had to shoot anything'?" He did that tongue smacking thing again. "You gals probably don't remember the incident we had here a while back do you?"

"What incident?" I asked.

"Well, let's just say it involved something rabid, a 10–45. You ask your parents. They'll remember. Now, get them soda pop bottles cleaned up before I issue a citation. I don't think your parents would like that. Am I right or am I right?"

"Yes sir, you're right."

"10–4 then." He saluted us and our bottles and drove off. For some reason his LPD pickup didn't have a tailgate. In east Texas that was like walking around with your fly unzipped. It was embarrassing. Pine straw, cow manure and old Dairy Queen sacks flew out of the pickup bed as he sped through town. Talk about a 10–15. And that flashing, orange light on top of his truck. I bet he slept with that light. It was always on. He was notorious for leaving the engine running and lights flashing while he ate lunch at the Lion's Den.

Mrs. Snodgrass, the third Mrs. Snodgrass by the way, was just as embarrassing as Mr. Snodgrass. I'd seen her—I don't know how many times—in Piggly Wiggly wearing a pink hairnet over brush rollers. If that wasn't bad enough, she usually had a cigarette hanging out of her mouth. This troubled me as an eleven year old girl. A God–fearing woman wouldn't shop at Piggly Wiggly with her hair in curlers and a cigarette stuck to her lower lip. That was like painting a target on your back during deer season. She was asking for trouble. Miss Mattie had installed café curtains on her House of Hair windows so passers–by couldn't see the ladies sitting under the hair dryers. No lady would be caught dead in public like that.

"Well, BJ, you ready to take your soda pop bottle and go home before we get a 10–15? Am I right or am I right?" We giggled as we loaded our litter and rode toward town. The green Coke bottles rattled in my basket as I steered my bicycle over uneven ground. "I have to get home in time for church. You want to come to the revival meeting tonight?"

"I don't know. I've never been to a revival. What do y'all do there?"

"It's a lot like Sunday mornings. You know, preaching and all. But there's a famous evangelist coming all the way from Ft. Worth. He draws Bible story pictures while he preaches and the kid who brings the most friends gets to keep the picture."

"How long does it last?"

"About two hours."

"If I come, will you win the picture?" she asked.

"I doubt it. Joey Fontaine won last night because Mr. Fontaine brought his Boy Scout Troop. I thought you might want to help out your best friend." I clasped my hands together like a beggar and continued, "Please? I hate sitting by Nita Sue. She's so mean."

"Speaking of your sister, why is she always cutting out pictures of wine and beer bottles?"

"She glues them on wooden boxes and sells them as purses. The high school girls in Lone Tree love them. Nita Sue can't make them fast enough. I think every girl in their Pep Squad probably has one." I swatted at a mosquito and continued. "Believe it or not but Momma and Daddy don't know she makes them. They'd really kill her if they knew she was selling them."

"Wow. Where does she get all the pictures of wine bottles?" We rode past the movie theater and waved at Mr. Nichols. He nodded as he swept the sidewalk.

"Well, the best pictures of liquor and wine bottles are in *Playboy* magazine."

"How do you know that?"

"Because that's what Uncle Ed told Nita Sue. He buys *Playboy* to read the sports stories. The biggest advertisers for sports magazines are liquor companies. So when Uncle Ed is finished reading the sports stories, he cuts out the ads for Nita Sue. It takes two

Playboys to make one purse. Aunt Betty didn't want him giving liquor bottle ads to Nita Sue but Uncle Ed told Aunt Betty that Nita Sue is an entrepreneur—whatever that is. They had a big argument about it. Aunt Betty forgot I was in the storeroom and I heard every word. You should have heard Aunt Betty yelling at him."

I steered my bike toward BJ and raised my voice as I imitated Aunt Betty. "'God–fearing Baptist girls shouldn't be cutting liquor bottles pictures out of any magazines. Especially *Playboy*. And shame on you, Ed Lawson.'"

"What did he say?"

"Well, he pushed her finger toward the floor and told her she better quit waving that thing at him. Then he told her to stop worrying about what other people thought and that she should be proud to have a niece who might be the next Helen Gurley Brown."

"Who's Helen Gurley Brown?"

"I'm not sure but I saw her picture in *Cosmopolitan* magazine."

"Your momma lets y'all read *Cosmopolitan*?" BJ's front tire hit the curb by Shores Funeral Parlor.

"Heck no! She'd snatch us baldheaded if she knew. Nita Sue has one hidden in the box springs of her bed along with the album cover to *In-A-Gadda-Da-Vida*."

"Inna who?" BJ wasn't up to speed on hippie music like I was. Nita Sue preferred hard core rock to my Bobby Sherman.

"*In-A-Gadda-Da-Vida*. That album by Iron Butterfly. Anyway, Momma says that young ladies shouldn't listen to that kind of music. Brother Paul preached about rock and roll a couple of Sundays ago. Momma and Daddy got so worked up that they made Nita Sue take down her zodiac poster. Nita Sue told them that her Capricorn poster didn't have anything to do with rock and roll, but they made her take it off the wall just the same. Then Momma threatened to throw away her albums so Nita Sue hid all of her album covers then slipped the records into my Bobby Sherman jackets. Now every time I want to hear *Julie, Do You Love Me?* I make sure I'm not playing Iron Butterfly or the Rolling Stones."

"Why do your parents get so worked up about that stuff?"

"I guess because Brother Paul says it's the devil's music and Momma and Daddy believe everything Brother Paul says. 'The voice of the Lord' they call him. All I know is that he is long–

winded. Last Sunday half the choir fell asleep before he finished his sermon."

"I'm glad we're Methodists. Reverend Finney doesn't get too worked up about anything. Bubba's MYF group has dances every Sunday night in Wesley Hall."

"What's MYF?" I asked.

"Methodist Youth Fellowship," she answered.

I made a circle eight with my bike as I tried to picture Nita Sue and her teenage friends dancing to the Rolling Stones in Fellowship Hall.

"Mom and Dad think it's great that he and his friends are at church instead of riding around and hanging out at the Dairy Dip. The Dairy Dip sounds like more fun to me but his girlfriend's parents won't let her hang out there, so he goes to her church on Sunday nights."

We continued to ride through our neighborhood as we discussed Nita Sue's blatant disregard of all things alcohol related and Baptist's disapproval of dancing.

"Wow. You are so lucky. I think the roof would cave in if First Baptist had a dance. We can't even use dice to play our Bible games. Our Sunday School teacher says it promotes gambling and card playing. Last Sunday, we had to make our own spinners for the Ten Commandments board game because she wouldn't let us use dice. I asked her why it was okay for church ladies to play bridge but we couldn't use cards or dice to play Bible games."

"What did she say?"

"She told me not to talk back to my elders. I didn't tell her that her grandson stole half of her S&H Green Stamps to buy the Tripoli gambling game. She'd probably die on the spot and I would get blamed for her early trip to heaven."

"Who's your Sunday School teacher?"

"Mrs. Morris, who else? She's been our teacher for three years now. I wish she would teach one grade and quit moving up with us. Every year on Promotion Sunday they ask all the teachers to stand up. I cross my fingers and pray that I won't see her blue hair rise up from that pew, but, up it comes. This year she turned and waved at me to let me know that she would be my teacher once again."

"Why do they let her keep moving up with y'all?"

"Because she went to Baylor University. I guess they figure anyone who went to Baylor probably knows the Bible better than anybody. Plus, she has her 25 year WMU pin. That's right up there with getting saved."

"What's WMU?"

"Women's Missionary Union. Please, please, please come with me tonight? You can see Mrs. Morris' blue hair and watch a man draw pictures. Please?" We coasted toward her front yard.

"Sorry. No way am I sitting through two hours of preaching." She jumped off her bike and ran up the steps to her front porch. "Have fun tonight!" She waved and disappeared behind the screen door.

No sooner had the sentence left her mouth, it began to rain.

Revival: n. (ri–vī–vəl) an often emotional evangelistic meeting or series of meetings

The humidity hung in the night air like a thick blanket. Sometimes I couldn't catch my breath because the air was so heavy. I longed to live up north in places like Minnesota or Massachusetts; states we had studied about in geography.

My World Book Encyclopedia was full of photographs with snow. Lots of snow. People were bundled up in wool sweaters, toboggans and mittens—just like my hero, Mary Richards, on the *Mary Tyler Moore Show*.

That was the kind of life I dreamed of, a fancy job, a bachelorette pad and a cool car. I could envision myself as a twenty-five year old woman speeding down the freeway in a new dress and matching boots with the radio tuned to the coolest rock and roll station. I would park in my own parking space, lazily exit my car, ride the elevator to the WJM newsroom and throw open the door to the sounds of, "Good morning, Carol Ann. Here, sign this. Sign that. We can't go on the air until you approve this." I would be one important, independent woman with no one telling me what to do, where to go, or what kind of oil to put in my car.

Reality set in when someone announced Ritchie Fontaine as the winner of the evangelist's hand–drawn pastel. Judging by the sea of blue uniforms, Ritchie's Cub Scout Troop had, indeed, fulfilled their commitment to help a fellow Cub Scout. Oh well, I didn't care. His momma would confiscate it anyway. He'd never see that special drawing again.

I bet Mary Richards never had to sit through Sunday morning and evening church services. I bet she and Rhoda could pick and choose whether or not they went to revival meetings, too. Heck, I bet they didn't even *have* revival meetings. The way Aunt Betty talks, Yankees don't go to church as much or know the Bible like we do down here.

I imagined Mary Richards and Rhoda Morgenstern spending their evenings shopping at Macy's and Neiman's just like BJ's mom. What a life.

Mrs. Dodge and Mrs. Campbell were notorious for their shopping trips. I overheard Aunt Betty talking to Momma about them driving to Dallas and about how much money they spent on their clothes. Aunt Betty said it was a sin to spend that kind of money on something that had to be washed and ironed every week. Momma reminded her that Mrs. Dodge employed Bertie to wash and iron and clean their house. And what business was it of hers if Mrs. Dodge had a dozen maids to launder her expensive clothes? Everyone knew that the Dodges were fine, Christian people.

Aunt Betty just shook her head and mumbled something about storing up riches in heaven. She was always quoting Scripture. Half the time she misquoted not only the Scripture, but the chapter and verse. I knew most of the important verses in the Bible because we spent so much time memorizing them in Training Union.

In fact, I was pretty talented when it came to Bible Drills. I would have made it to the state convention finals if Mrs. Morris hadn't let that snotty Michelle Conner enter instead of me. I know I out-drilled her but that was the Sunday after the Longhorns beat the tar out of Baylor. I made sure everyone in Training Union knew that I had rooted for the Longhorns and not for the Bears. I made sure Mrs. Morris knew it, too.

Momma nudged me with her elbow. It was time to stop daydreaming about snow and Mary Tyler Moore and pay attention to the service.

"Open your hymnals to hymn No. 483. That's four, eight, three. We'll sing the first, second and last stanzas," Brother Eddie Earl Eaton announced. I reached for the green hymnal and obediently turned to page 483. With both palms aimed at heaven, Brother Eddie Earl motioned for us to stand. I stood while trying to keep my new pantyhose from snagging on the pew. Why couldn't we have pew pads like other churches? It would save Momma a bundle. She was always complaining about the money she spent on pantyhose and feminine hygiene products.

As Brother EdEarl's (his name ran together sometimes) right hand kept time to the music, we lifted our voices to the Lord and sang of Jesus' wondrous love:

"Sing His mer–cy and His grace
In the man–sions bright and bless–ed,
He'll pre–pare for us a place."

Like clockwork, Brother EdEarl used both hands to direct the chorus. It was his way of telling us to sing a little louder and a whole lot faster. I took a deep breath just to keep up with him.

"When we all get to heaven,
What a day of rejoicing that will be!
When we all see Je–sus,
We'll sing and shout the vic–to–ry!"

Brother EdEarl rotated his palms down and pointed both index fingers at the accompanists. This was their cue to remain silent and our cue to repeat the chorus softly and slowly.

"When we all,
    when we all (The men in our church reached deep within their souls as they sang the echo)
Get to heaven,
What a day of rejoicing that will be! (Re–joicing that will be!)
When we all (when we all) see Je–sus,
    We'll sing and shout the vic–to–ry (shout the vic–to–ry)."

Followed by a roomful of amens and the sound of hymn books being returned to the racks, Brother EdEarl took his rightful place beside Brother Paul in the red velveteen podium chairs. He wiped his brow with a blue bandana. He was sweating something fierce. Mr. Arnold of Arnold's Tires slowly climbed the four steps to the podium to present the offertory prayer.

"Let us pray," he announced. After asking God to help us return to Him what was rightfully His, we sat down for Brother Romone's evangelistic sermon and sketching.

Nita Sue and I placed bets on which choir member would fall asleep first—the loser had to make the winner's bed for a week. My pick? Mr. Burch. He snoozed more than anyone else. Nita Sue chose Mrs. Drummond. She slept a lot, too, but Mrs. Winnenborg usually nudged her about the time her jaw dropped.

"Today, brothers and sisters, we are going to study what I believe is one of the greatest passages in the New Testament. Open your Bibles to the fourth chapter of John's gospel. We'll begin with verse four." The rubber band popped off the colored pencils. Pastels appeared out of thin air.

I proudly opened my new red letter edition of the King James Version that Momma and Daddy had given me on my last birthday. I was the only one in my Sunday School class who owned a red leather Bible. I didn't understand how it could be red and leather. Momma's was brown leather and Daddy's black. Surely there weren't red cows—at least not in east Texas. If there were, I'd certainly not seen one. I bet they came from one of those Communist countries we had studied about in civics class.

"Remember who Jesus is talking to here, folks—a Samaritan woman." He emphasized the word "woman" as he sketched a woman next to a well.

"In those days," he continued, "Jews didn't walk through Samaria, much less talk to one of their womenfolk. You see, Jesus knew that this particular woman would be at that particular well.

"Jacob's well." A pause.

"To draw water." Another pause.

"He made it a point to ask her for a drink." He drew Jesus standing beside the well.

It was about this time that I noticed Mr. Burch's chin slowly making its way to the gold collar on his choir robe. About two minutes into Brother Paul's Sunday sermons, Mr. Burch would close his eyes and before you could say "Texas Fight" he was sawing logs. It was no different that night. Like clockwork, Mr. Fischer began drawing house plans on his bulletin like he did every Sunday when Brother Paul began preaching. Perhaps all church-going architects did that. Looked like I won another week of bed-making freedom.

As I gazed around the sanctuary, I noticed that many of the older men had their hands cupped behind their ears. By pushing the right ear forward and turning the head slightly to the left it was amazing how much clearer one could hear the sermon. I knew this to be true because I'd tried it several times while eavesdropping on Nita Sue and Randy.

"...and now verse seven. 'There cometh a woman of Samaria to draw water: Jesus saith unto her, Give me to drink.' Notice that his disciples have disappeared from the scene. They walked to town to buy food for Jesus and themselves to eat."

Speaking of something to eat, my stomach was growling. All this talk of eating was making me hungry.

He resumed, "You've had five husbands and the man you are living with is not your husband." Another pause and he sketched the woman drawing water from the well. "How many of you, here tonight, think that free sex is something new?"

Did he actually say "sex?" Mr. Burch was awake now.

"All of this free love and sex is nothing new, folks. It's been going on for two thousand years. The hippies renamed it, that's all." Everyone sat up a little straighter.

"Now then, I know some of you are sitting there saying to yourselves 'This here is Lake View, Brother Romone. We don't have any hippies or free sex going on in our God–fearing town.'" There it was again: "sex." Mr. Courtney had both hands cupped to his head.

"It's coming, folks. It's *lurking* on the borders of Lake View just waiting to come in through your television sets, magazines and record albums." Frantically, he added color to Jesus. "That rock and roll music that some of your teenagers own; have you parents really *listened* to the words of those songs?"

I didn't think *Julie, Do You Love Me?* qualified as a lurker.

"Jesus knows what is coming. Just like He knew what was coming out of that Samaritan woman's mouth. He knows what the devil is planning folks, but more importantly, He knows what's in our hearts." He drew clouds and added blue pastels to the sky. Folks seemed to relax a bit. Mr. Courtney was down to one, cupped hand. Brother Romone was preaching about something familiar to all Baptists: the devil.

"Have you ever stopped to think what it must have been like for that Samaritan woman to meet Jesus? How embarrassing it must have been for her to have a complete stranger tell her about her sinful, sexual deeds?" Two hands again.

"Jesus loves you just as you are. Warts and all. He knows none of us is perfect. He's the only perfect one! But you can't wait to change your sinful ways before you come to Him!" A few amens and stones appeared on the outside of the well. "He wants you to come just as you are!" More amens and stones. "Just like that Samaritan woman and her sexual sins."

Mr. Burch was adjusting the collar of his choir robe. It must have gotten too tight.

"Look at verse eighteen." Brother Romone pivoted to his left and gazed at the choir loft. I saw sweat beading on one man's forehead. "Notice how Jesus gently answers the woman. He knows she doesn't have a husband. He knows she has had five husbands." Five men were drawn into the background—each progressively smaller as they were sketched away from the well.

"But Jesus doesn't beat her over the head with this information. No! He simply points out her sin to her." Mr. Burch's hairy eyebrows were going up and down.

"Folks, I have preached on this passage many times. But it wasn't until last night as I knelt by my bed that the Holy Ghost pointed out something to me. This woman was obviously comfortable enough around Jesus to have a conversation with him and a very personal one at that. What does that tell us about Him?" BAM! Brother Romone's fist slammed into the palm of his other hand. Everyone who wasn't asleep, jumped in their pew.

"It tells me that Jesus was and still is the one person we can turn to. He already knows everything anyway. So why do we try to hide our sins from him? Why don't we just come out in the open with them? Who better to confess to? *Je-sus* is the one who loves us in spite of our sins. Sexual and nonsexual alike." A few coughs. More color appeared on the drawing. I looked around for Mr. Grimes.

"Repent of your sins before it is too late." He snapped a pencil in half. "*Je-sus* wants you to come just as you are. Just like the woman at the well. Admit that you are a sinner and you need *Je-sus*. Come on down here before it's too late!"

He waved his Bible in the air. I looked over at Nita Sue. She was writing "Mrs. Nita Sue Mitchell" over and over again. What a drip. She hadn't heard a thing Brother Romone had said.

"That devil is planning things here in Lake View, folks. Some of you have already fallen captive to his schemes! You come on down here before it's too late!"

Mr. Grimes was nowhere in sight. *Just As I Am* drifted through the church.

> *"...And that Thou bidd'st me come to Thee,*
> *O Lamb of God, I come!*
> *I come!"*

At First Baptist we sang four stanzas of *Just As I Am* waiting on people to walk the aisle. During last year's revival, we sang a record seven stanzas. Nita Sue said she almost went forward just to shut everybody up.

A familiar orange light flashed through the bottom half of the stained glass window closest to our pew. Within seconds it was gone. Mr. Snodgrass probably heard about the liver and onions special at the Lion's Den.

Brother EdEarl watched Brother Paul out of the corner of his eye for the signal…that secret sign that Baptist preachers give Baptist music directors when it's time to stop the invitation singing. A few Cub Scouts gathered at the altar as Mrs. Fontaine made her way to the front. I thought she was there to counsel the young boys. Instead, she rolled Jesus and the Samaritan woman up and stuck the artwork under her arm like a general marching to war with his bazooka. Ritchie could forget his prize. His momma would have it framed and hanging in their pawn shop before Sunday.

"When the moon is in the seventh house, and Jupiter aligns with Mars, then peace will guide the planets, and love will steer the stars."

The Fifth Dimension

7:00 a.m.

I hated mornings. I hated them mostly because it meant I had to get up and get ready for school. When I was in the middle of a good dream, Momma would come in, grab my big toe, and say, 'This is the day that the Lord has made. Rejoice and be glad in it!'

This morning, the first day of school, Momma wasn't rejoicing which was unusual for Hazel Jean Lawson. The clothes that Nita Sue left on the clothesline last night were soaked by the rain. Momma was muttering under her breath about how she was going to spend the entire afternoon washing the Baptist Belles hand bell tablecloths again when she had planned on ironing them this afternoon. After all, it was ironing day. Everybody knew that washing took place on Monday and ironing on Tuesday. Plus, she had the PTA coffee first thing this morning.

Personally, I didn't see what the big deal was. If your clothes were clean and ironed and you could wear them, who cared if happened on Monday or Tuesday? When Momma got out of sorts, it was usually over housework. *Cleanliness is next to godliness.* That's what was embroidered on the hand towel in the kitchen. I didn't know if God cared that much about my personal hygiene, but I was going to stay clean just in case.

Nita Sue and I headed out the door for school. Me, with my school supplies and new Bewitched lunch box and Nita Sue with another liquor bottle purse hidden under her raincoat. We began our three block hike up Kennedy Lane when I saw Uncle Ed's car out of the corner of my eye. How many other custom–orange, longhorn–hood–ornament Cadillacs were there in Lake View? Uncle Ed hollered for us to get in the car.

"Looks like rain," he yelled as he pulled in the driveway. "Climb in while I put the top up."

Oh, man. My stomach turned cartwheels. I did not like riding in the car with Uncle Ed.

He was a maniac behind the wheel and I was his prisoner. Riding with him was like riding The Big Bend at Six Flags, but at least you knew what to expect when you rode Big Bend.

Walking as if the Lord himself had summoned me to the burnt orange convertible, I slid across the front seat and took my rightful place beside Uncle Ed, my feet planted firmly on either side of the hump. Nita Sue sat on the passenger side twirling her hair with her finger and humming a Neil Diamond song. She was oblivious to what was about to take place. How a five-block ride to school could turn into the car ride from you–know–where, I didn't know, but it always did.

Uncle Ed lit his Roi–Tan with the Zippo lighter we had given him for Christmas. His thumb snapped the chrome top in place, he put the car in drive, blew a smoke ring, looked over at me, and said, 'and away we go!' Somehow it sounded better when Jackie Gleason said it.

In a matter of seconds, my stomach gave way to the anxiety that was flowing from my brain to my sweaty palms and, finally, to my bottom side. We were backing out of the driveway and onto the road when he yelled his first obscenity. An ash from his cigar had landed on his pant leg. He quickly slapped his lap, brushing the ember to the floorboard.

"Whew! That was a close call, girls!"

The torture began. The first block wasn't so bad but around block number two it all broke loose. A woman pulled out in front of Uncle Ed and wasn't driving as fast as he thought she should be. After he called her a woman driver, he rolled down his window so he could yell at her if he needed to. At that moment it began to rain.

With clouds of cigar smoke circling his head, he took his eyes off the road to find the windshield wiper switch. At the same time the lady in front of us came to a complete stop. Uncle Ed jerked the wheel, jumped the curb, and passed the lady on the sidewalk. When we squealed by the passenger side of her car, he yelled another obscenity and muttered something under his breath about those danged Democrats giving women the right to drive. I thought it was the right to vote; not drive. We never studied about the right to drive in civics class.

I thought I might vomit right then and there. Between his cigar smoke and Momma's biscuits, I was sure the lake of fire had found a resting place in my belly. The amazing part of riding with Uncle Ed was that he never seemed to notice that his behavior was different than that of other drivers. One minute he was honking, yelling and swerving. The next minute he was singing his version of *Just a Closer Walk with Thee.*

"A closer walk, indeed," I whispered to myself.

"Uncle Ed? Would you mind if I walked the rest of the way? I see some of my friends right there." I pointed to a group of kids walking to school. I couldn't tell if I knew any of them or not—I didn't care—I just wanted out of his orange, death trap.

"Sure thing. I know how it is at your age. I was young, too, you know."

He stopped the car to let me out, smiled, and told me to have a nice day.

Sure. Right after I puked.

I slid from my spot and stepped out of the car—nauseous, I might add—when he peeled out, waved his left hand and honked his horn. Activated, actually. *Texas Fight* blared through the neighborhood. I thought I might fall over dead from humiliation. Clutching my lunchbox as if my very life depended on it, I walked toward school.

Truth be told, I was glad to be walking today. Momma had insisted on rolling my hair in those awful, pink sponge rollers for the first day of school. I preferred to wear my hair straight, and told her as much, right to her face, which was a big mistake.

So the two of us (me and my hair) continued to walk toward JFK Elementary. I knew if I timed it just right, the mist would relax most of the curls and I could brush the rest of them out in the bathroom between the first and second bells.

"Hey, Curly Girly!" Oh no. It was that idiot, Lamar Webb.

"Shut up, Lamar," I yelled and continued walking.

"Stick your finger in the light socket, did you?" he cackled.

I put my thumb to my ear and my little finger to my mouth like I was talking on the phone. The moron continued to ride circles around me. "The cave men are calling and they want their brains back," I yelled in return.

"Oh yeah? Well, the...HEY!"

I turned. Lamar had stopped dead in his tracks and was trying to regain his balance on his bike. Someone had hurled a pinecone at his head and hit it dead on.

"What do you think you're doing?" he cried.

For a moment time stood still. Standing behind me was a girl in the shortest skirt I'd seen this side of the television set. "I am protecting the rights of this woman, you male chauvinist pig," she said.

Who was this girl and how did she know Lamar so well? I stared at her long, black, Cher–Bono–like hair. Obviously, her mother hadn't stuck pink rollers in her hair at bedtime.

"What are you looking at?" she barked at Lamar. He was trying to get his rear end back on his bike.

"Uh, nothing. I guess." And with that he rode as fast as he could to school.

"Hello. I'm Roxanne, but you can call me Roxy." She extended her hand. I took it but couldn't take my eyes off her face. She was wearing make–up. And her eyelashes—they must have been two inches long. I leaned in to get a better look. I bet it took thirty minutes to put on all that mascara.

"Hi there. I'm Carol Ann Lawson but you can call me Carol Ann. Do you live around here?" I asked.

She swept her hair back with her hand and answered, "I do now."

I stared at this specimen of womanhood. She couldn't live here in Lake View. No one like her lived in Lake View.

"We just moved here from Boston. You know, Boston, Massachusetts? Surely you guys have heard of it." She continued to walk down the sidewalk like a model on a runway.

"Oh, yeah. Sure, we've heard of it. We've even studied about Massachusetts in geography class." I answered as if I had actually taught the lesson on Massachusetts that day.

"I see."

"Uh, yes. How long have you lived here?"

"Exactly eighteen hours and," she looked at her watch, "thirty-eight minutes."

We continued toward the school. I guess she saw me admiring her black go-go boots because she said, "Back in Boston, no one wears penny loafers."

I looked at my shoes: penny loafers.

"Oh, yeah, I didn't wear my boots today. My mother wanted me to break–in these new shoes for fall." Ugh. I could have slapped myself for saying that. *Stupid, stupid, stupid.*

"You guys walk to school every day around here?" I replayed her question in my head. It sounded like she said "Yooseguys." Maybe that's how they talk in Boston.

"We walk or ride the school bus," I replied.

"I see. Are all the guys like *that* one?" She gestured in Lamar's direction.

"Nah…that's Lamar Webb. He's a first class moron. Nobody pays attention to him."

"I certainly hope the other guys aren't as crass as that pig."

"Oh no. No. Not at all." I wasn't sure what crass meant, but if she was using it to describe Lamar, it couldn't be good.

"Back in Boston women are liberated. We stand up for ourselves. We consider ourselves equals with men."

With a name like Roxanne and an arm like Tom Seaver, I guess she was equal to any man. To Lamar Webb anyway.

"Thank you for taking up for me back there," I said.

"No problem C.A." I looked around for a C.A.—whatever that was. I didn't see one.

"What's a C.A.?" I asked sheepishly.

"You. Consider yourself C.A. Lawson, a liberated woman."

Holy Moly Batman! Me, a women's libber! Yes sir, things were finally looking up around here.

We approached the circle drive of the school. Heads whipped around like nobody's business. Everyone was staring at the new girl and her liberated friend.

Cher: "They say we're young and we don't know, we won't find out until we grow."
Sonny: "Well I don't know if all that's true, 'cause you got me and baby I got you."

Sonny and Cher

"Have you seen the new girl?" BJ asked.

"Oh, you mean Roxy?"

"Roxy?" BJ's head spun around.

"Yeah, Roxanne Wojowitz from Boston, Massachusetts. I've seen her alright. I walked to school with her this morning as a matter–of–fact." Suddenly I had everyone's attention at the lunch table. I focused on the green peas that had magically walked over the divider of my lunch tray and taken up camp in my apple betty. I acted as if plucking up those peas and putting them back in their rightful place was of the utmost importance.

'What? Roxy who? You know her?' was all I heard from my fellow lunch mates. I delicately positioned the last pea where it belonged with the other disgusting ones. One thing's for certain, you'd never see a green pea in C.A. Lawson's mouth.

"Yes, I know her. I've met her anyway," I replied.

"Did you see her hair?" someone asked. "It looks just like Cher Bono's. And her dress! I'd give anything to wear a dress like that. My momma would tie my tail in a knot if she ever caught me in something that short."

"Yeah. Me, too," BJ answered. "I'd give my left arm for those boots. I've never seen go-go boots in black patent leather, have you Carol Ann?"

I considered asking BJ to refer to me as C.A. from now on, but I thought it might hurt her feelings if she knew that Roxy and I had such a close, personal friendship. "No, I've only seen them in the Sears and Roebuck catalog." The conversation took on a life of its own as word spread down the table that I actually knew the Cher Bono girl.

Then… silence. The kind of silence you hear when–you're–passing–a–note–in–class–and–it–gets–very–quiet–and–you–realize–that–the–teacher–is–standing–right–behind–you–and–everyone–can–see–her–except–you–of–course kind of silence. Roxanne Wojowitz had entered the cafetorium. (Someone in PTA thought it would be hip to combine cafeteria and auditorium) She walked to the other end of the table next to ours. She paraded through the room like a woman destined for greatness. Even the lunch ladies stopped spooning peas with their ice cream scoops long enough to stare.

Roxy pushed back her black silky hair and sat down in a rusted, folding chair with JFK stenciled on the back. Now all we needed was a Sonny Bono look–alike to walk through the door and break out singing *I Got You Babe*. This gal got cooler by the minute. In a flash she produced a hot pink Josie and the Pussycats lunchbox complete with matching thermos. Wow! None of us guys had ever seen one of those.

Talking resumed as Roxy proceeded to eat her lunch. From where I sat I couldn't see everything she was eating, but I knew this much—it wasn't peanut butter and jelly. Her sandwich looked like it had grass sticking out on all four sides. She produced fresh broccoli and carrots and actually ate them raw. Around here mothers packed potato chips, Twinkies and Ding Dongs in their kids' lunchboxes. I was forced to eat cafeteria food. For 31¢ a day JFK provided a well balanced, nutritious meal straight from the Food Pyramid and I hated every bite of it.

Mrs. Greene blew her whistle announcing that it was time for our grade to leave the cafetorium and head to recess. The line was slower than usual because everyone stared at Roxy as they passed her table. I overhead that idiot, Lamar Webb, discussing the tastiest parts of armadillo. Gross me out. That guy and his eight brothers and sisters had to be the most disgusting people in east Texas. Maybe in all of Texas. Maybe the world.

Banging my tray against the inside of the trash can, I tried not to smell the hundreds of leftover green peas. Evidently, the majority of my fellow students felt the same way about peas as I did.

As soon as I stepped outside, the humidity slapped me upside the face. Normally I would gripe about having to go outside on a day like today, but the air had flattened Momma's curls straight as a board.

"Hey, Carol Ann, want to run down to the well house and back?" BJ asked.

"Not today. I really don't feel like it, but you guys go ahead."

"What did you say?"

"You guys go ahead." I pronounced each word exactly as it should be.

"Okay. Suit yourself." She and two other girls ran toward the square, stone structure screaming their lungs out while my other friends pushed pine needles in tiny holes on the playground trying to catch chicken chokers.

"C.A.?" It was Roxy. Even her voice was like Cher Bono's.

"Yes?"

"What are those guys doing?" She nodded toward BJ and the other girls. Most girls my age would have pointed, but Roxy's arms were folded across her chest; her right heel anchored at the instep of her left boot giving her that I–am–Miss–Texas–posing–for–photo–ops–look.

"Oh, they're just running up to the well house, that's all."

"Why are they screaming?"

"You see that house across the street from the well house? The one with the faded For Sale sign?"

She nodded.

"Well, Lennie Loyd Backstrom murdered his parents in that house. People say you can still see the bloodstains on the carpet and the walls. Their graves are right over there." I pointed to the Catholic cemetery beside the Backstrom house. "I don't know if you can or not. I'm too scared to look in the window. Students aren't supposed to cross the street so we like…" I cleared my throat and corrected myself, "we *guys* like to pretend his ghost is chasing after us with a hatchet. That's what he used to cut up his parents."

Roxanne stood there. Staring. "Interesting. What happened to the boy?"

"They took him to Terrell. Locked him up for life." I, too, folded my arms and stared toward the house of murder.

"Very in-ter-est-ing," Roxy muttered under her breath. "Father teaches Psychology at Berkeley. He loves this sort of thing."

"Is Berkeley in Texas?" I asked.

Roxanne turned her gaze from the well house to me. "Berkeley is in California. It's a prestigious university."

"Oh." *Silly me.* "Well, if your father lives in California, why did you move to Lake View?" This gal was a bundle of contradictions. "Parents divorced. The courts dictate that I live with Mother until I turn sixteen. Then I can move back to California."

Roxanne Wojowitz was more fascinating than ever. I'd never met anyone who lived in Texas, Massachusetts and California. Come to think of it, I'd never met anyone who'd *been* to Texas, Massachusetts and California. My Uncle Claude and Aunt Vestal lived in California, but they don't count—they're family.

She turned those two inch eyelashes my way, exhaled rather loudly and said, "Mother and Father used to live in California, but they divorced and Mother moved to Boston to be near her parents. My grandparents, of course."

"Of course," I said to myself.

"Mother met Louis—Louis Sabatini—when we lived in Boston. They fell in love. So when he transferred here, we came with him. It's as simple as that." Roxanne was inspecting her hair for split ends. I doubted if she found any.

"So, Mr. Sabatini is your stepfather?"

"No, Louis Sabatini is *not* my stepfather. Louis Sabatini is my mother's live–in lover." That being said, she tossed her hair behind her head and walked off.

Wow.

I knew of one, maybe two girls whose parents were divorced, but I sure didn't know anyone whose momma had a live–in boyfriend. I hoped they weren't Baptists. I didn't think Baptists believed in living together before you got married. As a matter–of–fact, I knew they didn't. Brother Paul preached on it a couple of weeks after the movie *Love Story* came out.

BJ would never believe this!

Homecoming: (hōm̒-kə-min) the return of a group of people usually on a special occasion to a place formerly frequented or regarded as home

The school bell rang and I waited around to see if Roxy needed someone to walk home with. Momma pulled up before I had the chance to really look for her.

"Hi, honey. How was your day?" Momma asked through the car window.

"Okay, I guess. Why are you picking me up? I thought I was supposed to walk home." I got in the decrepit station wagon, but kept looking for Roxy. The car jerked a couple of times, then lurched forward.

"Aunt Betty needs you at the flower shop," Momma said as both our heads lunged forward and snapped back again with the car. "The high school coaches moved homecoming to September, and Betty only has a few weeks to get ready. I told her that you and Nita Sue would come over after school and help her get everything organized."

I continued to stare out the window hoping for a glimpse of my new friend. No luck.

"Carol Ann? Is something bothering you, honey?"

"Ma'am?"

"You seem preoccupied. Is everything all right?"

"Yes, ma'am. I was just looking for this new girl that I met today. She's in my class but she's already turned twelve. Roxanne Wojowitz—isn't that a cool name?" I pressed my nose against the window thinking it might stabilize my face when the car sputtered again.

"Wojowitz? I wonder if she belongs to the young woman I met this morning at the PTA coffee?" Momma was focused on driving the speed limit because Sheriff Whitehall was notorious for handing out speeding tickets the first week of the school year.

"I don't know. I didn't see her mother," I answered, "but I know they just moved here from Boston, Massachusetts."

I pictured her mother as an older version of Roxanne, like the women who graced the cover of *Cosmopolitan*. I bet she wasn't dressed like my mom, that's for sure. When Momma dressed for church or PTA she looked like a female sailor reporting for duty. "Always buy quality clothing that you can mix and match, Carol Ann," she would say, "and stick with navy, black and white. You can't go wrong with those. Plus, you can always accessorize with red."

Having to dress like Momma and Chatty Kathy was taking its toll. I longed for psychedelic mini-skirts and hot pants. But, as Nita Sue said, hell would freeze over before that happened at the Lawson house.

"Well, here we are. Leave your school things in the car, honey. I don't want to make another trip tonight because you or your sister left something at the flower shop. Tell Betty I'm going to get Nita Sue and I'll be back in a jiff." I slammed the door on our old clunker and headed toward the shop.

I wished we could own a decent car like everyone else on the planet. But no…Daddy believed in saving your money until you had enough to buy whatever it was you had been saving it for. I dreamed of a Dodge Charger, but Daddy said they were too expensive. Nita Sue wanted a Volkswagen bus, but that was out of the question. We would probably ride in this loser cruiser until I got married.

The Eyes of Texas played as I opened the door to Betty's Bloomers. It was time to get to work and listen to Aunt Betty talk to herself.

My aunt was the sole owner of the only flower shop in Lake View. Everyone in town bought their wedding flowers, funeral flowers and prom flowers from Aunt Betty. "We wed 'em or dead 'em" was her favorite expression, but not in front of the customers. She just said that to Nita Sue, me and the part–time delivery boy, Luther Tripp.

Running my hand across the wall that was lined with potted plants, I entered the real world of Betty's Bloomers, the work room. I wasn't talking about floral design. I was talking about real, back–breaking work. And guess who did the majority of it? Me, Carol Ann Lawson.

I bet I'd hauled ten thousand buckets of water back and forth among the cooler, the work room, and the back door. I'd pounded enough flower stems to last me a life time, yet I wasn't even old enough to use Secret: "Strong enough for a man, but made for a woman."

The one and only time I got to do something creative was when Mrs. Erlichson gave birth to twin boys and Aunt Betty let me design the door decoration for her hospital room. I loaded it up with so many plastic baby bottles and rattles that the hospital maintenance man had to bolt it to the door thus ending my short career as a floral designer.

"Hi there, Aunt Betty," I said.

"Well, look what the armadillo dragged in. How was your first day of school?" She blotted her forehead and neck with a hankie.

"It was great. I met the coolest new girl from…"

She cut me off mid–sentence. "Grab an apron and get to work, young un. We'll talk about your new friend later."

I grabbed an apron and walked to the six foot table covered in last year's homecoming supplies.

"How many cowbells we got, Carol Ann?" she hollered from across the room.

"Which ones? Texas–sized or miniature?"

"The little ones we tie on streamers. And what about gold glitter, is there enough of it? Lordy, Lordy, I can't run out like I did last year. Those Burton girls cried for days because their boyfriend's jersey numbers weren't written in gold glitter. And see how many orange pipe cleaners we got leftover from last year. I'm already two weeks behind making LHSes."

Lake View held dear the tradition of homecoming mums; no ordinary corsage would do for homecoming weekend. When Susie Allen returned from the University of Texas wearing her UT mum, women stood for hours admiring it. The church foyer was lined with women and girls of all ages gazing at the orange and white streamers dangling from the corsage. Aunt Betty couldn't take her eyes off it. She whispered "Lordy, Lordy" over and over until Uncle Ed ushered her out of the church. Nita Sue said you could see dollar signs in her eyes, just like those cartoon characters on Saturday morning television. That year, homecoming mums got bigger and gaudier all because of Susie Allen.

If you dated a football player you were practically guaranteed that your homecoming corsage would be even bigger and gaudier than all the other big and gaudy corsages—which was why every girl at Lake View High dreamed of going to the dance with a football player. It was considered an honor to have the following scripted in gold glitter on your corsage streamers:

1. Your name
2. Your date's name (preferably a football player)
3. His position on the team (quarterback, lineman)
4. Your status (cheerleader, majorette, maid)
5. The year (this was particularly important, because you didn't want to confuse last year's dried bulletin board decoration with the current dried bulletin board decoration.)
6. Go Lions, Beat (the opposing team)
7. Lake View High School
8. LHS pipe cleaner logo glued to the middle of the mum

If your date's mother was willing to spare no expense, she could spring for small plastic footballs, lions, and miniature cowbells. The more noise, the more expensive the corsage. If you were lucky, you had a five pound corsage attached at your collarbone with streamers and other paraphernalia hanging well below your waistline.

Aunt Betty was so busy jawing about the homecoming supplies—or lack of—she didn't notice that Nita Sue and another woman had arrived.

"Yoo-hoo, Betty! Where's my favorite florist?" *Texas Fight* played once again.

Oh, no. It was Mrs. Martin, the town busybody. She knew more gossip than Aunt Betty, and Aunt Betty knew a lot. She could out–talk, out–gossip, out–everything and everybody until the cows came home. She was sure to quiz Aunt Betty about whose corsages were the biggest this year. Heaven forbid her Margo's mum might not be the size of downtown Dallas. Nita Sue and I made a beeline for the walk–in cooler.

Once inside, Nita Sue began imitating Mrs. Martin. She could mimic her perfectly. I was laughing so hard I thought I might pee in my pants. She pranced between the gladiolas and carnations and mocked in her best Mae West voice, "Betty, dahling, how big is your biggest mum? Make mine a double." Nita Sue pretended to blow smoke rings in the cold air. I could see her breath as she cocked her head.

"Do it again!" I laughed so hard I could barely get the words past my now–turning–blue–lips. Nita Sue broke off the tip of a carnation and stuck it behind her left ear. Then she stuck out her chest and pranced around the cooler. She looked just like Mrs. Martin. So much, in fact, that when Aunt Betty knocked on the glass window Nita Sue jumped into a bucket of yellow roses and spilled water all over the floor. We forgot that customers could view the flowers from the lobby. Evidently, Mrs. Martin didn't see the humor in Nita Sue's comedic abilities. Come to think of it, she didn't see the humor in much of anything.

We scrambled out of the cooler still giggling as we made a beeline to the storeroom. I hoped Momma didn't hear about this— we'd be dead meat.

"Okay, you can come out girls." Opening the storeroom door, Aunt Betty stood armed with a stapler and she wasn't afraid to use it.

"Lordy, that woman is going to send me to an early grave. She was nosing around here to see if anyone else had a double mum this year." All this talk about double mums caused Aunt Betty to forget about Nita Sue and me.

"Do they?" I asked.

"I don't know yet! I could shoot them coaches. Just shoot them!" Aunt Betty got off track sometimes. She blamed it on menopause. "Margo is so tiny she's going to look like she grew extra boobies with that big old thang hanging off her shoulder." Aunt Betty was disgusted. She took great pride in her homecoming corsages and Mrs. Martin just rained on her parade.

"Why don't we just hang a big, old cowbell around her neck? Then everyone could see and hear her coming." Nita Sue said this with such authority that I almost saluted her.

"I wish I could hang one on her mother, that's for sure." Aunt Betty set the stapler on the work bench and resumed fretting over the pipe cleaners. "Let's get back to work here. I got more work orders than Borden's got cows."

Aunt Betty took homecoming seriously. It was one of the most profitable events at Betty's Bloomers. Only an Episcopal funeral brought in more money than Lake View High School homecoming.

"Phone for you, Aunt Betty," Nita Sue said as she covered the mouthpiece. "It's Mrs. Campbell."

"Which Mrs. Campbell?" Aunt Betty asked.

"The rich one with the big hair," Nita Sue answered. Aunt Betty practically ran for the phone. Rich customers got special treatment.

"Luther," Aunt Betty instructed, "start folding corsage boxes and counting corsage pins. Put three to a box. I don't want any of these mothers saying they didn't have enough pins to hold up their daughter's mums." She dabbed her upper lip with her hankie. "Why good afternoon, Mrs. Campbell. What can I do you for today?"

Armed with Elmer's glue and gold glitter, Nita Sue and I began the boring, yearly task of printing names, ranks, and football numbers on pre–cut orange and white streamers.

Hippie: n. (hi-pē) a long–haired unconventionally dressed person

The cowbells clanged (I had unplugged the fight song) as another customer walked under the giant, red bloomers bolted atop the front doors of Betty's Bloomers. Aunt Betty got the idea from Mrs. Bertram's front yard. Mrs. Bertram had several yard art cut–outs strategically placed around her mobile home. I think it was meant to scare the birds away from her vegetable gardens, but all they did was create a shortage of plywood at Strong's Lawn and Garden. Pretty soon, half the residents of Lake View were also the proud owners of a woman's wooden derriere staked in their yards.

The older ladies were particularly fond of them and tried to outdo each other. One woman on Front Street painted cherries on her bloomers while someone on Block Street decorated her bloomers with orange butterflies. She was the same woman who had plastic butterflies attached to her house, trees, porch, mailbox, and birdbaths. If it was in her yard, a monarch butterfly was stuck to it.

I thought they were kind of tacky myself and didn't pay that much attention to them until vandals began painting what Baptist ladies called "unthinkable pictures" on them. I suspected it was the same group from Lone Tree who'd decorated our statue of James Bowie, but Sheriff Whitehall had never caught them.

"Carol Ann, get out front and see who it is," Aunt Betty ordered.

"Yes, ma'am." I peeked through the opening in the curtains and saw a man I'd never seen before. "I don't know who it is, Aunt Betty—some man."

"Lordy, Carol Ann, get on out there and wait on the customer for crying out loud." Moving the homecoming date was getting the best of Aunt Betty.

"May I help you, sir?" I asked politely. I had been instructed to always walk around the sales counter and approach the customer in a friendly manner.

"Yes, I was wondering if you had any protea in stock?" he asked. Now, I'm sure this fellow thought I was strange because I stood there staring at his feet. He was wearing shoes that looked like women's sandals. And with socks! "Miss? Are you okay?" His ponytail flopped on his shoulder.

I knew he had asked a question, but for the life of me I couldn't take my eyes off his feet. I'd never seen a man in sandals.

"Uh-huh. Do what?" I mumbled.

"Perhaps you should sit," he replied gently.

I sat.

"Are you okay?"

"Yes sir, I'm fine. Thank you. What did you say again?" I couldn't help but stare at the weirdest looking fellow I'd come across in my lifetime. Where did he come from? Couldn't be Lake View or Texas, for that matter. A man could get himself shot for dressing like that.

"I asked if you had any protea." His smile was nice even if the rest of him was weird.

"I'm not sure. Are they flowers?"

"Yes, they're African flowers. Is there a florist here today? Perhaps he could help me."

"He?" I giggled out loud. "There is no "he" florist." *If there was, I bet he was pushing up daisies.* "No sir, only a she. My Aunt Betty of Betty's Bloomers."

"Do you think I might speak with her?"

"Yes, sir. I'll go fetch her. Stay right there. Don't go anywhere." I scrambled around the sales counter and managed to knock the rack of sympathy cards onto the floor.

"Do you need some help?" he asked.

"No thanks. I got it. Don't go anywhere now." I eased my way through the curtains and pulled them together, all the while smiling and nodding at our new customer.

"Aunt Betty, Nita Sue. Get over here. You're not going to believe the man that just came through the front door." I was talking so fast that Aunt Betty made me start over. "The man out front," I said as I tried to contain my excitement, "is wearing sandals with socks and just asked if we have any protein flowers. You gotta see this!"

Quick as a wink, Aunt Betty was peeking between the gap in the curtain while Nita Sue and I peered out a few inches below.

"Shoot–a–monkey!" Aunt Betty hollered. "He's got his hair in a ponytail!" (Aunt Betty pronounced it hay yur) She could make one syllable words stretch into two, three, sometimes four syllables.

"Cool," Nita Sue chimed in.

"Did you say he's looking for protein flowers?" Aunt Betty asked.

"Yes, ma'am. That's what the man said."

"Well," she stated, "there's only one way to find out. You girls get back to those corsages, I'll handle this." After all, Aunt Betty was a certified FTD florist. She proudly displayed the coveted gold decal in the front window.

She removed a pencil from behind her ear, pinched her cheeks a couple of times and straightened her green florist apron as she walked confidently to the front of the shop. Nita Sue and I peeked through the curtain and watched Aunt Betty do what she does best: extract information from anyone naïve enough to tell it to her. She nodded her head as he talked. And let me tell you, he talked. I couldn't make out a word he said because Luther was counting corsage pins out loud. How hard could it be to count to three for goodness sakes?

"Shh." Nita Sue waved her hand at him.

"What's up?" asked Luther. "Who's out front?"

"Shut up, Luther, I can't hear."

Once Luther stopped making noise, we could hear this man telling Aunt Betty something about a new job and a new house. We heard Aunt Betty saying "bless your heart" over and over again. Then she began her secondary task—taking the man's order. By this time, all the good stuff was over and there was nothing more to hear. Or so I thought.

"S-A-B-A-T-I-N-I. Sabatini."

Aunt Betty was still writing. "What a lovely name." She had turned up the charm now, "Australian is it?"

"No, Italian," he replied as he produced something that looked more like a lady's purse than a man's wallet.

"Italian? (she pronounced it eye–tal–yun) Why, shoot–a–monkey! You're the first *I*talian to step foot in Betty's Bloomers. Wait until Mattie and the girls hear about this."

"Is there a problem?"

"Land sakes alive, no. It's just a first for me, that's all. Why, I bet you make a mean spaghetti dish!" Aunt Betty was pretty excited. I guess it was unusual to have a real *I*talian in the shop. "That'll be two dollars and fifty cents, Mr. Sabatini."

"Sabatini? Did she say 'Sabatini,' Nita Sue?" We were still peering through the slit in the curtain.

"Uh huh. Why?"

"Because that's the name of the new girl's mom's live–in boyfriend."

"What are you talking about?"

"The new girl at school. She's a Yankee from Boston. California, actually. Her mom is divorced and she lives with her boyfriend named Louis Sabatini. The mother, not the new girl."

"Cool. Check out that ponytail. I love a man with a ponytail." Nita Sue drooled all over the curtain.

"You've never seen a man with a ponytail."

"I have too."

"You have not."

"Have too."

"Not."

"Ouch…that hurt!" Nita Sue yelled as Aunt Betty barged through the curtain and practically knocked her over.

"Lordy, lordy. An *I*talian right here in Lake View. Mattie and the girls will never believe this." Aunt Betty was on a roll. Her mind was off homecoming and onto the new *I*talian man.

"What kind of flowers did he want?" Nita Sue asked.

"Some kind of exotic thang that no one around here ever heard of. I talked him into carnations. I told him they were every bit as exotic as those other thangs and cheaper, too."

Now was the time to see if he mentioned Roxanne. "Did he say the flowers were for his wife?"

"Not that I recollect," she answered. She dabbed at her neck again. I guess her hot flashes were back.

"So… he didn't say anything about a wife, or a daughter, or a job, or anything?" Good grief. She talked to the man long enough to know his dentist's name and phone number. What would a tiny bit of information hurt?

"The man is a social worker at the prison and bought the flowers for his girlfriend's housewarming. See there, girls? Now some people, and I won't name names, would think he was a nut case or a moral derelict because he wears his hair like a woman. But, I, Betty Lawson, am not a prejudging person. I can tell you that this man is a gentleman trying to be thoughtful and brighten up his girl's new house."

Nita Sue cut her eyes toward me and blurted out, "Aunt Betty, he lives with his...ouch!" My right hand clamped over her big mouth. "Cut it out you moron," Nita Sue said under her breath, "you'll smear my lip gloss."

"Shut up. You'll ruin everything," I whispered, "I'm invited to a party at that house and I don't want Momma and Daddy to know that it's a house of sin."

"All right all ready," she whispered as she rubbed her lips together, "but you owe me, big time." Nita Sue's mischievous grin reached from ear to ear.

"Okay. Just keep quiet about it." My mind was already on Saturday's party at Roxy's house and what I was going to wear.

The new, improved Flicker Razor. It shaves you closer than ever because, this year, your legs are being looked at closer than ever.

Flicker advertisement

Saturday couldn't get here fast enough. I hadn't slept all week thinking about Roxy's party. Last night Nita Sue threatened me with death if I didn't quit rolling around in my bed. She said it was bad enough sharing a bedroom with a sister who had a poodle lamp on our nightstand, but she didn't know how much more she could take of my tossing and turning. My response was simple: Liquor Bottle Purses. That shut her up.

***

Saturday afternoon I worked on my new look—the one I'd dreamed about while tossing and turning all night. I'd searched Nita Sue's *Cosmopolitan* and decided I needed bigger boobies. At that point I would have taken anything since I was completely flat chested.

I stood in front of the bathroom mirror admiring my new chest. I never knew a box of Kleenex tissues could come in so handy. I bet I was at least a C cup or bigger. I twisted to the left and gazed at my profile between the mirrors on the medicine cabinet. One side looked a little bigger than the other so I shoved my hand inside my bra (it was Nita Sue's old one that I took from her drawer) and gently readjusted.

I retrieved the Slicker that BJ had loaned me for the occasion. These razors were guaranteed not to cut a woman's sensitive legs, at least that's what the TV commercial said. I hoped it was true because Momma had forbidden me to shave my legs until I was in junior high school. But I figured I could get away with it just this once and she would never know the difference.

Boobies in place, I slipped off my jeans and sat on the edge of our bathtub. I watched Nita Sue shave her legs last night so I knew exactly what to do. She started at the bottom of her right leg and stopped at the knee. I took the Slicker and slowly worked my way up one substantially hairy leg. It wasn't as easy as it looked. Something was missing. I realized my legs were totally dry. I needed shaving cream. I looked around the tub but it was nowhere in sight.

Daddy used shaving cream, right?

I hobbled over to the medicine cabinet and grabbed Daddy's can of Barbisol. It should do the trick. Thick, creamy lather oozed out of the red, white and blue can like ice cream being shoved through a barber's pole. The clean smell reminded me of my grandfather.

I lathered my right leg and took aim.

No more hair, at least not for now, anyway. I could grow the strawberry blonde fuzz back after Roxanne's party and Momma would never know.

One leg down, one to go.

Halfway up the left leg, the razor quit working. It was grabbing hair and yanking it out by the roots. I couldn't go to the party with one shaved leg and one hairy leg. What would everyone think?

Daddy shaved every day, right?

I grabbed his razor and went to work. Before I could stop myself, I dragged a six inch piece of skin (hair still attached) up to my knee. Blood poured off Daddy's razor. I grabbed the dangling piece of skin thinking that I could somehow, magically glue it on my bleeding shin; only to discover that I had sliced the ends of my fingers and they were bleeding all over the bath tub, too.

"Honey, are you in there?" Pause. "I need to use the bathroom." Another pause. "Carol Ann?" Momma knocked on the bathroom door, her voice filled with a sense of urgency.

"Yes, ma'am. I'll be right out. Just a minute." I grabbed the nearest towel and wiped the blood off my leg. It kept bleeding. She knocked again.

"Carol Ann, I really need to go, honey. Now."

"Yes, ma'am. Coming." I wrapped the towel around my waist thinking that I could hide the blood. I grabbed another one and wrapped it around my head like I had just washed my hair. That would explain the water around the tub.

I threw open the door as if I had just stepped from the shower.

"Sorry, Momma. Just getting ready for tonight's party," I lied as I walked down the hall thinking that I had actually gotten away with it.

Then I heard 'Carol Ann Lawson!'

Busted. I was definitely busted.

"Go to your room this minute, young lady, and wait for me."

Had she smelled Daddy's Barbisol?

I heard the toilet flush and the bathroom faucet turn on and then off. The towel rack clanked against the tile. The bathroom door squeaked as it opened.

I never noticed all the sounds that came from the bathroom...

Momma headed my way, her slippers clicking at full speed.

"What do you think you're doing, young lady?" she asked.

"Uh, sitting on my bed, waiting for you?" I drew out the waiting for you part so I could make a more pathetic face.

"Did you shave your legs, Carol Ann?"

"What makes you think I would do that?" I answered innocently.

"Well, the puddle of blood dripping onto my carpet for starters." I looked down and, sure enough, there was a big old puddle of blood dripping on her carpet alright. I was so busy listening to her in the bathroom that I forgot to keep the towel on my leg.

"Oh...that."

"My second clue was your father's razor and shaving cream. I believe you left some skin in it."

Oops. I did, didn't I?

"And for heaven's sakes, take off that ridiculous bra. Where did you get it anyway?" She leaned in for a closer look. "Is that Nita Sue's? Why are you wearing your sister's bra?"

"Well, you see, it's like this..." but before I could finish my sentence, she held her hand up like the school crossing guard.

"Stop right there. I don't *even* want to hear it. You get dressed this minute, Carol Ann Lawson. Then you march yourself straight to the kitchen and take two slips out of the grounding jar. Your father and I will have a long talk with you later this evening." Her face was red and she was doing her one–eyebrow–higher–than–the–other–thing.

"Two? That's not fair!" I yelled. "Nita Sue snuck out with Randy Mitchell and she only got one. I shave my legs and I get two?"

"Yes, young lady. One for shaving your legs when I distinctly remember telling you not to, and another one for lying about it. And don't even think about going to the new girl's party tonight."

I stomped toward the kitchen using the new curse word I learned from Nita Sue. Luckily, Momma was cleaning up my mess in the bathroom and couldn't hear it. I retrieved two slips of paper from the grounding jar. Whenever Momma or Daddy grounded us, our punishment was the chore we pulled out of the pig's feet jar.

I mumbled, "Scrub the baseboards? Dust the light fixtures? What is this, Cinderella's house?"

"Is there a problem, Carol Ann?" I heard from the bathroom.

"No, ma'am. No problem."

Stepmother.

*"Who can turn the world on with her smile?
Who can take a nothing day and suddenly
make it all seem worthwhile?"*
The Mary Tyler Moore Show theme song

Saturday evening came around just like every other Saturday night at the dull, boring, nothing–ever–happens–here–house–of–Lawson. Since I was grounded from Roxanne's party, I performed my usual Saturday night ritual. I showered like always, with one hairy leg and one carved–up leg, while Daddy spent the entire hour of the Lawrence Welk show combing through the tangles in my hair. He was the only one in our family who had enough patience to work through the knots that appeared every time I shampooed with Prell. I used Prell on Saturday nights because it gave my hair bounce and it smelled good. Besides, it was nice having Daddy all to myself.

Tangles out, I popped some Jiffy Pop popcorn on our electric stove. Daddy and I shared a bowl of Jiffy Pop every Saturday night while we watched our favorite shows: The Bob Newhart Show, The Carol Burnett Show and the Mary Tyler Moore Show. The Mary Tyler Moore Show was the highlight of my week. Oh how I longed to be like Mary Richards! I sat on the couch waiting for it to begin.

"Carol Ann, remember to set out your Bible and your quarterly tonight. I don't want to be rushed in the morning," Momma yelled from the kitchen.

"10–4, backdoor," I answered. She shook her head and continued rolling Nita Sue's thick, curly hair on orange juice cans.

"Can Hershey have popcorn, Daddy?"

"I suppose one or two won't hurt anything." Hershey, our chocolate Labrador, had been lying at Daddy's feet until she heard the Jiffy Pop container scraping across the burner. She was slobbering all over the floor just waiting for a nibble.

"Sit," I commanded. She sat and I lofted a piece of popcorn in the air. She caught it every time. Her tail wagged ninety–to–nothing.

"Daddy, why does Bob Newhart live in an apartment? I thought psychiatrists were rich," I asked before I crammed another handful of popcorn in my mouth.

"Well, he's a psychologist not a psychiatrist. I think in big cities like Chicago, most folks live in apartment buildings. It's so crowded that they build up instead of out like us. They don't have as much land as we do here. And, remember, it's just a television show." He smiled. "Get ready, your favorite show is about to begin."

Finally, *The Mary Tyler Moore Show.*

Mary Richards was about to toss her blue and black hat into the air in downtown Minneapolis. Chicago and Minneapolis. One day I would live up north where it snowed, and I would wear genuine wool mufflers, not the cotton kind that Momma crammed in our Christmas stockings every year. So what if I had to live among Yankees? I mean, how bad could they be? Roxanne was a Yankee and she was fast becoming one of my best friends. I bet Yankees were every bit as nice as us, no matter what Aunt Betty said.

"Who can turn the world on with her smile?" I sang along as Mary Richards drove her mustang through Minneapolis. I knew every, single word of the theme song. *"Who can take a nothing day, and suddenly make it all seem worthwhile. Well it's..."*

"Carol Ann?" Momma interrupted, "did you lay out your clothes like I asked? Your Bible? You know you can't watch Mary Tyler Moore until everything is ready for tomorrow."

"Yes, ma'am. I'm doing it right now." I jumped off the couch, performed my Saturday night duties and was back in time to hear Ted say, 'Morning, Mary.'"

Daddy and I laughed as Murray Slaughter made fun of Ted Baxter. Murray was Daddy's favorite character—probably because they were both bald. Daddy's motto was no plugs, drugs or rugs as he was especially disgusted by toupees. He would never tell anyone besides Momma, but we knew he didn't approve of Brother EdEarl's toupee. Nita Sue overheard Momma and Daddy laughing about his toupee one night. When I quizzed Nita Sue about how she overheard these things, she produced a stethoscope from her sock drawer.

"Mo–ther!" Nita Sue hollered, "Please don't make me wear that dress tomorrow. It's so…yesterday."

"Well, it may be *yesterday* but it's not going to fit much longer, and I want to get my money's worth out of it."

"But Mo–ther, I…"

"Nita Sue, mind you mother," said Daddy.

"Yes, sir." Looking defeated, Nita Sue huffed and puffed her way right into our bedroom, where she undoubtedly unleashed a mouthful of her newly learned curse words.

The telephone rang. "It's for you, Carol Ann." Momma put the receiver on the table and continued folding a load of laundry at the kitchen table. Baptists didn't do laundry on the Sabbath.

"Hello?"

"C.A.? Roxy here. What are you guys doing?" My eyes lit up.

"Oh, hi there! We're watching TV. What are you guys doing?"

Momma stopped mid–air with her towel folding and stared at me while I listened to Roxy's response. "Oh really?" I said. "How's the party? Sorry I couldn't come."

"The party is simply c-o-o-l. We just finished round two of Spin the Bottle. All the guys are asking about you." I could picture it: incense, black lamps and zodiac posters.

"Oh, really?" I had to be careful. Momma didn't know that boys were invited, and I sure didn't want her finding out. I'd be power washing the entire house if I wasn't careful.

"You asked me to call, remember?" If I didn't know better I'd think Cher Bono was on the other end of my party line.

"Oh. Uh, yes. I did, didn't I?" Why did I ask her to call me? I couldn't remember. Momma was eyeing Daddy and Daddy was eyeing me. I had to come up with something fast. "Would you guys like to come with us to church and Sunday School tomorrow?"

"No," she replied flatly, "we're atheists."

"You're what?"

"Atheists. We don't believe in God," Roxy answered. I nearly dropped our new harvest gold telephone. How could anyone not believe in God? I never heard of such a thing. If Momma and

Daddy caught wind of this, I'd be banned from her parties forever. Heck, I'd be banned from her.

"Okay, I see. I understand. Uh… I guess I'll be seeing you guys on Monday. Thanks again for calling." I hung up the phone and made a beeline toward the bedroom.

"Just a minute, Carol Ann," Daddy said. "Who was that on the phone?"

"It was my new friend from school."

"Does this new friend have a name?" he asked.

"Roxanne. Roxanne Wojowitz from Boston, Massachusetts *and* California."

Momma chimed in, "Is this girl the one you were looking for after school the other day? The same one who was having the party tonight?"

"Yes, ma'am." I was trying to go to bed in order to avoid the Lawson court of law even if it meant missing Ted Baxter botch another newscast. I was halfway down the hall when Momma piped up.

"Just a minute, young lady. Why are you in such a hurry to go to bed all of a sudden?" Judge Momma asked. Didn't she have some more laundry somewhere?

"Oh I'm not in a hurry, does it look like I'm in a hurry, because I'm definitely not in a hurry, no ma'am, not in a hurry at all." Dadgummit, I had stuck my foot clear down my throat.

"Sit down, Carol Ann," Daddy said.

I sat down.

"This new friend of yours, Roxanne is it?" He shifted his weight in his Lazy Boy as Momma took a seat on the couch. She held the same yellow towel in her hands.

"Yes, sir. Her name is Roxy. Roxanne Wojowitz from Boston, Massachusetts."

Momma asked, "Was her party still going on? At 9:30 on a Saturday night?" This was not turning out at all like it should. As far as Mr. and Mrs. Dan Lawson were concerned, all activities should cease by 9:30 p.m. on Saturday evening so everyone could get the appropriate rest required for worship on Sunday morning.

"Uh, well, I'm not exactly sure if her official party was still going on, but I know she was still awake." This wasn't the response they wanted to hear.

"What did Roxanne say when you invited her to church?" Daddy asked.

"She said she couldn't come. Can I please go to bed now?" I faked a yawn. "I'm really tired."

"Yes, you can go to bed." Daddy stood up and stretched his arms over his head. I had him yawning, too. "Good night, Carol Ann." He leaned over and kissed my head.

"Good night, Daddy."

Momma chimed in, "You go ahead, Carol Ann. I'll be there in a minute."

Great. This was just great. Now, I'd have to think of something to distract her from asking questions about my new I–don't–believe–in–God–friend.

***

"Good night, honey."

"Good night, Momma," I said in a rather quiet voice.

"Is something bothering you?"

"Kind of," I replied.

"Do you want to talk about it?"

I looked over at Nita Sue's bed. It was empty. I didn't want her to hear what I was about to tell Momma. "I do, but I'm afraid it'll make you mad. Do you promise not to get mad if I tell you something?"

"I promise." Momma hesitated a bit as she set the laundry basket on Nita Sue's twin bed, then sat on the edge of mine. Now was the time to divert her attention away from Roxy and on something else.

"It's like this. I really want to buy an album with the money I made at Aunt Betty's. But, if I tithe, I won't have enough."

Before the word "enough" was out of my mouth she said, "Don't tithe, then." She never even slowed down.

"Ma'am?"

"Don't tithe then. God doesn't *need* your money, Carol Ann. He wants to bless you when you tithe, but He certainly doesn't *need* it. Go ahead and buy your record. He can accomplish His plan without your ten percent."

She stood and rearranged the towels in the basket. I wanted to respond, but I couldn't. Momma just told me not to give ten percent of my earnings to God and she even suggested that He didn't need it.

I lay there listening to her hoof it across the hall and into the bathroom. Could I really not tithe? Was it optional? I was under the impression that miraculous things happened to those who tithed. Everything from finding twenty dollar bills stuck in last year's coat pocket to paying off the church's bills on time and all because we Baptists believed in tithing. Well, it sounded like Hazel Jean McClanahan Lawson just gave me the go–ahead on the Fifth Dimension's latest album.

**Tithe: v. (tīth) to pay or give a tenth part of—
especially for the support of the church**

The following morning we awakened early, as usual, we dressed, and were ready to make the two block hike to God's house. I was wearing the brand new waffle stomper shoes that Momma had ordered from the Sears and Roebuck catalog. I loved walking through the dirt and looking back to see the shoe's imprint. No one else in my Sunday School class owned a pair of waffle stompers; I was the only one.

The best part of my new outfit, however, was my cape. Our seamstress, Mrs. Frazier, had sewed it to look exactly like the sketch on front of the Simplicity pattern, navy blue with red trim. I'd begged for the psychedelic fabric on the "Just Arrived" table at Murphy's but Momma would have no part of it. "Quality clothing in navy, black or white" was her response to my plea.

I felt a little like Barnabas Collins as the wind blew the cape over my shoulder. It reminded me of the summer that Nita Sue and I watched *Dark Shadows* in the afternoons when we weren't slaving for Aunt Betty. That is, until Brother Paul preached a sermon on vampires and vampire movies. That ended our venture into all things vampire related. Later that summer, he preached on the immorality of soap operas which ended our summertime viewing pleasure of the newest soap opera, *All My Children*. We were sick about it, too, since Erica Kane was the topic of most teenage conversations in the summer of 1971. We were forced to watch at friends' houses whenever we could.

"Carol Ann, don't dillydally after Sunday School. Come straight to the sanctuary, okay?" instructed Momma.

"Yes, ma'am."

"You sure look nice today, honey."

"Thank you."

With my red leather Bible in one hand and my purse in the other, I knew I would be the talk of Mrs. Morris's Sunday School class today. When we arrived, four deacons were standing in the parking lot greeting church members. I think their real purpose for hanging out in the parking lot was to nab any visitors who might sneak through the door without registering. Baptists were famous for their record keeping. Not only did we keep a list of every person who had ever visited First Baptist, but we invaded their homes on Wednesday nights, whether they wanted company or not, and called it visitation.

The usual group of smokers were huddled by the side door of the church—all men, of course. One time, the WMU president told Momma that it was downright sinful the way those men stood outside and smoked after everyone else went to their Sunday School rooms. They should be ashamed, she had said, smoking on God's property. What would the unsaved think if they drove by and witnessed that?

Climbing the brown speckled linoleum stairs to the second floor, I was disappointed that there wasn't any dirt or sand for my waffle stompers. As I approached Mrs. Morris's class, I tossed my cape over my right shoulder with panache. I wasn't sure what panache was but I had read it in a copy of Nita Sue's *Cosmopolitan* and vowed to add it to my vocabulary list. After all, news anchors needed a diverse vocabulary.

"Good morning, Carol Ann. How are you today?" Mrs. Morris asked.

"Fine, thank you." I replied.

"My, my, what a darling outfit. Shannon Grubbs is wearing one just like it, only hers is cornflower blue instead of navy."

What? Cornflower blue? Like the cornflower blue in the 64 box of Crayola Crayons? It couldn't be. Momma paid good money for me to have this new outfit—complete with Barnabas Collins cape—and Shannon Grubbs shows up wearing one in cornflower blue?

"Hi, Carol Ann," Shannon said. "We're twinsies, see?" She twirled around on one foot like a pixie doll as her cornflower blue cape spun out of control. "I saw you looking at this pattern at Murphy's and Mother thought it would be cute if we had the same outfit. Do you like the color?"

Of course I liked the color. It made my cape look like I worked for the United States Post Office. "Yours is pretty, Shannon. Real pretty."

A crowd formed to watch Shannon twirl her cape while I dug around my Bible for my envelope. Where was it? I knew I put it in my Bible. Turning the gold tipped pages toward the floor, I gave it a good shake and out it plopped.

"Excellent!" Mrs. Morris began, "You remembered your envelope. You know, Carol Ann, you are the only one of my girls who can check each box on her envelope every week. I just bet you get the 100% pin this year! Let's see, now." She took my envelope and compared it with the boxes on her mimeographed roll. "Lesson studied? Check. Bible brought? Check. Tithe? Carol Ann, you didn't check tithe box. Did you forget your money today?"

Oh boy. There it was in black and white—the unchecked tithe box. What should I do? I had received the 100% pin for the last four years and I wanted to make it five. Momma said God didn't need my money and I had believed her, or did I? I'd breezed through that conversation, all right, but now I felt guilty.

"Carol Ann? Did you forget to put the money in?" Her blue hair looked purple today.

"Uh, yes, ma'am. I forgot, that's right, I simply forgot," I lied between my teeth. She held my envelope up to the fluorescent light. At least ten flies had met their death inside the plastic fixture.

"I don't see anything in it. Could it have fallen out on your way to Sunday School?"

Oh no. How was I going to explain that I had not only forgotten to check the tithe box, but that I had forgotten to put the money in the envelope, too? "Uh, well, you see, I, uh, I had it and I laid it down on the bar to fill out my envelope, and I guess I forgot to put it in. Maybe Mother or Daddy picked it up so that I can put it in the offering plate in big church." I was going to hell for sure.

"Don't use the word *bar*, honey, always say *counter*," she whispered, "it sounds much nicer."

"Yes, ma'am," I replied. Sweat broke out on my forehead and under my arms. My cape stuck to me like a fly on a No Pest Fly Strip.

All the sixth and seventh grade girls were busy examining Shannon's silver clasp on her cornflower blue cape. It made a clicking noise when it opened and closed.

"Does yours have a clasp, too?" Marybeth Mobley inquired. Suddenly, all the attention was focused on me.

"No, mine has a big snap on the inside. See?" I unsnapped the cape with panache. As soon as I did, it hit the floor and everyone's hands hit their noses. What was that smell?

"Ew, gross! Have you ever heard of deodorant?" asked Marybeth.

Body Odor: n. an unpleasant odor from a perspiring or unclean person

My eyes stung from holding back the tears. I wanted to crawl under a rock and disappear. I had never been so embarrassed in my life. If word got around that I had b.o. I would never live it down. Only those girls from the other side of the railroad tracks had body odor. I told Momma that I needed to shave my legs and use deodorant but, no, I wasn't old enough. Well, how old does a girl have to be before she can use Secret, 79?

"Praise God from whom all blessing flow.
Praise Him all creatures here below..."

The choir sang the Doxology. I stood beside Daddy contemplating how I could manage to shave my other leg and use deodorant without Momma noticing.

"Praise Him above ye heavenly host."

I could wear jeans the rest my life so she couldn't see my legs. Or I could just shave them and say "tough" when she noticed.

"Praise Father, Son and Holy Ghost. Amen."

I could blackmail Nita Sue into letting me use her Secret since I helped her sneak back into the house that night. Daddy tapped my Bible. It was his polite way of telling me to open up and pay attention. Today's sermon title: Ten Percent.

"...so what is God saying here?" Brother Paul was in the pulpit pounding the podium. Today's sermon and invitation would be shorter than usual because Roger Staubach was being interviewed before the noon kick–off on channel six. "God clearly tells us to bring one–tenth of our goods to the storehouse. In our case the storehouse is the local church." Pause. "I believe in the local church, folks. And not just because I am the pastor here. And I believe God is clearly telling His followers to give ten percent of what is His in the first place. Have you ever thought about how little ten percent is? Ten percent, folks. If you are practicing biblical tithing, then you get to keep ninety percent of your income!"

He turned toward the choir loft. "That's right, ninety percent of what is God's in the first place is what He allows you to keep for yourself!" Brother Paul was on a roll today, sweating something fierce. He kept wiping his forehead with his handkerchief. Maybe he had hot flashes, too.

Brother Paul Mitchell was one of the finest preachers I had ever known, not that I knew that many, being eleven and all, but he had a real sweet way about him. He didn't seem too concerned about his clothes or what kind of pickup he drove. He stood up when ladies entered the room—even girls my age. He was the first to arrive and the last to leave the church every Sunday morning. He called each lamb in his flock by his first name. He knew the names of all the children and most of their pets. When Scooter died last year Brother Paul sent me a sympathy card. It was a fancy one, too, with a glitter–covered dove and a poem inside. As far as I was concerned, he was the perfect preacher.

My thoughts were interrupted as he embarked on his weekly ritual. It began with a furrowed brow (a sign of intense thought) followed by pursing of the lips (he was choosing his words carefully) and, finally, his pacing back and forth across the platform. He had a habit of tugging at his coat pockets as if they might sneak off during his sermon. Today was no different. After a quick pocket check, he returned his hands to their regular position—clasped—with his right hand rubbing his left thumb.

"Now, understand something here folks. When it comes to money I don't know who gives what in our church and I don't want to know. But I asked Mrs. Higginbotham for some numbers this past week." He must have hit a nerve because Mrs. Rutledge was doing her nervous cough thing.

"And I must say that I am very concerned about our congregation. Our records indicate that the average church member at Lake View's First Baptist Church only earned two thousand, five hundred dollars last year." Men were adjusting their ties and shrugging their shoulders. Mr. Burch's collar must have been extra tight because he was using two hands today.

"You heard me right. If our records are accurate, and you are tithing, most of you are in the poor house."

I felt something in my lap and looked down to see what it was. Nita Sue had eased the bulletin under my hand. I opened it only to find a drawing of a girl in a cape with outstretched arms standing over a bunch of dead bodies.

The caption read:

GIRL WITH B.O. KILLS ENTIRE SUNDAY SCHOOL CLASS. MORE AT TEN

The tears returned. Only now they were tears of anger and revenge coated with body odor.

"Just listen to this, folks." Brother Paul was still harping on our finances. "Last year alone, eighty percent of our congregation gave twenty percent of the money." You could have heard an atom split. "Our children set a better example of tithing than our adults."

Go Brother Paul! It's about time we got credit for something around here.

"One Sunday School class had four children who gave faithfully last year. Those four children gave each week and one of those precious children was able to check 100% on her envelope every week for a year."

Uh oh. Was he talking about me? I thought he just said he didn't know *who* gave *what*.

"Listen to me now, I know what you're thinking. You're thinking, 'sure a child can give each week because he doesn't earn that much money and doesn't have my mortgage' and you are correct. Children don't have the same responsibilities. But when our children are willing to give the Lord the very money they use to shop at the five and dime, shouldn't we do the same? Shouldn't we set the example here, folks?"

My legs went numb. It was as if I had a red neon sign on my forehead flashing:

LIAR...PHONY...KEEPER OF GOD'S 10%

My neck burned. Sweat poured down my back. I fanned myself with Nita Sue's bulletin. Body odor filled the surrounding pews.

"Remember the words of our Lord," Brother Paul continued. "Bring the whole tithe into the storehouse."

I would remember them, alright, they would be the very words paving my road of good intentions. All I wanted to do was go home, crawl in my bed and never show my face, or armpits, again.

Then I remembered that the Cowboys were playing the Redskins today and I'd have to get up if I wanted to watch the game. Maybe I could eavesdrop on our party line and finally hear some juicy gossip. Who was I kidding? I'd never do any of those things. Momma's WMU group had funeral duty tomorrow night and I knew I'd be sitting in front of the TV watching the game while I peeled two bags of potatoes for potato salad.

I didn't understand why the WMU ladies always took potato salad to funeral meals. Did it calm the nerves or help in the grieving process? Why couldn't Momma take a green salad? And, more importantly, why was it always my job to peel the potatoes? This had turned out to be a rotten weekend—all my plans down the drain and fragranced with body odor.

Brother EdEarl watched Brother Paul out of the corner of his eye for the signal during the invitation singing. The signal was probably taught at the Fort Worth Seminary since every Baptist preacher seemed to use it. I was inwardly thrilled for the signal, today, because I was getting hungry and not for potato salad. Mrs. Morris didn't bring snacks because it was sprinkling and she didn't want to get her hair wet making two trips from her car to our Sunday School room.

Brother Paul wound things up by making a few announcements. Heads bowed, eyes closed, and each of us blessed for the upcoming week, we were free to make the two block walk home from church, rain or shine. Last Sunday, Brother Paul was so fired up that we sang *Just As I Am* (as always), but then he asked us to bow our heads and pray while Mrs. Herron played four stanzas. I thought we'd never get out of there. On the walk home Nita Sue told me that no one ever got saved past noon. I wasn't sure if that was true or not since Brother Paul often preached past noon but only if the Cowboys weren't on TV.

Momma, Daddy and Nita Sue headed for home. I lagged behind so my b.o. wouldn't knock them out. I bet Roxy used deodorant, and tampons, too, for that matter, although I still wasn't sure what they were for. Truth be told, I didn't know that much about a lot of things. But I hoped that would change. Sooner rather than later…

Exaggerate: v. (ig–za–jə–rāt) To enlarge beyond bounds or truth

Someone was honking their horn outside our house—probably Mrs. Peterson. "You girls hurry up with those dishes," Momma said, slipping on her black high heels. "Mrs. Peterson and I are going to the funeral home to sit with the Hughes family for a few hours. When I get home, I better find a clean kitchen.

"How much homework do you have tonight, Nita Sue?" Momma was barking orders as she gathered the Kleenex boxes. One couldn't be too prepared for funeral watch. "Oh, fiddle…where's my cardigan? I just had it."

"It's right there, Mo–ther." Nita Sue had a way of turning Momma's name inside out.

"Thank you, honey. I'll see you girls when I get home. If you need something, call the funeral home. It's under Shores in the white pages. I'll probably make it home before your daddy since he has a deacon's meeting tonight." With a *quality* black cardigan draped across her shoulders, she was halfway out the door when she turned and said, "No television until you finish the dishes and homework." She blew a kiss as she closed the door.

"Well, that's just great," I said with disgust. "Why can't these dead people have their visitations during the day while we're at school? Why do they always have them at night? I want to watch *Truth or Consequences* and there's no way we'll finish these stupid dishes before it comes on."

"You can do the dishes, now, if you want to, but I'm watching TV. She won't know when we did them. We can wash them later. Come on, we've got the house to ourselves." Nita Sue said this as she shoved another piece of Super Bubble in her mouth and stretched out on the couch.

It made perfect sense to me. Momma wouldn't know if we washed the dishes now or after the show. So I, too, plopped down in Daddy's chair and reached for the orange plastic bucket filled with Halloween candy. Momma believed in bargain shopping. We were eating last year's candy.

Satisfied with the black, wrapped peanut butter delight, I anxiously awaited Mr. Bob Barker. He entered our living room every night at the same time. My favorite part of the show was when he reunited a wife with her soldier husband. Most of the soldiers were stationed in Vietnam. I knew this because I had written my six weeks report about Vietnam in my civics class.

We settled in for another half hour with Bob. When the last consequence was complete, I stood up and stretched my arms above my head. "Come on," I said, "let's get this over with."

"Hey, dirt–for–brains, the Monday night movie is about to start. If we wash a few during each commercial, we'll be finished by the time she gets home. She said she'd be gone a couple of hours, remember?" Nita Sue smiled her up–to–no–good smile.

"I don't know, Nita Sue. I don't want her mad at me."

"Okay, Miss Goody Two Shoes, you can start but I'm watching the movie."

I figured a few more minutes couldn't hurt. If we hurried during the breaks, we could easily finish before Momma returned home from funeral duty.

The movie music began, and I unwrapped another peanut butter delight (with an orange wrapper this time). Tonight's movie was about a private detective whose wife had been killed by mistake. He had exactly two hours and several commercial breaks to catch her killers. The first commercial appeared.

"Okay, let's get started," I said.

"Don't get your panties in a wad. Those dishes aren't going anywhere." Nita Sue repositioned her legs on the back of the couch. She was right. It wasn't as if they could multiply in the sink or anything. Ten peanut butter delights and four commercial breaks later, we headed for the kitchen. Momma had been gone for an hour and a half and we had a sink full of dishes calling our names.

Nita Sue started washing the glasses as I scraped the leftover food into the trash can. I'd just wiped the table when I heard something.

"Did you hear that?" I asked Nita Sue.

"Hear what?"

"THAT!" I screamed. A car pulled into our driveway, its headlights flashed across the TV screen. "Momma's home and we haven't even washed the plates yet!" I was about to panic. We stared at the three dinner plates stacked next to the soapy water. There wasn't enough time to get them washed, dried and put away before she got inside the house.

"Here. Start licking!" Nita Sue shoved a plate at me.

"WHAT?" I screamed. Her tongue was licking the middle, side and edge of the plate.

"Hurry up!" Plate in hands, I frantically licked the remains of pork chops, mashed potatoes and fried okra. It wasn't as good the second time around. Nita Sue shoved her plate in the cupboard with the others and began licking plate number three. I inspected mine and stacked it on top of the first one.

"The glasses," she stated matter–of–factly. I glanced at three glasses turned upside down in the drying rack. Every pot, pan and glass—anything that was used for supper—had to be put away before we could watch TV. I placed the glasses in the china cabinet and hurried back for more. Nita Sue finished licking and practically threw plate number three in the cupboard as I tossed silverware in the drawer. I could hear Momma thanking Mrs. Peterson for the ride. Perhaps they would have a word of prayer before she came inside.

"THE TELEVISION!" I screamed. I whirled around the corner looking for the clicker. It was nowhere in sight, of course, so I opened the panel and turned it off. I ran back to the kitchen, sliding on the freshly–waxed linoleum, only to see Nita Sue drying the counter with a tea towel. Within seconds Momma walked through the living room. I heard her purse drop on the couch.

Click, click, click. Those high heels were louder than I remembered.

With her head summoning me to the icebox, Nita Sue opened the door and bent down as if she were looking for something to eat.

"Well, hello there. What are you two doing up? I thought you'd be in bed by now," Momma said as she removed her high heels.

"We thought we might have some cake and milk before we went to bed. Can I get you a piece, Mother?" Nita Sue inquired with an innocence that fooled even me; almost.

"That sounds nice." Momma opened the cupboard and reached for a plate. Holy Moly Batman! Momma's hand gripped the edge of plate number three. Nita Sue slammed the icebox door and announced with a fake yawn, "I changed my mind. I'm ready for bed after all; it's been a long night. Doing all that homework made me sleepy. Goodnight, Mother."

Momma's hand retreated and closed the cupboard. "Good night, sweetie. Thank you for doing such a good job on the kitchen. It was a long night for me, too."

Nita Sue was halfway to the bedroom when Momma looked at me and asked, "What is it, Carol Ann? You look like the cat that ate the canary."

More like the pork chop. "Oh, nothing. I'm just tired. I had a lot of homework, too."

"Goodnight, honey. Don't forget to say your prayers," she reminded.

"Don't worry, I will. Goodnight, Momma."

"I have a lot of confessing to do tonight," I whispered to myself.

My thoughts drifted away from the dinner dishes as I got ready for bed. Not knowing about tampons had been a humiliating experience for me. Girls on the playground had started talking about things I knew nothing about and when I asked Momma she told me not to concern myself with those things that someday, soon, we would have a long talk about the birds and the bees when the time was right.

Suddenly, it wasn't that much fun to outrun Lamar Webb, or Greg and Al and the other boys I'd played football with since the first grade. Even the well house had lost its appeal.

I longed for excitement. For adventure. For anything that would take my mind off the boredom that stuck to our house like flies in molasses. But everything I longed for was off limits. Momma and Daddy acted like we still lived in the Stone Age or something. People all over the world were talking about women's rights and the ERA and we were still talking about PTA candy sales.

Roxanne Wojowitz had arrived and, because of her, life looked different. She had the look that we longed for while watching *Laugh–In*. She had the clothes, make–up, boots, everything. And she could speak French! How many other girls in Lake View, Texas could order a hot dog and Coke in French?

Unhappy with my current state of mind, I crawled in bed and turned on my poodle lamp. Nancy Drew would have to help me get to sleep tonight.

"Turn it off! I'm trying to sleep," Nita Sue said in a groggy voice.

"Nita Sue, do you feel bad about tonight?"

"Tonight?" She sat up in bed looking like an ad for a Florida orange juice commercial.

"You know, lying to Momma about the dishes and everything."

"You woke me up to ask me if I feel bad about lying? First of all, we didn't really lie about the dishes. We washed ninety–seven percent of them. It was the three percent that we didn't get around to that we fibbed about and I plan on washing them at breakfast before Mother sees them. So, no, I don't feel bad about it at all. Now would you please put that poodle to sleep? Get it? Put your poodle to sleep?" She slapped her covers a few times and lay back down.

"I get it all right. And it's not very funny," I said as I reached over and turned out the light. I opened the nightstand and retrieved my flashlight. Nancy Drew better find that mysterious clock and fast.

"All the leaves are brown and the sky is grey, I've been for a walk on a winter's day. I'd be safe and warm if I was in L.A., California dreamin' on such a winter's day.
The Mamas & The Papas

"Help me! The chickens are coming! Someone…please help me!" I screamed. Bits of pink fur fluttered through the air as I clung to a tree branch. I was holding on for dear life with one arm while slinging Grandma's Christmas china with the other. My hot pink, furry, bacon–covered vest must have been what attracted the rabid chickens that were chasing me. Thousands of them filled the streets of downtown Lake View. I plucked dinner plates, bread plates, and salad plates from the mimosa tree as fast as I could and slung them at a giant rooster. Just as I ran out of Christmas china, I sat straight up in my bed.

The sheets were wrapped around my legs and sweat poured down my sides. Luckily, for all humans within a mile radius, I snuck Nita Sue's can of Secret and sprayed my armpits. I knew I was in my bedroom when I saw orange juice cans on the floor. I'd had some pretty weird dreams before but none like this one.

It must have been the herbal tea we drank at Roxy's house. Momma let me go to the Wojowitz's house after school yesterday since parties were out of the question for now. I had found a recipe for making papier–mâché and thought that Roxy, BJ and I could make piñatas, but BJ had a cold so Dr. Dodge made her stay home in bed.

The piñatas were fun to make. I made an elephant like a good Republican and Roxy made something I'd never seen before. She said it symbolized world peace. When we finished our piñatas and set them outside to dry, Roxy produced a Ouija Board.

"I don't know about this, Roxy. I'm not allowed to mess around with stuff like this."

She cracked her knuckles and let out a huge sigh. "Like what?"

I timidly answered, "You know, Ouija Boards and Magic Eight Balls and Terror cars. Evil stuff."

She laughed. "You mean Tarot Cards? And who exactly told you that these things were evil, mon ami?"

"Momma for starters. She says these things open the way for evil spirits to come around and that we shouldn't mess with them. I could be grounded for the rest of my life if she found out. We can do something else, can't we?"

Roxanne Wojowitz stared a hole through my brown and purple poncho and said, "When you are at *my* house we do what *I* want to do. When we're at *your* house, we do what *you* want to do. Ça va?"

I wasn't sure how Yankees viewed hospitality rules but we Southerners let guests do what *they* wanted to do, not the other way around.

"Well, okay then."

"Now," she said, "put your fingers here." She pointed to a teardrop shaped object. "Now, as I call on the spirits, he or she will communicate with us by moving this from letter to letter, spelling out the message to us mortals."

I started giggling. "You're joking, right?"

"I never joke about such matters," Roxy answered. "Who would you like to communicate with?"

I racked my brain trying to think of someone who might want to communicate with a couple of girls from Lake View, Texas. "How about Greg Brady? I'd really like to talk to him."

Roxanne pulled her hands away and glared at me. "Greg Brady is a–l–i–v–e. Alive."

"Yeah, I know. That's why I want to talk to him."

"We can only communicate with spirits. Dead people. Isn't there some dead person you'd like to talk to?"

"Well, there's my grandmother. But, she's probably too busy talking to Ruth and Naomi and all those other Old Testament women. She probably doesn't have time to commune with us living folks." I thought a bit longer. "I know! How about James Bowie or Sam Houston? They're deader than doornails. I bet they'd talk to us."

So, we beckoned the spirit of James Bowie. Of course, nothing happened. I was relieved, too. Momma would have plucked my eyeballs out and fed them to the crows if she knew that I'd been in the same room with a Ouija Board. Ouija Boards were strictly forbidden at our house.

Roxy didn't even know who James and Sam were. I had to explain that these were famous Texas heroes. She wanted to know if they were Democrats because Democrats were the only real heroes in her opinion. I told her not to say that too loudly around town since most of the upstanding citizens of our community were Republicans. She said something in French and we returned to our herbal tea and cinnamon toothpicks.

Her mom and Mr. Sabatini had spent the better part of the day in their beanbag chairs dozing on and off. The only time I saw her mom move was to braid Mr. Sabitini's hair. Incense filled the house with a steady stream of purple smoke. It spiraled upward and weaved in and out of the colorful beads that separated the kitchen from the den. When they weren't chanting, they listened to hippie music. Later that day, Mr. Sabatini played a musical instrument that looked a lot like a guitar but was twice as long. I'd never seen one in Lake View and sure didn't want to look stupid by asking what it was.

Roxy taught me a few French words and I taught her a bit of Texas history. All in all, it had been a good end to a crummy week, and now I was sweating in my bed.

I untangled my legs and pulled the covers to my chin. Saturday was the only day we were allowed to sleep in late but, for some reason, I could smell bacon frying in the kitchen. I tried hiding my head beneath my pillow to block the smell of sizzling, crispy bacon but my nose won. And, thanks to Secret, I could smell something other than body odor.

I slid from my warm bed and walked—half asleep—to the kitchen. It wasn't until I was in the middle of the kitchen that I noticed it wasn't even daylight.

"What time is it?" I asked Momma trying to adjust to the light over the stove.

"It's 5:30, honey," she answered.

"Why are you up this early on Saturday?" I asked. Had she lost her mind? This was her one day to sleep in, too.

"Aunt Betty just called," she said while she muffled a yawn. "Mrs. Atkinson died last night and she's going to need us to help her at the shop today." Another yawn. I noticed she had turned over the same piece of bacon about four times.

"Who is us?" Same piece of bacon five times now.

"The three of us. Dan has to work at the store today while Ed's gone." Her eyes twitched up and watered as she yawned.

"So, what time do we have to be there? The shop doesn't open until 10:00 on Saturday. Right?" I asked the question even though I knew the answer.

"Aunt Betty wants us there by 7:00 sharp. She ordered a fresh shipment of flowers for this funeral, and she needs us to be there early to prep all the flowers."

Great. Another Saturday ruined because of some rich, haughty–taughty–old–blue–haired–woman–sucking–in–her–last–breath on my favorite day of the week.

"Momma, do I have to go? Please don't make me go. Roxanne wanted me to come over and paint our piñatas. Please, please, pleeease?"

"Carol Ann, if it were up to me you could sleep until noon. But you know your Aunt Betty needs our help with the big funerals. And it sounds like this will be a big one. Maybe you can finish up early and head over to Roxanne's house later in the day." She didn't sound very confident. "Now go wake Nita Sue and you two get dressed and ready to go. I'll have the grits ready quick as a wink." Her half–hearted smile didn't fool me. Nothing should be quick as a wink this time of the day, especially on Saturday.

Eyes half open, I walked to our bedroom to do the impossible; wake Nita Sue.

"Nita Sue, get up." I rocked her shoulder back and forth. "Come on, get up. We have to dead 'em today. Aunt Betty needs us at the shop."

Nita Sue's arm flung in the direction of the alarm clock. Her hand was bouncing off everything on the nightstand including my poodle lamp.

"What time is it? I can't see the clock."

"It's 5:45. Now get up, Momma's frying bacon." I said that last part with authority as if I, too, had been frying bacon.

"Who the hell gets up at 5:45 on Saturdays?" she yelled at me.

Nita Sue had started cursing last year. Her vocabulary was limited to "Who the hell?" "What the hell?" "When in the hell?" and "Where the hell?" This happened only in the privacy of our bedroom. She cursed the most when she couldn't find her makeup and would call each cosmetic item by name. "Where the hell is my powder?" she'd yell. Or "Who the hell has my lip gloss?" And my personal favorite: "Why in the hell do I _____?" She was quite convincing. If I didn't know her better, I would think she had been cursing for a lifetime.

"Who the hell died?" she asked.

"Mrs. Atkinson," I answered.

"Do we know her?"

"No, but she must be an Episcopalian because Aunt Betty ordered a truckload of flowers last night when she heard."

"She's dead," Nita mumbled, "she's not going to care when the hell we get up." My thoughts exactly.

Slave labor: n. forced labor performed under duress by slaves

I stood at the prep table beating spider mum stems with a rubber mallet when Aunt Betty breezed by talking to herself. She was all worked up because the orders weren't coming in quite as fast as she had anticipated. I guess Mrs. Atkinson wasn't the most popular Episcopalian after all. So far, I counted four standing sprays, three potted plants, two arrangements, and one sash spray.

I didn't understand the need for sash sprays. I mean, if you were sitting at someone's funeral wouldn't you know whether or not that person was your brother, aunt, uncle, or grandparent without some big ribbon across the front spelling the relation out in glitter? Still, this was a tradition in Lake View, in fact, most of the South, and it meant big funeral flower business. Aunt Betty was known across three counties for her sash sprays.

"Aunt Betty, can I take a break? My hands are tired," I asked with my head tilted to one side. This seemed to evoke sympathy from adults with no children, but it never worked on mothers or teachers because they'd seen it too many times.

"Why, sure thang. Get a Coke out of the Coke box and sit out on the back step for a minute. The sun'll do you some good." She patted my hand as she answered.

I slid the Coke bottle to the end of the row and pulled. Like magic, it popped right up. I stuck the cap in the opener and listened to it drop to the bottom with the other bottle caps. Aunt Betty was right. A Coke and some sunshine were all I needed to endure the rest of my Saturday. As far as I was concerned, free Cokes and spending money were the only benefits of working at Betty's Bloomers.

The east Texas sun felt warm on my face. I closed my eyes and listened. Not much was happening on the square this early, but the afternoon would be a different story. Old men would rock the day away in front of The Lion's Mane barbershop exchanging gossip and spitting tobacco and Skoal juice into empty Styrofoam coffee cups. Checkers games would be won and lost and bragger's rights would be secured for the upcoming week.

Today was, hands down, the busiest day of the week at Miss Mattie's House of Hair. Ladies would get their hair set on Saturday so they could wear Texas hair to church on Sunday. It was downright disgraceful to worship with flat hair. I knew this to be the gospel because, oftentimes, Nita Sue and I would try to pick out the ladies who had set their own hair during the worship service on Sunday mornings. We could tell by the indention marks left behind from the pink, plastic picks that dug into the scalp while securing brush rollers.

Daddy's store would be full of avid fishermen practicing their casting techniques in the back room. Daddy and Uncle Ed inflated my old baby pool, filled it with water, and used it to teach customers how to cast. Daddy was good, but Uncle Ed was the best. He could land his lure inside the floating ring every time.

Murphy's Five and Dime would be crawling with kids itching to spend their allowance, but I wouldn't be part of that group. Instead I slaved over a work table pounding away on flower stems that probably wouldn't be used for this so–called high dollar Episcopal funeral.

"Break time's over, Carol Ann. I need more foam when you finish with the mums," Aunt Betty hollered.

"Okay, I'm coming," I answered. So much for the sun.

A car pulled into the parking space marked "BEREAVE." It was Mr. Odell Shores. He and his brother, Orten, owned the local funeral parlor. The parking space was reserved for funeral folks and family members of the deceased. Mr. Shores was probably stopping by to talk to Aunt Betty about the funeral flowers.

"Why, hello, Miss Carol Ann," Mr. Odell shouted my way. "Your aunt gotcha working today, huh?"

"Yes, sir," I replied.

"I know how much she appreciates you and Nita Sue pitching in."

"Yes, sir," I replied again.

"Is Dan here?"

"No, sir. Daddy's at the store. Just Momma and me. Nita Sue's sick." I blocked the sun with my hand so I could see his face.

"I'm sorry to hear about Nita Sue. Nothing serious, I hope," he added politely.

"No, sir. Just a little bug, that's all." I smiled the fakest smile I could muster under the circumstances. That lying, no good sister of mine had weaseled her way out of another day of work by lying through her perfectly straightened teeth. And here I sat, wasting a sunny Saturday cooped up in Betty's Bloomers. A little bug, my foot. Anyone could stick their finger down their throat and puke. Maybe I'd go in the bathroom right now and...

"...of course, Odell," I heard Aunt Betty say, "not a word to anyone. You can trust me."

Oh, boy. I wasn't sure what Aunt Betty was promising to keep quiet about, but I'd bet the farm we were about to hear the juicy details as soon as the door closed behind Mr. Shores.

"Shoot–a–monkey! You better sit down, Hazel Jean. You won't believe this one! Lordy, lordy." Aunt Betty was as white as a freshly Cloroxed sheet. Momma, Luther Tripp and I huddled around the worktable for the latest breaking news.

The color was making its way back in Aunt Betty's face as she announced,

"Carol Ann, you and Luther finish up in the cooler. I don't want the roses standing in day old water."

What? And miss the latest gossip? Who did she think she was, summoning me to the cooler? And with Luther! He could barely follow directions much less understand the magnitude of what might be the best gossip in years. No way was I missing this. No, no, no. I didn't get up at 5:30 a.m. for nothing.

I strolled toward the cooler all right, but I took a left and hid behind the boxes of floral foam stacked neck high by the cooler door. Luther could change the ice cold water, I wasn't missing this.

"Hazel Jean, you just won't believe this. In all my born days I never heard of anythang like this in Lake View—maybe Hollywood or up north—but not right here in our own backyard." Aunt Betty was getting to the good part. I could tell because she was whispering. She always whispered when the gossip was juicy.

"Well, spit it out, Betty. For goodness sakes, what is it?" Momma was getting irritated. I could tell because she always raised her voice when she was tired and irritable.

"You'll never believe where Mrs. Atkinson died."

"Where?" Momma was practically shouting.

"Well, it wasn't in *her* bed!"

"So, which roses get fresh water? All of them or just the red ones?"

"All of them!" I yelled from behind the boxes, "every stinking one. Now hurry up!"

"Carol Ann!" Momma exclaimed, "Get yourself out here this minute!" I slithered from behind the boxes and made myself known.

"What do you think you're doing, young lady?" Momma asked.

"I'm trying to hear whose bed Mrs. Atkinson died in!"

"She died in someone else's bed?" Mr. Dirt–for–Brains asked.

"Carol Ann Lawson, you march yourself right out that door and wait for me. Do you hear me?"

Oops. Whenever Momma asked, "Do you hear me?" we were dead meat. Of course we could hear her. She was screaming for Pete's sake, the dead could hear her. *Hey, maybe one of them could fill me in on whose bed Mrs. Atkinson died in.*

I marched myself right out the door, as requested, crossed the street, and sat down under a pine. Who did they think they were anyway? I had rolled out of bed before sunrise to help them, for crying out loud. I was chewing on a pine needle when I saw Momma cross the street. The four horsemen had nothing on her when she was mad.

"Carol Ann, I am *extremely* upset with you. *Did* Aunt Betty or *did she not* tell you to change the water in the cooler?"

"I know that, but Momma…"

"Don't you but Momma me, young lady. When an adult tells you to do something I expect you to comply. Do you understand?"

"Yes, ma'am. But I just want to know what all the fuss is about, that's all. I mean, she made it sound like a Hollywood movie or something, and I knew that if I didn't hide outside the cooler, I'd never know." I was practically in tears.

"I understand, honey. But this is adult business, Carol Ann. Not the business of a girl your age. Now, I want you to go home and have an early lunch. Stop by the drugstore on your way, they have a package for Nita Sue."

"Yes, ma'am." My chin rested on my knees as I stared at the pine needles sticking up around my Keds. Oh, well. It would come out sooner or later. BJ would know as soon as anyone. Her mom knew everything.

Moon Pie: a pastry which consists of two round graham cracker cookies, with marshmallow filling in the center, dipped in a chocolate coating

I took my sweet time walking to McDeaver's Drugstore. They could make me go to lunch, but they couldn't make me come back. Well, actually they could. Who was I kidding? I'd be back within an hour to beat the heck out of more stems.

"Good morning, Carol Ann. How's your sister feeling? Better?" I started to tell Mrs. Breeland that my sorry sister was just fine and that she simply had a case of the finger–down–the–throat–to–get–out–of–work bug.

"I'm sure she's better," I said instead. "Momma let her sleep while I went to work at Aunt Betty's this morning. There's a big funeral coming up." If Nita Sue was going get the sympathy votes around this town I could let folks know that *I* was the dependable Lawson girl.

Unbeknownst to me, Mrs. Breeland had taken a Coke out of the icebox and was in the process of trying to locate her bottle opener. "I heard something about that. Do you know who died?" she asked. There was something in her voice that told me she knew more than she let on.

"Uh, I think her name is Mrs. uh, uh," she handed me the bottle. "Oh, thank you. Mrs. Atkinson, maybe? I didn't know her."

I turned up the Coke and drank it in.

Mrs. Breeland leaned across the counter. Boxes of dusting powder were stacked next to each of her elbows. McDeaver's was where Momma shopped when she bought make–up and panty-hose.

"Did your Aunt Betty say when or *where* she died?" Bingo. That's why she gave me a free Coke. If I played my cards right maybe I could get a free moon pie or a package of peanuts to go with it.

"No, ma'am. At least not to me, anyway. Mr. Shores was over this morning talking to Aunt Betty about the funeral flowers. Come to think of it, I believe I did hear him say something but I had to leave because I got real hungry." Without looking, Mrs. Breeland reached behind her and pulled a bag of peanuts off the red Tom's display and handed it to me.

"For me?" I asked innocently. I don't think she heard the question because she launched right back into her interrogation.

"Did you hear Mr. Shores say whether or not they were having a viewing?" Bingo again.

"Well," I began as I poured the package of peanuts into my bottle, "I don't know if he said anything about the viewing part, but I reckon it's going to be an open casket because the family ordered her a corsage."

Mrs. Breeland's fake eyelashes shot up to the bottom of her painted eyebrows.

"I see," she said.

"I don't mean to be rude, but do you have a package for Nita Sue? I have to get home and then back to Aunt Betty's by noon."

"Oh sure, hon. You wait right here. I'm fixin' to get it for you."

"Thank you very much for the Coke and peanuts, Mrs. Breeland. They hit the spot." I rubbed my stomach in a circular motion as if I hadn't eaten for months. A little acting couldn't hurt anything, could it?

Mrs. Breeland returned with a sack for Nita Sue. She passed it over the counter then whispered, "Carol Ann, if you hear anything *unusual* about Mrs. Atkinson, you come right back over here and we can talk about it over a Co–Cola. You hear?" She kept a firm grip on the sack until she finished her sentence.

"Yes, ma'am. Thanks again." The bells clanged against the door as I skipped out of the drugstore. I'd keep my ears open alright. I had a sneaking suspicion that I was fixing to eat and drink my weight in Cokes, moon pies, and peanuts.

***

The screen door slammed as I walked into the kitchen carrying Nita Sue's package. "Nita Sue, I'm home, you flea bag," I muttered under my breath.

I plopped the Pepto–Bismol on the kitchen table and went straight for the icebox. Leftovers. Why couldn't we have Chinese takeout or pizza like everyone else in the world? Just once, I would like to open the icebox and find food from any other store but the Lake View Piggly Wiggly.

I wasn't that hungry after the peanuts, but I knew I'd better eat or I would be hungry all afternoon. With cold, fried chicken and grape juice in hand, I walked down the hallway to our bedroom. What was that smell?

I opened the bedroom door and saw Nita Sue and Margaret huddled over a long, skinny, smoking stick.

"What's that?" I asked. Margaret jumped so high that she knocked the stick onto the carpet.

Nita Sue yelled, "Quick! Put it out before it burns a hole in the carpet!" Margaret jumped up and saw my glass of juice. Next thing I knew, she was pouring grape juice on the carpet.

"You idiot! You'll ruin the carpet!" Nita Sue was sure enough screaming now. She ran to the bathroom and came back with a towel. "Here. Start scrubbing." Margaret obeyed. She was scrubbing that purple juice back and forth and sideways until the stain was as big as my new Fifth Dimension album. "Look what you did! You made it bigger!"

Oh, man. They were in some kind of trouble now. Momma would have their hides. Daddy, too, for that matter. We weren't allowed to eat or drink anywhere except in the kitchen.

"What is that thing?" I asked after I bit off another piece of chicken.

"It's incense, you moron, and if you hadn't barged in here like you did, we'd still be sitting here smelling it. What is your problem?"

"My problem? My problem?" I laughed. "You don't see me standing over a big purple stain with half–burned hippie sticks everywhere." Nita Sue looked down at the enormous spot on the carpet.

"Okay, what's it going to cost me to keep you quiet?"

I rolled the drumstick over and bit off another hunk of meat. "Actually, there is something," I said with a grin. Bring on the free Cokes and moon pies.

"You and I must make a pact, we must bring salvation back. Where there is love, I'll be there."
The Jackson 5

"...of the United States of America, and to the republic for which it stands, one nation under God, indivisible, with liberty and justice for all." I had recited the Pledge of Allegiance every morning since the first grade. Today was no different.

Mrs. Wood asked everyone to sit down and open their Texas History books. Being the ever–obedient Lawson girl, I reached inside the bottom of my desk and brought forth the seventeen pound book with the Texas flag flourishing on its cover.

"Page 83, class," chimed Mrs. Wood, "I believe we left off at the Alamo on Friday." I flipped to page 83 and, sure enough, there was a color photo of the Alamo.

"Now, who can tell me why Texas lost against Santa Anna's army at the Alamo?"

Lamar Webb spoke first, "Because there weren't no back door?"

Laughter erupted in the classroom. Everyone was howling except Clara Wood. She took this Texas history jazz rather seriously. Her shiny, white Cadillac had a NATIVE bumper sticker on it. If some folks might wonder what kind of native, the Texas flag pasted on the other side of her bumper was their first clue. It was my understanding that only certain people were granted native status, but I didn't know how one became a member of that club.

"Actually, Lamar, if you look closely in your book, you won't see the words back door anywhere in the text. Now, who can answer my question?"

"Excusez–moi Madame Wood?"

"Yes, Roxanne? And speak in English, si vous plait?"

Whoa.Clara Wood spoke French? I knew she spoke Spanish but not French.

"Weren't the Texans really scavengers? I mean, weren't they just taking Mexico's land and depriving them of their civil rights?"

I thought Mrs. Wood might just grab her autographed Darrell Royal photo and run for cover. No one spoke ill of Texas in her class.

"No, Roxanne. Texas did not deprive Mexico's people of anything. Now who can answer my question?"

Shannon Grubbs' hand shot up first. Surprise, surprise. As Shannon launched into her dissertation of Colonel Travis' loss, my thought process turned elsewhere.

Hershey would give birth to her puppies today. Daddy said we could probably expect three or four chocolate Labrador pups this afternoon after school. Daddy had eased a box under his rolltop desk last night. I lined it with old bath towels and shredded newspapers. This would be Hershey's third and last litter. Watching Hershey with her pups was one of the best parts of owning a dog.

Uncle Ed and Aunt Betty owned Cocoa, the puppies' father. Lawson Brothers sold the finest hunting dogs in Bowie County. Daddy and Uncle Ed let Nita Sue and me keep the money from the sales. I gave ten percent to the church (I'd learned my lesson) and put the rest in the bank. I was determined to go to college. Hopefully, in Minnesota.

"Carol Ann, do you know the answer?"

There was a long pause.

"Carol Ann? Are we daydreaming again?" asked Mrs. Wood. I didn't know about her, but I sure as heck was.

"I'm sorry, Mrs. Wood. What was the question again?"

"I asked why the Alamo is so important to Texans?"

I should know this. I'd had three years of Texas History. Come to think of it, I'd had more Texas history than American history. Was that legal? Could they do that?

"Carol Ann? Please come see me after class," I heard.

"Yes, ma'am."

***

Mrs. Wood's cat eye glasses were perched on her long, sunburned nose. I stared at the chain looped around the back of her skinny neck and attached to her glasses. What were those little things hanging off the chain? Oh, please, not cowbells. Was this woman living in the real world or what? She should move into

Darrell Royal's house and set up shop. I'm sure no one would mind, especially me.

"Carol Ann, is there something bothering you? Your school work is suffering and you seem distracted," she asked.

Come to think of it, I had been a little distracted. "Ma'am?"

She repeated, "Is there something bothering you?"

"To tell you the truth, Mrs. Wood, I am a little distracted. I've worked the last couple of Saturdays for Aunt Betty. I guess I'm tired."

Clara's eyes peered over the glasses as her body angled toward mine. "So," she said rather slowly, "you worked at your aunt's flower shop last week?"

"Yes, ma'am." What was this, *Perry Mason*?

"Did you help your aunt with the Atkinson funeral by any chance?" And there you have it. Your witness, counselor.

"Yes, ma'am. As a matter–of–fact, I did work the weekend of Mrs. Atkinson's funeral. It was really sad."

"Yes indeed, God rest her soul. Very sad indeed." The old Clara-meister was nodding her head with the kind of sympathy reserved for those in mourning.

She continued, "So, Carol Ann is there anything about that Saturday that caused your schoolwork to suffer? Anything at all?" If she leaned any closer, I could count the fillings in her teeth.

"Now that I think about it I was somewhat distracted that day. Nita Sue was sick and it was just Luther and me working on the flowers." A wet blanket could have answered with more panache.

"So, did you hear anything about how Mrs. Atkinson passed, dear?"

"I don't understand the question."

"Well, I just wondered if you knew *how* she died. Was she ill? Or in an accident, perhaps?"

"Now that you mention it I believe I did hear Aunt Betty and Momma talking about some kind of accident."

"What kind of accident?" Her nostrils flared with each inquiry.

"Mrs. Wood, I don't think it would be Christian of me to talk about it. Momma says that gossiping is a sin."

"Your mother is right as rain! But this isn't gossip, dear, this is factual information."

"Like the Alamo?"

"Exactly! Think of this as a fact finding mission!" she declared with the enthusiasm of a Dallas Cowboy cheerleader.

"A fact finding mission," I repeated. "The fact is…" I planted both elbows on her desk and cupped my hands around my mouth, "that she died in someone else's…," I glanced around the room looking for eavesdroppers, "someone else's…," she was practically foaming at the mouth, "someone else's bed!"

"LORD, HAVE MERCY ON MY SOUL!" Clara Wood clutched at her bosom as if her heart might beat right out of her chest.

"That's right," I reiterated, "in someone else's bed." Perry Mason couldn't have done better.

"I feel the earth move under my feet, I feel the sky tumbling down."

Carole King

I was more than ready for Nita Sue to keep her end of our agreement. If I wanted to keep the Cokes flowing, I needed some cold, hard facts pronto. Between Margaret Mathison and Randy Mitchell, Nita Sue should be able to obtain the information I needed. I wondered what all the fuss was about. Surely people died in other people's homes, right? I mean, if BJ spent the night with me and happened to croak, she would die in someone else's bed.

Thank goodness school was over and I could go home. Momma would probably know the scoop on Mrs. Atkinson, but I knew better than to ask her. Momma put up with a lot from Nita Sue and me, however, she did not put up with gossip. She would send us straight to our room if we so much as hinted that we might bear false witness against our neighbor. Nope, Nita Sue and BJ were my best bets in the Atkinson scandal.

When I walked through the sliding glass door, I could hear the new puppies. Momma and Nita Sue were sitting on the floor admiring the contents in the cardboard box. Kneeling behind Nita Sue, I peeked beneath the old desk and saw four of the cutest Labrador puppies ever. Their eyes were still closed, but they were nestled up to Hershey's tummy eating away.

"What do you think, Carol Ann?" Momma's face beamed.

"I think they're even cuter than the last litter!" Hershey raised her head and looked at me. "Sorry, girl," I whispered.

"Me, too," Nita Sue replied. "But look at the runt, she's so tiny. Do you think she'll make it?"

"Oh, I think so, honey. Nature has a way of taking care of its own." Momma stroked Hershey's head as she answered. Momma was the only human Hershey would tolerate while she gave birth. She had been beside her during each delivery.

Secretly, I was glad I wasn't around for the other part. I'd seen a video in P.E. class of a cat having kittens and it made me nauseous but not as nauseous as Pam Moore. When the momma cat started licking and eating all of the slimy stuff on the kittens, Pam puked all over the floor. I was the one Mrs. Borcherdine sent to the janitor's closet to retrieve the InstaVomi. We watched as Mrs. Borcherdine poured orange pellets onto Pam's upchucked breakfast. She called it a teacher's best friend.

I motioned toward the bedroom with my head. Nita Sue rolled her eyes at me, but got up just the same. Once behind the closed door of our room I began my interrogation.

"Okay, what did you find out?" I probed.

"For starters, Miss Goody-Two-Shoes, your Mrs. Atkinson wasn't exactly a saint." Nita Sue plopped down on her bed and stared at the ceiling.

"So what? I don't care if she was a saint or not. I just want to know where she died and how."

"Well, I got the scoop from Margaret, who heard it from her mom, who heard it from some lady sitting next to her at Miss Mattie's House of Hair or something like that."

"So, we know it's accurate, right?"

"Yeah, of course."

"Okay, so what did you find out?" Nita Sue was dragging this thing out a little too long for my taste. I made a "V" with my fingers. "Two words big sister: incense."

"That's one word, you idiot."

"Oh, so what? Tell me then!" My patience was running thin. There were Cokes and moon pies calling my name.

"Well, it seems that your Mrs. Atkinson died in a motel room at the Lone Star Inn after a night of drinking at the Hay Loft." You would have thought we were playing a game of Clue the way she emphasized each word.

"No way. Why would an old woman, who lived in town, be at the local motel and bar? You must have gotten it wrong, Nita Sue. You know as well as I do that rednecks hang out at the Hay Loft."

"Believe what you want, little sister, but she died there all right. That's what everyone's been whispering about. The family is embarrassed."

Nita Sue dragged her hand through the air as if painting a newspaper headline. "Rich, local, seventy year old woman dies in motel room. See 10a for details."

"Wow. How embarrassing would that be?" I asked out loud. "I mean, I'm sure she's someone's grandma or mother or something."

"Of course, she's someone's mother, that's what makes it even better. Her son is a U.S. senator from Tyler, according to my sources."

"Right, like Miss Mattie's House of Hair is now as reliable as Huntley and Brinkley."

She continued, "This hotshot's mother, who was boozing it up at the Hay Loft, went to a motel room with some strange man and then croaked."

I knew I could depend on her to get the scoop.

"You're off the hook, Nita Sue. I won't breathe a word to Momma about the incense or you faking a stomach bug." And with that, I was off to deliver the good news.

Thou shalt not raise a false report. Exodus 23:1

As I pedaled toward the downtown square, I stretched my arms straight out from my body as if I were an airplane taking off for some exotic destination. The wind whipped my hair across my face as the sun's warmth enveloped me. Nothing could possibly go wrong today. Hopefully I had enough scoop on Mrs. Atkinson to merit at least one moon pie, perhaps a package of peanuts but definitely enough for a free Coke.

Where to first? I decided to stop by McDeaver's Drugstore and see if Mrs. Breeland and her fake eyelashes were working today. The bells clanged on the glass door as I entered the drugstore.

"May I help you?" I heard from behind the counter. Mrs. Breeland's head popped up behind a rack of nail polish.

"Hello, hon. What can I do for you today?" she asked.

"Well, I was just passing by and thought I might stop in for a few minutes. It sure is heating up out there." A little exaggeration couldn't hurt anything.

"Oh, uh huh," she answered. She was sorting pink bottles of nail polish from red ones. Based on the number of bottles sitting on the counter, she wasn't having a lot of luck. There must have been a hundred bottles of red fingernail polish alone.

"Revlon sent ten shipments of Crabapple Red instead of the one shipment I ordered last week. Lurleene opened every single carton while I was on my lunch break and now I can't send them back."

I couldn't tell if she was talking to me or if someone was behind the counter with her. I leaned over the glass counter top. She was sitting alone on the floor with one hundred bottles of Crabapple Red fingernail polish.

"Yes, ma'am. I can tell that you're real busy. Would you like some help?"

Glancing up at my torso hanging over the cosmetics counter, her fake eyelashes slapped her eyebrows a couple of times before she said, "Yes, hon, I could use some help."

I inched my way around the cosmetics counter. Revlon and Max Factor signs reflected in the mirrored wall behind the displays of make–up. Box after box of lipstick, dusting powder, and mascara lined the shelves. This place was a girl's paradise.

I sat down on the floor beside Mrs. Breeland. Wrapping bows filled a box under the dusting powder. Rolls of wrapping paper hovered above my head just waiting to be torn and used. Three pairs of scissors hung from one huge nail. They took gift wrapping seriously at McDeaver's Drugs.

"See if you can count out fifty bottles of the Crabapple Red. I'm fixin' to make me a Buy One, Get One Free sign and put it in the store window."

"Yes, ma'am. Anything else I can do for you?"

"Let's get them fifty bottles out of the way first," she replied.

Counting by twos, I cut my eyes toward her to see if it might be the time to announce the good news.

"So, Mrs. Breeland, remember when I was in here last Saturday? When Nita Sue was sick? When I picked up her package? When you gave me a Coke?"

"Yes, I remember. What about it?"

"Well, remember when you asked me to let you know if I heard anything about the Atkinson funeral?" Bingo. Those fake eyelashes shot up higher than her fake eyebrows. How was that possible?

"Why yes, hon, I do remember," she said as she turned her attention toward me and away from those pesky Cotton Candy and Crabapple bottles. "What did you find out?"

"Well," I coughed a little hoping she might respond with a Coke, "I heard that she," cough, cough, "that she…"

"Here! Have a Co-Cola." A Coke bottle materialized out of thin air and into my hand before I could get another fake cough out of my throat. She popped the cap without even looking. This woman was fast.

"Oh, thank you. I'm really thirsty today."

"Of course you are, God love ya, you just take your time, hon, and collect your thoughts."

"Well, the way I heard it is like this. Mrs. Atkinson died out at the Lone Star Inn on Highway 59. They found her in one of the motel rooms." I whispered that last part and took another swig of my Coke.

Her hand shot up to her mouth while bottles of nail polish spilled out onto the floor. "Why, I swannie! I never! Land sakes alive!"

As she went through her list of exclamations I leaned over her pile of sale items and whispered, "Do you know who her son is?"

"No, who?"

"A senator from Tyler."

"I swannie!"

"Do you think I might have a bag of peanuts for my Coke?" Without looking, her hand found its way to a box of peanuts stashed by the bows. Upon closer inspection, I noticed all kinds of snacks under there. A pack of Lance's finest fell in my lap.

"What was she doing at the Lone Star? Did you hear?"

"No, ma'am. That's all I know about that. But I *did* hear that her son is coming to town shortly." I took one of the three pairs of scissors and sliced off the top of the Lance's package. Fizz oozed up the green bottle as I emptied the package.

"Her son? Is he from Lake View?"

"No, ma'am. Just a senator from Tyler."

"Oh my! A Texas state senator right here in Lake View!" Her neck was actually turning red with excitement.

"Not a state senator, ma'am, but a United States senator who just happens to be from Tyler." And with that piece of news, she literally fell back against the shelf of junk food. I could see the wheels turning in her head. She had people to see! Places to go! There was big news in Lake View and she had the scoop! Forget the nail polish, this was far more important than some Buy One Get One Free sign.

"Uh, Carol Ann," she said as she straightened her skirt, "I have some other things I need to take care of in the back. Is there anything else I can get you? Anything at all?" It was my chance to cash in on some serious junk food that never graced the pantry of the Lawson home.

"It's getting pretty close to lunch. Do you think I could have one moon pie?"

"Hon, you eat anything you want. You need to keep up your strength, God love ya." Before I could thank her, she had hoofed it to the back of the drugstore. I filled my pockets with Super Bubble, Sugar Daddies, and two moon pies, then maneuvered my way from behind the cosmetics counter. The moon pies would hit the spot.

Dewey Decimal System: a proprietary library classification system created by Melvil Dewey in 1876

I rode around the square trying to decide whether or not to stop in at Aunt Betty's. I decided against it knowing that she might put me to work. I rode past the Paramount to see if a new movie was playing but it was still *Valley of the Dolls*. I thought about going to Roxy's house, but she and her mother were driving into Tyler to check for a natural food store or a farmer's market. Her mother's motto was: Know your farmer, know your food. They didn't eat foods that had been sprayed with bug spray. I didn't know that buying foods that hadn't been sprayed for bugs was even an option. It seemed to me that garden vegetables wouldn't taste very good with cut worms inside them. But who was I to question them? They were from Massachusetts and California, after all. Plus, Roxy wanted to look for more French albums. She had mastered French expressions and was ready to move on to more vocabulary words.

There was nothing left to do except ride to BJ's house and share my loot with my best friend, but I remembered that she was babysitting the two terrors today and there was no way was I going over there.

The library was always a possibility. I'd finished my last Nancy Drew book and needed something else to read. I smiled at the pile of goodies in my basket and pedaled toward the Lake View Public Library. Our library was one of the larger libraries in east Texas and was known for its selection of books.

Heaving open the huge oak door, I stepped inside one of my favorite places in the whole world. I closed my eyes and took in the aroma of oak, lemon oil and books. I wasn't sure if other libraries smelled of adventure, but ours sure did.

The circulation desk stood by the entrance to the adult section. To the right of it was a spiral staircase (like the one on the Dean Martin show) that led to the nonfiction adult books. One of my favorite pastimes was sneaking up the staircase and hiding in the corner with a good book. Miss Page didn't allow children to dawdle in the adult nonfiction area. She enforced the policy because she had caught too many boys looking at pictures in the art history books.

"Hello, Miss Lawson." Miss Page addressed everyone as Miss or Mister, it didn't matter if you were married or not.

"Hi, Miss Page."

"May I help you find something today?"

"No, thank you. I think I'm going to look around for a while."

"There are some new Carolyn Keene books, if you're interested."

"Yes, ma'am."

I walked past the Explorer's table dragging my finger across the selection of new science books. They were interesting but my first love was Miss Nancy Drew. I headed straight for Carolyn Keene's newest book. Taking it from the shelf, I waited for Miss Page to get busy with another patron so I could sneak up the spiral staircase. When the coast was clear, I darted upstairs and found a spot in the corner where I wouldn't be seen from the bottom level.

I dug a piece of Super Bubble from my pocket and opened the pages of another new adventure. The yellow spine creaked as I turned to page one. Several pages into Nancy's latest mystery, I overheard two female voices whispering a few aisles over. Several "you don't says" later, I heard one of the voices gasp. I laid my book on the floor and snuck over to the 629.28s. There was Mrs. Snodgrass, with her hair in curlers, and another lady whispering into each other's ears like grade school girls. I forgot I was chewing bubble gum and accidentally popped a bubble. Both women jumped like scared rabbits.

"Sorry, I was just looking for this book." I grabbed the nearest one—*A Beginner's Guide to Foreign Car Repair*—and rushed back to my hiding spot before either woman could get a good look at me. What on earth were those two talking about? And why were they in the automotive section? Something wasn't quite right.

I ducked down and snuck around the other side. I wouldn't make the same mistake twice; I stuck my gum underneath the bottom shelf of the 400.00s. They were whispering ninety–to–nothing. Mrs. Snodgrass was saying, 'Oh my God!' over and over. This woman was going straight to hell for sure. I backed up a little in case the Lord decided to take her right then and there.

The other lady was talking so low that I couldn't understand her. She held a book to her face and I couldn't tell who she was. But there was something very familiar about her. Was it the shoes? No. The dress? No. The necklace? Yes. It was the necklace. I knew that necklace. But how did I know that necklace? Was it a necklace? No, it was a chain used for glasses. Then it hit me. It was Clara Wood and her cowbells. What was she doing in the adult nonfiction part of the library chatting it up with Mrs. I-only-wear-my-hair-in-rollers-Snodgrass?

Upon closer inspection, I heard Mrs. Wood say 'U.S. senator' over and over again. Then Mrs. Snodgrass would respond with 'Joseph and Mary.' Joseph and Mary who? The only Joseph and Mary I knew about were Jesus' parents. Surely she wasn't talking about them.

I crawled toward the middle of the aisle. I could have touched Mrs. Wood's hem by sticking my hand through the 500.00s and scared the dickens out of them both, but I decided I would rather live, instead.

The longer I listened, the more I learned. It seemed that Senator Nowlin was coming to town for his mother's memorial service. According to Mrs. Wood, a lot of Texas officials were coming, too. She wondered if Lady Byrd or Pat Nixon would be in attendance. Mrs. Snodgrass wondered where they would have the memorial. Would it be at the Episcopal Church? Was there enough room? She also wondered if the Secret Service would be there. And what about the former president, LBJ? After all, this Senator was a Texan. Then Mrs. Snodgrass supposed that she had better get going because she really needed to get her nails done and probably should get a perm just in case this whole memorial service thing might make it in the newspapers, or, better yet, TV. Then Mrs. Wood anticipated that this would be a weekend to remember and she, too, should probably make an appointment with Mattie to get her hair and nails done. Having said all of that, they disappeared from behind the 500.00s.

*"And it's too late, baby, now it's too late. Though we
really did try to make it.
Something inside has died and I can't hide
and I just can't fake it.*

Carole King

So much information! So little time!

My basket was filled with enough junk food to last me a while. Clara Wood had the scoop on the whole Atkinson affair so there was no use trying to butter her up anymore. I guess the only thing left to do was share in my good fortune with my best friend, Belinda Jean Dodge. She should be home by now, I thought. I rode to her house, junk food in tow, and knocked on the screen door.

"Hello, Mrs. Dodge?" I hollered through the door, "is anyone home? BJ?"

"Hello, Carol Ann. Come on in. We just got home," Mrs. Dodge answered. "Belinda is upstairs."

"Thanks." I took the stairs two at a time. BJ would never believe this! Barging into her room, I could hear the Fifth Dimension floating up, up and away in their beautiful balloon while BJ painted her toenails.

"Hi there," I said as I tossed a package of Sugar Babies at her.

"Oh, hi. Check it out—Crabapple Red. I got it half price at McDeaver's. What do you think?" Five red toenails wiggled in the air.

"Let me guess, you also got a bottle of Cotton Candy for half price, too?"

"How did you know that?"

"I was there when Mrs. Breeland unpacked the one hundred bottles of nail polish that Lurleene opened by accident."

"Oh," she answered.

I fell on her bed and popped a handful of Sugar Babies in my mouth.

"Where did you get all the candy?"

"McDeaver's."

"Did you spend the whole day there or something?"

"You could say that. How were the two sheriffs?"

She turned her head and gave me the Evil Eye. "You don't *even* want to know."

"You're right, I probably don't. But that's not why I'm here. I've got the biggest scoop ever to hit Lake View, and... I've got the candy to prove it." I was rather proud of my detective skills and wanted BJ to enjoy my spoils with me. She began painting the other five toenails.

"Oh, you mean about that motel thing with the senator's momma? I already know about that, I overheard Daddy telling Momma all about it."

"What? When did you hear your daddy telling your momma?"

"Last night, I think. Why?"

"Why? Why? I'll tell you why! Because it's only the biggest story to ever hit Lake View, and I got the scoop before most other people around here, that's why! And because I *did*, I got lots of free candy for you and me. That's why!" I was furious. BJ knew about this thing before me and didn't even bother to call me with the details and here I was sharing my junk food with her.

"Calm down, it's not that big a deal, Carol Ann. Good grief." She resumed her toenail painting.

"Calm down? Calm down? Don't tell me to calm down. I can't believe you! I came straight to your house as soon as I knew the truth about the town's biggest scandal and you sit there painting your toenails and acting as if this whole thing is no big deal!" I was working myself into a tizzy.

"Get a grip, girl. You're going explode."

"Well, maybe I should explode! I can't believe you didn't call me last night, BJ. How do you think I feel? I come over here to share this news with my best friend and find out that you already know? And didn't think to call *me* first thing? How do you think that makes me feel, huh?" I was yelling but didn't realize it until Mrs. Dodge knocked on the door.

"Is everything alright, ladies?"

"Yes, ma'am. We're fine," BJ answered. "Geez Louise, what is wrong with you? You're acting like I forgot to tell you that I'm dying or something."

"Well, that's about how I feel, BJ." The Fifth Dimension was singing about going where you want to go and doing what you want to do.

"Look, I was in my room last night working on my scrapbook. I had stuff spread all over the floor when I heard Daddy answer the upstairs phone. I could tell it was serious because he pulled the phone to the other side of the landing. He always does that when one of his patients is really sick or someone's died. So, I stood by the door and listened. Next thing I know, Momma is on the landing asking Daddy if it's serious and he tells her about some senator's mother who died a few days ago at the motel and how he had to do all the paperwork and how it seemed there was a problem with it and that he'd be gone for a couple of hours. Then Momma said that she had heard something about it at her Circle meeting and how one of the ladies had asked the Circle to pray for the senator's family. Then Daddy said that he had to go and for her not to breathe a word about this to anyone and she said she wouldn't. And that's all I know."

The Fifth Dimension was no longer singing about anything. BJ shuffled over to the turntable. Cotton balls stuck out from between her Crabapple colored toenails.

"There's a lot more to it than that!" I yelled.

"Okay, like what?" she shot back.

"Okay, like this. For your information, Mrs. Atkinson died at the Hay Loft, or should I say the Lone Star Inn, in one of the motel room beds. Ha!" Take that.

"So what? I'm sure lots of old people die in motels rooms all across America."

"Oh yeah? Well, how many of them dropped dead in the local, no–tell motel when they live in the same town? And how many of them got caught boozing it up at the beer joint next door to the motel? Huh?"

BJ looked at me like I was crazy. "And who told you that she was boozing it up in the beer joint? And how do you know she wasn't at the motel visiting a friend who was passing through town or something? Huh?"

"Because I just do."

"Carol Ann, I don't know what you heard, but you better be careful about spreading rumors. Your momma will snatch you baldheaded and ground you for life if she catches you gossiping."

"I know," I said. I was feeling guilty now. The Holy Ghost was working on me good. "But nothing exciting ever happens around here. I mean, all over the world they're having sit–ins and love–ins and we're having sew–ins at the YWCA. Aren't you just a *wee bit* excited that something big is finally happening in our one horse town?"

I could hear the silver ball rattling against the nail polish bottle as she beat it on the palm of her hand. "No, not really. I happen to like Lake View the way it is. Not like those California towns where everybody's doing heroin and stuff. And you know what?" she said as she started painting her fingernails, "if you want to get in trouble for gossiping, you go right ahead. I don't want any part of it."

"Well, Miss No–Flies–On–You–Dodge, I'll just take my candy and go share it with someone who can appreciate some big city news in our crummy, little town." I gathered my loot and headed toward the door.

"Don't let the door hit you on the way out!" she screamed.

"Don't worry!" I yelled as I raced out the door.

Dadgummit. What had gotten into her? You'd think I was a Manson follower or something. All I did was keep my ears open to the latest news in town. I mean, isn't that what Mary Richards would do?

I was telling BJ off in my head for the hundredth time when I rode past Betty's Bloomers. She must have had a lot of customers today because her OPEN sign was hanging crooked. It only did that if the door had been opened and closed a lot. Mr. Odell Shores was walking toward his funeral car when he spotted me.

"Miss Carol Ann? Your Aunt Betty's been looking all over for you." I coasted up beside the hearse.

"Is something wrong?"

"No, she just needs some extra help this afternoon. First Baptist ordered a whole mess of extra flowers for tomorrow's services."

"Our church? Extra flowers?" No wonder Brother Paul was always badgering us about tithing.

"I believe so." He tipped his black hat and climbed into the Morgue Mobile. (That's what Nita Sue called his funeral car) I glanced at all the candy in my basket and decided I might have a hard time explaining handfuls of Sugar Babies and bubblegum to Aunt Betty and that doorknob on two legs, Luther Tripp, so I hid it inside the green Lake View Ledger newspaper tube. No one would see it there. The paper had been delivered already.

"Aunt Betty? You still here?" Wishful thinking on my part.

"Shoot–a–monkey! You nearly gave me a heart attack. Grab an apron and help me with these flowers. I got six big orders here and the good Lord only gave me two hands. Luther! Where is that boy?" she hollered. "Luther?"

While Aunt Betty was busy counting the only two hands the Lord gave her, I donned an apron and began looking through the orders. Mr. Shores was right; our church had ordered a huge altar arrangement plus five smaller arrangements for Fellowship Hall. The WMU must have had something planned for tomorrow. Upon closer inspection, I noticed Atkinson/Nowlin on all six orders.

"Aunt Bet…" I was interrupted for the umpteenth time in my life.

"Carol Ann, start cutting foam to fit inside those coffee cans. Remember to tape it to the sides of the cans real snug like. I don't want anyone griping about them being lopsided. Luther, hurry up with them glads. We ain't got all day, son."

Luther counted gladiolas while Aunt Betty started greening the containers. She used more leather leaf and baby's breath than any other florist on God's green earth but what did I know? I just did as I was told.

"Aunt Betty? What's with all the flowers? What's going on to-morrow?" She looked at me like I'd been drafted or something.

"Where have you been the last twenty–four hours? Under a rock?"

Luther blurted out, "Senator Nowlin is talking at your church tomorrow. Pretty cool, huh?"

A Folgers coffee can, full of water–soaked foam, slid out of my hands and spilled on the floor. Ice cold water drenched my legs, but I didn't feel it. I'd gone numb.

"Carol Ann, you're white as a ghost. You all right? Carol Ann?" Aunt Betty was asking me questions but I couldn't answer. I wanted to answer but nothing came out.

"Carol Ann? Carol Ann?" She was slapping my face with her cold, wet hands. "Luther, get a Coke out of the icebox. Hurry up."

Next thing I knew I was sitting on a stool drinking an ice cold Coke. Aunt Betty was in my face. "Carol Ann?"

"Ma'am?"

"You gave us a scare. Are you sick, child?" Luther's face was two inches too close to mine. I stood up and moved away from him. I knew his family was poor but even poor people should brush their teeth for crying out loud.

"No, ma'am. I guess the shock of a U.S. senator coming to town threw me for a loop, that's all."

"You're not the only one. I reckon every living, breathing soul in our little Peyton Place is a bit shook up—with all them awful rumors floating around. I heard that Senator's Nowlin's coming to town to put a stop to it."

I sat back down. "What rumors?"

"The rumors about his momma. You know, that Atkinson woman. Haven't you heard?" Aunt Betty stiffened up like a drill sergeant and barked an order. "Luther, go get the carnations out of the cooler."

She waited until he was inside before she turned to me and explained, "Now, don't you go telling Hazel Jean I told you any of this, you hear me?" I heard her alright. Her mouth was right next to my ear. "Evidently, someone started some kind of horrible rumor about his momma, Mrs. Atkinson."

"What kind of rumor?"

"Well, I don't know if I should be telling you this." She hesitated.

"Tell me. Tell me!"

"Well, I guess it won't hurt seeing how you're going to hear about it tomorrow anyway. Somebody started a rumor about her dying at the Lone Star Inn."

"She *did* die at the Lone Star Inn."

"Yes, she died there all right, but not the way everyone's been saying."

"Oh, yes she did. She died in the motel bed after she'd been boozing it up at the Hay Loft with all those rednecks!" How could anyone confuse these facts that I'd been so careful to collect? Aunt Betty's mouth dropped open. Her Poligrip must have quit working because her top dentures clacked a couple of times.

"Shoot–a–monkey! Where did you hear a thing like that?"

"Where? Where? Right here, that's where! The Saturday when Mr. Shores was in here and you and Momma were carrying on and you sent me to the drugstore and Mrs. Breeland said…" My head was spinning something awful. "You told Mr. Shores you could keep a secret. That you wouldn't breathe a word of it to anybody. Remember? Remember that?" My voice grew louder with each sentence.

"Of course I remember that. But that's not the secret I swore to keep."

"Yes it was! Yes it was!" I was off the stool now, swinging my Coke bottle around. "I heard you tell Momma 'she didn't die in her bed' which can only mean that she died in someone else's bed and we all know that Mr. Snodgrass saw the ambulance at the Lone Star Inn while they were taking her body away!" I slammed the bottle on the design table. Luther was back with carnations.

"Keep your voice down, young lady. Who do you think you're talking to, the hired help?" I should know. I *was* the hired help.

Aunt Betty continued, "For your information, everything you just said is one hundred percent wrong and I should know because Hazel Jean already got onto me about that bed thing. She just left here mad as a wet hen over this Atkinson mess. And what a mess it is! Now, I'm fixing to set you straight but you have to promise me that you won't let on that you know a thing. You hear?"

"Yes ma'am, I promise." Finally, we were getting somewhere around here. As soon as I learned the real story, I'd hoof it on over to McDeaver's and cash it in for another basket of moon pies.

The phone rang.

"It's for you." Luther handed me the telephone.

"Hello?" Daddy was calling from his store. Did I have my bike? Yes, I had my bike. Could I please ride my bike to the house to get his extra set of keys? The Erlichson twins had locked themselves in the bathroom again.

"Now?" I asked. Yes, right now. They kept flushing the toilet and he was afraid they would flood the entire store.

"Can't you just ask them to stop?" I asked. No, he couldn't just ask them to stop. And tell Nita Sue to get off the phone when you get there and hurry.

"Yes, sir." Dadgummit. Just when it was getting good, too.

"Aunt Betty, I'll be right back," I assured my new confidant. "We'll pick up where we left off, okay?"

I pedaled past McDeaver's Drugs. It looked like the two for one sale had been a success. Most of the Crabapple Red bottles were gone from the window display. I wondered if Lurleene got fired. Not likely...she was Mr. McDeaver's niece.

What a day.

But the tongue can no man tame; it is an unruly evil, full of deadly poison. James 3:8

We filed into our pew just like every other Sunday morning of our lives, yet, this was not like every other Sunday morning of our lives. For starters, the church was packed. Folding chairs were stuck in every nook and cranny of the sanctuary. Polite men offered their seats to old ladies. Even the nursery workers were here today which meant a lot of screaming babies.

Momma adjusted her pearl necklace with her left hand for the umpteenth time. Daddy wiped the dust off his wing tips for the umpteenth time. I looked around at all the people for the umpteenth time. When were we going to get this show on the road? The Pepsi Cola clock on the back wall showed that we were already five minutes late starting the service. I still couldn't believe Brother Paul would allow a Pepsi Cola clock in God's house. I mean, if you're going to allow advertising in the church, at least get a Coke clock.

Today was looking more like an Easter Sunday every minute. Tons of people poured into the building—people you only see once a year. Lots of hats and gloves and *lots* of perfume. Mrs. Breeland had extended another of her famous "Smell Twice as Nice" specials. If you bought a bottle of Jungle Gardenia you got a bottle of Emeraud free. I didn't know which perfume smelled worse, the Jungle Gardenia or Emeraud. Jungle Gardenia didn't remotely smell like the gardenias that filled our yard in summertime.

Emeraud disgusted Nita Sue. Whenever Momma wore it, Nita Sue would pinch her nostrils and say, 'Emeraud for the bod—when you can't get horse liniment'. I thought it was funny, but Momma didn't see the humor in Nita Sue comparing her choice of perfume to horse cream.

"Did you get a bulletin?" I heard Daddy ask Momma.

"No, I didn't see them. Did you check the back row? Sometimes they put the extras on that last pew by the door."

"I'll go check." Daddy quietly exited our pew. I guess Brother EdEarl didn't print enough. Of course, he had no way of knowing that the good senator would be speaking in the Sunday service and we would have twice as many folks. No one did. I just hoped Brother EdEarl's toupee stayed in place today. It would be awfully embarrassing if it slipped around.

A hush fell over the congregation. Mrs. Herron broke into her prelude on the organ. Brother Paul, Brother EdEarl and another man climbed the stairs to the podium. Wow, it was Senator Seth Nowlin. How this man could face the good, God–fearing people of Lake View was beyond me. Looked to me like he would be so embarrassed about his momma getting caught dead at the Lone Star Inn that he might consider not running for re–election. I know I would. Why, if Momma ever did something like that, I'd just pack up and move away. Now, there's a thought: perhaps Momma *would* do something like that and BJ and I could move to Minnesota. Fat chance. Hazel Jean Lawson was the godliest woman I knew.

Yesterday, when I got home to fetch the spare key to Daddy's store, she was waiting with the grounding jar in hand. By the time I'd made it home, she had already heard about me sharing information with other adults. After a long lecture on gossiping and, idle time being the devil's workshop, I spent the rest of the evening polishing what little silver we owned. Then I cleaned out Hershey's pen and ironed pillowcases until my hands cramped. No amount of gossip was worth all the work I'd done as penance. Worse yet, I didn't get to hear Aunt Betty's version of the truth. But I sure as hell (thank you Nita Sue) wasn't going to ask anyone about it. I'd cleaned enough to last me a lifetime.

"Here, take one and pass them down," Momma whispered. I took a bulletin and passed the others to Nita Sue. As the white stack passed from one set of hands to the next, I noticed that all the women's fingernails were red. Very red. Crabapple Red. I glanced at the row behind us. All the women on that row were sporting red nails, too. I leaned forward and did a quick inspection of the nails on that row: Crabapple Red. Wow, Lurleene may have messed up, but it looked like McDeaver's cashed in.

The choir was singing a song I'd never heard before in a language I'd never heard before. Nita Sue pointed to the bulletin. It was a song of praise in Latin. Didn't Brother EdEarl know that people don't speak Latin anymore? Those evil Romans were the last to use it and it didn't look like you'd want to start your worship service with the language of the people who beat up on the Apostle Paul all the time.

An elbow dug into my ribs. Nita Sue directed my attention to something she had written: SUCK–UPS. I frowned because I didn't understand. Was she calling me a suck–up? What did I do? I was just sitting here minding my own beeswax.

Then, another elbow. She had drawn a picture of a man in a toga with musical notes coming out of his mouth while a tall man smiled as he looked on. Brother EdEarl was sucking up to the senator by singing some fancy–schmancy thing that would impress him. I rolled my eyes. I wanted this service to be over so I could get back to being a carefree girl whose biggest worry in life was whether the man in the chicken costume chose Door Number One, Door Number Two or Door Number Three.

"…and it is with great pleasure that I turn the service over to the honorable Seth Nowlin." Brother Paul returned to his red, velveteen chair while Brother EdEarl wiped the sweat from his forehead. No toupee slippage today.

"Good morning," the Senator said.

"Good morning," we all replied.

"What a glorious day to be in the house of our Lord." His deep voice boomed across the sanctuary. Amens resonated.

"I asked Brother Mitchell if I might take five minutes of your time this morning."

I couldn't believe this guy. Had he no shame?

"As you know, I am one of your two United States senators from the great state of Texas." More amens. "I am humbled to be your servant and grateful for the opportunity to be here today. I love Texas. I love everything about it. But being a United States senator and a fellow Texan is not the reason I wanted to bend your ear this fine morning. No, today, I am here as a mother's son."

He continued, "Many of you know that my mother went to be with the Lord. While I am deeply saddened by the loss of the finest Christian woman I've ever known, I am confident that she is in the Lord's hands. Eating at the banquet table and visiting with the saints." More amens.

I looked at Nita Sue and she looked at me. Aunt Betty was three rows in front of us to the left. I saw her neck redden. Mr. Fischer was even listening, no house plans would be drawn today.

"One or two of you senior adults may remember my mother from way back when. However, most of you don't remember my mother because you weren't even born when she was a member of this church."

Aunt Betty gasped. Mother cleared her throat and glanced my way. Unless I wanted to play Cinderella for the rest of my life, I'd better sit quietly in my unpadded pew.

"Yes, my mother was a member of this church when she was a little girl. You see, Brother Harlan Berry, a former pastor, was my mother's father and my grandfather." Even the babies were silent. "Mother used to tell my brother and me the most wonderful stories about this church when we were growing up. How her family spent Sunday afternoons at Potter's Creek. How the ladies in WMU would bring pies to the house just because they loved my grandparents. But her favorite story about this church and this community was the hard work that went into the local missionary orphanage." He paused, took a sip of water and continued. "You don't remember the orphanage, do you?"

Nope, can't say that I do, Senator.

"Well, my grandparents and some of the other ministers in Lake View founded an orphanage that housed approximately twenty–five children. Evidently, Mother and her siblings spent a great deal of time there with the other kids. They assisted the older ladies with everything from the daily housekeeping chores to pulling weeds in the garden. Mother beamed when she told us these stories. She loved playing Red Rover with the little ones. She loved helping my grandfather repair the building. If there was anything that needed to be done at the orphanage, my mother was willing to do it.

"You see, God gave her a special talent. Mother could sense what people needed before they needed it. I believe God developed this gift in her at a very young age so she would be prepared for the tragedy that would come her way down the road."

What? Was he going to talk about the Lone Star Inn scandal, now?

"My grandfather was pastor here for eight years. Then God called him to south Texas to help with mission orphanages there. Mother spoke of her years in south Texas with fondness but not like the years spent here. Her heart was always here in Lake View. If she could have planned her life, I think she would have lived here forever.

"But God had other plans for her. When Mother completed her junior year in high school my grandparents were killed in an automobile accident. Being the oldest of six children, Mother became the parent to my aunts and uncles. They moved to south Louisiana where they lived with my great–grandparents. It was there that Mother met her future husband and my dad, James Nowlin."

If his dad was a Nowlin, why was her name Atkinson and what the heck was she doing at the Lone Star Inn?

"Mother and Daddy spent the first few years of their married life in south Louisiana where Dad worked on the oil rigs. Then tragedy struck again. My great–grandfather suffered a stroke and my grandmother simply couldn't take care of five children and her paralyzed husband alone. My parents agreed to take in the five brothers and sisters and rear them. Can you imagine the courage it took for my parents to say yes to *five* children? But they did. He and my mother became parents to her five siblings and raised them to be five of the finest Christian men and women I've ever known."

Wait a minute. How did this woman get from being like Lottie Moon to the Lone Star Inn?

"After four of the kids left home, Mother and Daddy decided they would like to have a child of their own, however, Mother wasn't able to conceive. She used to tell my brother and me that it was the biggest blessing God gave her because she and Daddy were able to return to Lake View and adopt two boys from the orphanage. One of those boys was me and the other was my brother, Luke. Mother used to joke that we were simply on loan from God and she took loans very seriously."

By this time, the women in the congregation were wiping their tears with their Sunday, linen handkerchiefs. I heard a few of the older men in the back blow their honkers.

"Ladies and gentlemen, I am here today because of that orphanage. I am here today because seventy years ago my grandfather and the Christians in this community heard God's call and obeyed.

I am here today because a very brave woman saw God's sovereignty in her life and chose to follow Him at all costs. I am here today," he paused and composed himself, "because a very special woman never allowed sorrow to invade her spirit."

I felt a big lump in my throat. My stomach did cartwheels. I knew how important orphanages were—heck, I would have lived in one if Momma and Daddy hadn't come along and adopted me. But, how did the woman end up in the back of an ambulance at the sleaziest place in town? I didn't understand.

"When my father died six years ago, Mother was doing mission work in south Austin where she and Daddy attended church. She met a man, Dr. Lloyd Atkinson, who was volunteering his medical skills at the local shelter. Widowed earlier in life, he and Mother fell in love and married. It was Dr. Lloyd who encouraged Mother to pursue what would ultimately be her dream come true: to rebuild the Lake View Orphanage."

Huh?

"I wish you could have heard her talk about coming home to Lake View. My wife and I listened to countless stories about how she and Dr. Lloyd were going to build the orphanage exactly as it had been when she was a little girl. His dreams of taking children to Potter's Creek and teaching them to fish. Her dreams of teaching the young girls how to sew and cook and how to plant their own garden. At seventy-eight, the thought of retiring never entered her mind."

Okay, already. But how did she wind up at the Lone Star—dead?

"Brothers and sisters, I am telling you that I owe *everything* to the Lord for placing me with such loving parents. The fact that I am a United States senator from Texas wouldn't mean anything if I didn't know Jesus Christ as my personal Savior. I want to thank this church for the vision it had years ago and the vision it has for the future. Thanks to your deacon board, you will have the opportunity to vote on providing support for the new Lone Star Boys and Girls Ranch.

"You see, what none of you know is that Mother and Dr. Lloyd had purchased the Lone Star Inn from its owner just last month. Mother was actually writing the check when she suffered her fatal heart attack."

Sobs were heard throughout the congregation. Mr. Burch was wide awake and blowing his nose something fierce. A Kleenex box passed among the choir members.

OH MY GOSH! She was buying the Lone Star Inn when she died?

Senator Nowlin gained control of his voice and continued. "And, while it grieves me that she won't see her dream realized, I know that she has already been rewarded for her tireless work among children all over the world. She wanted nothing more than to share the good news of Jesus Christ with as many people as humanly possible, while trying to help orphans understand that we are all orphans until we are adopted by Christ."

Aunt Betty bowed her head and wept.

"So, thank you all for the love and support you've shown me and my family this past week. I apologize for the confusion with the flowers. Several of her older friends assumed that we would hold funeral services here in Lake View, but Dr. Lloyd thought it best to have the funeral in Austin where so many of their friends reside. Miss Betty, I want to extend my gratitude to you and your dedicated staff for all your hard work."

Aunt Betty was wailing.

"And I thank you, brothers and sisters, for allowing me to take time out of your worship service today to share a few thoughts about Virginia Nowlin Atkinson. Lake View was near and dear to my sweet mother's heart. I'm just sorry that she didn't get to see her dream come true. But together, and with God's help, we can work toward making her dream a reality. God bless each and every one of you. Thank you."

The only sound in the entire sanctuary was the squeaking of the senator's shoes as he walked down the stairs. Brother EdEarl stared into space. Even Nita Sue was still.

Finally, Brother Paul walked to the pulpit. He grasped the sides of the podium so hard that his knuckles turned white.

"Folks, I would like to skip the singing today and go straight to the sermon. I think it's a message that we all need to hear. Open your Bibles to the book of James, chapter three. I'll be preaching from verses two through ten. I've titled my sermon *Wait 'til You Hear What I Heard.*"

As Brother Paul preached I noticed that everyone, old and young alike, listened. On our pew, each lap held an open Bible. In the choir loft, every single choir member was alert including Mr. Burch. For the first time in my short life I understood what Brother Paul was talking about as he preached the sermon.

The tongue was a small thing but it could do so much damage. He compared the damage of the tongue to that of a raging fire—all it takes is a spark. That spark's source? Hell itself. Left unchecked, the uncontrolled tongue could cause irreversible damage. Satan uses the tongue to divide people and bring harm to them without people even knowing it. He also uses it to hurt God's servants.

In our case, I think he used our small town to hurt a godly woman and the good that she wanted to do here in our community. I guess Momma was right about gossip, nothing good comes of it. No wonder she harped on it all the time.

Brother Paul concluded his sermon with a time of repentance. Not just the usual *Have Thine Own Way, Lord* invitation but a time of REAL repentance. He invited folks to come up and kneel before the altar and make things right with the Lord. He asked folks to look deep into their hearts and beseech the Holy Ghost to convict them where they needed convicting. He asked us to go to our brothers and sisters and make things right with each other.

People were flocking to the altar. Aunt Betty made a beeline to the senator and threw her arms around his neck. Her short, squat body shook against his tall frame. I watched his tanned hands pat her back like a mother consoling her baby. As I viewed this image of forgiveness, I was suddenly reminded of my own sin.

I'd spent weeks spreading false rumors about someone I didn't even know. I'd even encouraged others to do the same then shunned my best friend when she tried to help me. What had gotten into me?

Before I could answer my own question, my hands grasped the pew in front of me while my feet sidestepped those of my parents. I made my way to the altar and knelt in front of Brother Paul. I asked Jesus to forgive me for all the horrible things I had done. My mind was suddenly filled with a list of my wrongs: bad-mouthing Mrs. Morris, making fun of Mrs. Snodgrass, wanting to throttle Shannon Grubbs, lying to Momma about the dishes, lying about my tithe, lying for Nita Sue and Randy. As I prayed for forgiveness, peace flowed through my body. My heart felt light. My spirit lifted. I opened my eyes long enough to see Momma's navy pumps and Daddy's wingtips on either side of me. Daddy offered his handkerchief while Momma rubbed my back. Nita Sue's head rested on my shoulder.

"Remember this moment," I said to myself, "Remember this moment, because this is the love of Christ."

Baptism: n. (bap-ti-zəm) a Christian sacrament marked by ritual use of water and admitting the recipient to the Christian community

The smell of pine sap wrapped around my face like a warm blanket as the sun shone from above. On the seat in front of me BJ sang,

"Just like a sleeping giant,
Sprawling in the sun;
In one big hand, the Rio Grande
In the other, Galveston.
My ma was born in Dallas, father in Fort Worth;
You can bet your boots, I got my roots in the
good ole Texas earth!
For this land is Texas! The Lone Star state of Texas!
This is the giant; Land I love!"

I joined in the chorus and sang as loud as I could. I imagine we looked pretty silly—two stringy haired girls singing at the top of their lungs on a bicycle built for two.

But, for BJ and me, this was about as good as it could get.

Pulling into Potter's Creek, BJ fetched the two Cokes and two bags of peanuts from her basket and we headed toward the water.

"You're coming to my baptism, aren't you?" I asked.

"Yep. Our whole family is. Momma says it's a glorious thing to see a new Christian get baptized." The Coke cap bent in half as BJ opened yet another bottle of the Real Thing.

"Hey, get this. Pops is coming all the way from Mississippi." She handed my bottle to me.

"Y'all get dunked, right? Not sprinkled?"

"Oh, yeah. Brother Paul pushes us all the way under. You're supposed to bend your knees and let him do all the work on the dunking part. I just hope my feet don't come up and hit the little window like Nita Sue's did…it was pretty embarrassing." Another swig of the Real Thing. "Water splashed over the side and got half the choir wet. I thought it was hilarious and laughed out loud. Daddy thumped the back of my head so hard that a knot came up. I haven't laughed during a baptism since."

"Do you hold your nose when he pushes you under?" she asked.

"No, Brother Paul puts a white handkerchief over your nose. He explained all that stuff when I went to talk to him about getting saved."

"Oh." BJ answered.

My back arched upward as I rearranged a small cluster of pine straw. Easing into the sticky green and brown pile, I nestled in and took a deep breath. With fingers clasped behind my head, I listened to the familiar sounds of Potter's Creek—water trickling across the slick, moss-covered rocks and the distant caw of Mr. Hitchcock's blackbird. Before long Mr. Snodgrass's orange light would flicker in between the tall pine trees and the bull pines wrapped in tangled strands of poison ivy. The crickets would begin their serenade once again as the lightning bugs danced a graceful ballet signaling the end of August.

Finally! Carol Ann Lawson's life was back to normal. I had one thing and only one thing to worry about—being baptized without embarrassing myself or my family. Surely, I could handle that...

Mooch: v. (müch) to take surreptitiously; freeload

"Hurry! They're pulling in the driveway!" Pops hollered.

"I'm trying but my jeans are caught on something—I can't get my leg out!" I yelled. Pops managed to untangle the wad of denim from the spokes of his motorcycle. Trying not to laugh at my sixty-three-year-old grandfather as he stooped over his new bike was proving harder than I thought. A pot–bellied, retired Baptist preacher, Pops was wearing a red and black motorcycle helmet which covered a head of gray hair.

"They're almost up the hill," I said, "rip it out if you have to, I don't care."

"Got it!" he said and released the handful of denim. "Help me push the bike behind the retaining wall; we can hide there," he said half–laughing, half–yelling.

I grabbed one handlebar and he grabbed the other. Together we managed to push the motorcycle down the incline and finally behind the brick retaining wall.

"Shh…they're coming around the house." Sure enough, we heard Aunt Ada and Uncle Elmer walking around the side yard toward the front of my house.

"Would you look at Hazel Jean's camellias? There must be fifty blooms hanging on that bush. And that woman never lifts a finger to them," Aunt Ada muttered.

"Oh, shut your yap, Ada. I doubt if Hazel Jean has time to garden with two girls and all. Besides, that camouflage–selling brother of yours ought to be doing the yard work, not her."

"Keep your voice down, Elmer. You want them to hear us? Lord, I just want a hot bath, a free meal and a place to lay my head tonight. You can criticize my baby brother after breakfast tomorrow morning."

Pops rolled his eyes as I placed my hand over my mouth, trying to suppress my laughter. We must have looked pretty silly squatting in the thick grass beside his black motorcycle. I prayed my aunt and uncle wouldn't look over the hedges that grew on top of that wall.

"Ring it again," Aunt Ada ordered.

"I rung it twice, Ada. Either they're here or they ain't. Ringing the danged doorbell ain't going make them magically appear." He spit his disgusting tobacco juice in momma's freshly cut grass. Gross.

"Well where in tarnation can they be? You'd think at least one of them would be home." She stepped toward the door and began banging on it.

"Banging on the door ain't going help nothing, Ada. Let's go. They must be down at Dan and Ed's store or something."

"Where are those two girls of theirs? I don't want to go to Betty's shop and ask if we can stay with them. Their house is filthy. I'd just as soon sleep in the car as one of her beds. Would you look at that? The car's in the driveway. Somebody's home, I just know it. They're not answering the door, that's all."

She proceeded to pound on our front door. Then she stuck her ear to the door to see if she could hear anything. "You know, Hazel Jean never has liked me. The only reason she's nice to me is because of Dan and Ed."

She pinned her hat back in place. I could see enough of her calves (between the shrubs) to take note of the cheap nylons knotted above her knees. I never understood the logic behind her knotted nylons. I mean, if she's going wear nylons, she should wear them without a knot peeking out from under the hem of her dress screaming *Look here! I'm too lazy to put on a girdle!* or not wear them at all.

Aunt Ada and Uncle Elmer were the biggest moochers in our family. They showed up at our doorstep all the time—usually around dinnertime and always on an empty stomach. Uncle Elmer sold uniforms to the prisons and jails in east Texas which meant they stayed with us when he called on his jailbird accounts.

"I need to take a leak," Uncle Elmer broadcast. "You keep your eyes open."

Before we knew it, Uncle Elmer was relieving himself close to one of momma's gardenia bushes. Urine shot through the air and splashed close to the front wheel of the motorcycle. I knew better than to look at Pops. If our eyes met, we would crack up and how on earth would we explain our presence? I mean, it's not every day that a grandfather and granddaughter are hiding five feet from the family's only prison uniform salesman and his whiny wife. BJ would never believe this one.

"Elmer D., I cannot believe you just urinated on my brother's lawn. That's disgusting. Matthew 1:11"

"Dogs do it. Besides, no one's at home, they'll never know. And don't go quoting the Bible to me, woman." And with that, we heard Uncle Elmer zip up. He and Aunt Ada turned and headed toward their car but not before Aunt Ada picked several camellias and gardenias and shoved them in her purse. The nerve of that woman! I could hear her jawing all the way to their car. Uncle Elmer was telling her to shut her yap or he'd shut it for her.

Dirt and gravel spun on the driveway as the twosome drove away.

"We did it, Carol Ann." Pops said. "We just saved your momma from two days of non–stop Ada and Elmer."

I was laughing so hard my sides hurt. I'd rolled on the grass when I heard the car door slam. Pops picked up his helmet and shook his head. "Camouflage–selling brother, huh? Did he actually call my son-in-law a camouflage–selling brother?"

"Yes sir, he did," I answered as I shook my head of hair, "right before he took a leak on your daughter's gardenia bush."

Pops and I pushed the motorcycle up the incline toward the sidewalk. The thing was heavier than it looked. Wiping the sweat from my forehead I said, "Pops, can I talk to you about something?"

"Why of course you can. You can talk to me about anything— you know that, don't you?"

I nodded. "I don't get them," I said. "I mean, I know this sounds terrible but I hate it when they show up on our doorstep. Uncle Elmer goes out on his sales calls and Aunt Ada sits on our couch all day filing her fingernails and yelling answers at the TV game shows. She stays in her pajamas until noon while Momma cleans house and does laundry. Last time they were here she didn't lift a finger to help with the dinner dishes or anything." I was huffing and puffing something fierce trying to help with his motorcycle.

I continued, "And they take over our bedroom. Nita Sue and I have to sleep on the couch or the floor while they push our twin beds together and gripe about us not having a double bed for them." I was getting worked up just talking about it.

"I know it's frustrating, Carol Ann, but they are your aunt and uncle after all." Pops was working extra hard to keep a straight face.

"Yes sir, I know. And I know that I shouldn't speak ill of my elders, but I hate the way they just show up without calling." We parked the motorcycle by the door. "Uncle Elmer smokes like a chimney even though Momma and Daddy ask him not to smoke inside. We have to air out the house when they leave. And Aunt Ada," I said as I set my helmet on the seat, "she unloads her bag of Merle Norman makeup in the bathroom like she's the only one who lives here." Pops was nodding in agreement. I guess preachers get used to people complaining all the time.

"But the thing that bothers me the most is the way she treats Momma—like her own personal slave." I sat down on the grass and pretended to paint my fingernails. "'Hazel Jean, could you bring me another cup of coffee please? My nails are wet. And, Hazel Jean, could you please come change the channel? *The Price is Right* is starting. And Hazel Jean, remember that Elmer is allergic to peanut oil. Not a drop'. It makes me want to scream."

Pops continued to nod his head. "You know what I learned a long time ago?"

"What's that?"

"There are some people who are harder to love than others. It's like being asked to saddle up next to a porcupine when you'd much rather sit next to a mink. But when it comes to families, there's usually a whole mess of porcupines and not a lot of minks. And that's a fact.

"Just remember the words of a very wise man," Pops said as he tucked his thumbs under imaginary suspender straps, "You can pick your friends but you can't pick your family." His prolonged look told me it was time to stop complaining and change the topic of our conversation.

"Yes, sir."

"So, tell me about your baptism. I didn't ride two hundred miles on my new bike to hear about Elmer and Ada." Pops twisted his back and smiled as his spine popped.

"Well, I'm supposed to leave Sunday School fifteen minutes early and Deacon Wilder will take me to the baptistery changing room where I'll put on a white robe. Then I'll go to the baptistery and wait for Brother Paul to call my name."

Pops asked, "Do you say anything to the congregation? I know our church, people do that sometimes."

I thought about this for a minute. What would I say? Sorry that I stirred up the entire town with my gossiping and I hope you can forgive me like Jesus?

"I don't know, Pops. I don't think so. I'm kind of nervous about the whole thing as it is. Remember when Nita Sue was baptized and her..." he put his hand up.

"There's nothing to be worried about. Nita Sue lost her footing, that's all. But just because it happened to her doesn't mean it will happen to you. Besides, I brought something to help you with that. Come on in here." Pops motioned for me to follow him through the sliding glass door. He picked up his duffel bag, reached inside and produced a pair of socks. "Here you go. Straight from the Sears and Roebuck catalog." He handed them to me. "What do you think?"

I took the socks and rubbed them between my fingers a couple of times. They looked like ordinary pink socks. "They're nice, Pops. Thanks."

"Look at the bottom. They have rubber soles so you won't slip in the baptistery. See?"

He was right. There were little dots of rubber on the bottoms of the socks. "Oh, thank you, Pops." I hugged his neck. He smelled of Old Spice aftershave, wind and the Texas sun. I loved the way his scratchy beard felt against my face.

"So, what do you say we do a little work around here and get a head start on supper? That'd make my daughter happy, don't you think?"

"Yes sir," I replied. "Pops?"

"Yes?"

"Are we going to tell Momma about Aunt Ada and Uncle Elmer? I mean, she and Daddy might get a little upset with us."

He laughed. "Don't worry. I'll talk to Hazel Jean and Dan, myself. I happen to know that your momma and daddy don't have time to entertain Ada and Elmer this week. Besides, after supper,

I'm going to need some time to look through my dictionary word lists if I'm going beat your momma in a game of Scrabble tonight."

"I don't know," I giggled, "she's pretty good. None of us can beat her. Not even Daddy."

"Well, just remember who taught her how to play," he answered.

"I do; Grandma."

"Hey, wait a minute! You better scuttle you derriere right back here before I deliberately and with great anticipation knock you upside your cranium. Right about here." He pointed at my head and said, "Yes, right there. Right around the medulla oblongata." I rolled my eyes. He popped my leg with the dishtowel.

"Don't make me spell all those long words."

"Okay, just the last one."

"Oh, no. Not a medical word. They're the worst."

"That's right. And if you play your tiles just right, it's worth fifty extra points."

Funeral parlor: n. an establishment with facilities for the preparation of the dead for burial or cremation, for the viewing of the body, and for funerals

The following Friday, I rode my bike to the square thinking about all of the relatives who were coming to town for the family reunion and baptism. I had hoped for a calm, immediate–family–only kind of baptism, but Momma and Daddy were so excited that they called everyone—even Uncle Elmer and Aunt Ada—and asked if they would like to see me get baptized on the Sunday of the family reunion. Naturally, they all agreed.

Because of Senator Nowlin's generosity, all the relatives were staying at the Lone Star Inn, free of charge. This man had to be the nicest fellow alive. When he learned that Aunt Betty had ordered the ill–fated truckload of flowers, he bought every last one of them and sent them to the local nursing home, the VFW lodge, and the Senior Center. He even sent me an autographed picture of himself standing on the steps of the Capitol Building in Washington, D.C. along with a letter on his very own Senate stationery.

I was still nervous about Brother Paul pulling me under the water, but Pops assured me that the no–slip socks would work. He should know; he had baptized over eight hundred people in his lifetime as a Baptist preacher. He had some pretty funny stories which would be told, again, when everyone arrived. Nita Sue and I heard the same stories every year. My personal favorite was the one about the pregnant lady who floated. He said her belly added too much buoyancy, and that he couldn't shove her head under without snapping her neck like a chicken bone. He finally had to ask her to turn around and lay face down in the water, so he could push her and her buoyant belly under. The congregation actually applauded at that one. I laughed out loud as I tried to picture Pops pushing a pregnant lady under the water in the baptistery.

Betty's Bloomers came into view as I rode past the statue of Mr. James Bowie.

You'd think I'd get the day off from Betty's Bloomers since the elementary school was out today but, no, Carol Ann Lawson worked hard and cheap. I dismounted my bike and leaned it against the green newspaper tube as always. Work before play, right?

"Carol Ann, I need you to walk this over to Shores Funeral Parlor for me. The family will be there in thirty minutes and that corpse ain't wearing her corsage. While you're there, tell Orten that all the flowers are finished and that Betty will be there today and on time as promised!" Occasionally, Aunt Betty referred to herself in the third person when she was under a deadline (no pun intended).

"Yes ma'am," I answered. I might just stop by McDeaver's on the way back and see if Mrs. Breeland was in. A moon pie would hit the spot right about now. "Aunt Betty? Do you mind me taking a Coke and drinking in on the way? It's awfully hot today," I asked.

"Yes, yes, yes. Just get on over there before the family," she answered.

I grabbed a Coke and the corsage box and headed toward the funeral parlor. Lake View had one funeral parlor that served two groups of people: whites and coloreds. One side was designed for the dead white folks in town (large and elaborate), while the other was for the coloreds (small and plain). You had to be very careful to deliver flowers to the right side. White folks weren't too happy to have their flowers sitting on the colored side and vice versa.

Passing by Daddy's store, I peeked in the window and saw him dusting the twelve point buck mounted on the wall. Uncle Ed was chatting it up with a customer. I rapped on the window and waved hello. Before I knew it, Daddy was at the front door calling my name. "Well now, how is my favorite redhead?" he asked as he bopped me on the head with the feather duster.

"Hi Daddy," I answered, "I'm your only redhead and I'm a *strawberry blonde*, remember? Just delivering this corsage to Shores."

"I don't recall anyone dying this week." His forefinger rubbed the cleft in his chin. He did that when he tried to remember something—usually a rule that Nita Sue and I had broken.

I read the ticket upside down. "Says 'Thornton Funeral' on here."

"Huh. Well what do you know? Your old Daddy doesn't know everything after all." We both laughed. "You better get on over there before Betty sends Luther after you," he said with a twinkle in his eye.

"Yes, sir. See you tonight."

"Bye now. Don't take any wooden nickels." The bells clanged as the door shut.

I half–skipped, half–walked my way to Shores. I was trying to remember the cheers that BJ and I had learned by watching Nita Sue and the other junior high cheerleaders. I knew half of it:

"Sar–dines. And pork–n–beans." Step, step.
"Sar–dines. And pork–n–beans." Step, step.
"I can tell by the way the li–ons going play;
"Sar–dines. And pork–n–beans."

I was chanting the second verse when I arrived at the funeral parlor but decided it probably wasn't a good idea to waltz into the funeral parlor chanting a cheer about sardines and pork and beans.

The front door of Shores was imposing. A remodeled, three–story Victorian home, Lake View's only mortuary was one of four buildings on the Historical Register. Something important happened there, although I couldn't remember what it was but it had something to do with James Bowie.

The door was so heavy that I had to park my Coke bottle on the stoop and use my Coke–carrying hand to open the massive door. It read:

<blockquote>
Shore's Mortuary
Our Family Serving Yours
from
Shore to Sho e
</blockquote>

If they were talking about the shores of Lake Lone Star, they weren't serving very many people. I could skip a stone from one shore to the other. Maybe the Shore family had a chain of funeral parlors from California to the east coast and that was the reason their door read *Shore to Shore*, but it read Shore to Shoe since someone had scratched the "r" from the last word.

Parlor room A was reserved for white families. Parlor room B was for colored families. I looked around the lobby of the stately home but didn't see any employees. I stood in the foyer staring at the enormous hand–carved staircase trying to decide what to do. *Should I leave it on the desk or should I holler for someone to come help me?* I decided to go the holler and help route since Aunt Betty was intent on this woman having her corsage before the viewing.

"Hello? Is anybody here?" My voice echoed in the still house. "Hello?" I repeated, "Mr. Orten? Anybody?"

"Yoohoo! Back here, Luther." Oh no. It was Mrs. Martin. What was she doing here? She should be at home perming Margo's hair or something. The large–busted, platinum blonde woman prissed her way into the lobby. "Oh, it's you, Carol Ann. Where's Luther? I thought he was bringing the corsage."

"No, ma'am. Aunt Betty asked me to deliver the corsage. Uh, I don't mean to be impolite, Mrs. Martin, but is Mr. Orten here? Aunt Betty said to be sure that this corsage got pinned on the cor…uh, I mean, the uh…"

"Corpse, Carol Ann? Really? For your information, young lady, that corpse has a name." She was getting flustered. Maybe she had hot flashes, too. "Mrs. Somebody…I forget," she said. The pencil she stuck behind her ear disappeared. A box of No 2 pencils could get lost in her hair. I bet Miss Mattie sold her Dippity Do by the case. "For your information, Orten and staff are attending a convention in Ft. Worth. Odell and I are the only ones in town and he put *me* in charge of the viewing today." The fake fingernail on her index finger also disappeared as she scratched the top of her head.

"Oh, how nice for you, Mrs. Martin," I said. "Well, here's the corsage. I best be getting back to work." I tried to hand the corsage box to her but she wouldn't take it. She grabbed my arm instead.

"Hold on there, missy. You are going to pin that corsage on Mrs. What's–her–name before you go back to work."

"Do *what*?"

"You heard me. You are going to pin *that* corsage," her fake nail drummed the corsage box, "on *that* woman before the family gets here." I noticed a bright green mood ring on one of her fingers. If she thought I was touching some corpse she had another thing coming and it would turn her mood ring black.

"Mrs. Martin, I don't know who told you that I was the one doing the pinning but it's my understanding that I'm supposed to deliver the corsage and get Mr. Shores' signature on the ticket. Nothing more, ma'am." Her leopard skin, platform shoes practically came off the floor when I suggested that I had no intention of pinning the corsage on the dead woman.

"Listen here, Carol Ann Lawson. You and I are the only two *living* human beings in this house of death. You understand me? And there is no way on God's green earth that I am touching Mrs....," she looked at the ticket, "Thornton in there. So I suggest you march your skinny little self on in that room and get *that* flower on *that* woman's lapel before the family arrives in..." she looked at the clock, "three minutes."

Oh my gosh! What was I going to do? Mrs. Martin was notorious for spreading gossip all over town. There's no telling what she would say about me if I didn't obey her. And to tell you the truth, I was a little scared standing next to someone who referred to God the way she did. She was going to hell for sure and I didn't want to be standing next to her when she started her trip. She might just end up like Mrs. Thornton in there. But when Aunt Betty got wind of the way she treated me, she wouldn't be wearing a corsage— that was for sure.

I was trying to figure a way out of this morbid nightmare when I heard the door heave open. Mrs. Martin grabbed my right ear and whispered, "Get in there and get that flower pinned on her before I step on it and tell Betty *you* did it."

As much as I hated to, I nodded my head and asked, "Which room?"

"The one on the right," she answered.

I could hear feet shuffling in the foyer and Mrs. Martin practically slobbering on the grieving family. Someone was crying pretty loud! I walked to the room on my right and saw the casket. One standing spray and one potted plant lined the wall which was odd for someone important. Usually, there were a dozen or so plants and lots of flowers. I guess Mrs. Thornton wasn't that popular after all.

Half of the lid was up. I inched my way toward the casket. The box shook in my Coke–carrying hand.

"What is the verse Momma taught me to say when I am scared?" I asked myself out loud. "*The Lord is my shepherd*? No, that's the one they say at funerals. *Blessed are the meek*? No, that's not it either." My legs began to shake as I got closer. "*At times when I am afraid*? Yes, that's the one!"

I closed my eyes and prayed out loud as hard as I knew how. "At times when I am afraid I will trust in Thee. At times when I am afraid I will trust in Thee. At times when I am afraid I will trust in Thee." My hands shook so hard that I had trouble slipping the ribbon off the outside of the clear box. I told myself to slow down and breathe. "Breathe. At times when I'm afraid. Breathe…"

I opened the box and grabbed the corsage. It was time to do it and get out of this nightmare. The gardenia's aroma filled my nostrils.

"Take a deep breath and get it over with," I said. I dropped the corsage box on the floor and walked toward the casket. Trying not to look at the face, I closed my left eye. Using my right eye, I found a spot on the lapel and attached the corsage the best way I knew how. But something wasn't quite right. The lapel looked like it belonged to a man's suit, not a lady's jacket.

So, I did the only thing I knew to do. I looked at the face. It was a *man*; a *colored* man.

"Oh my gosh, oh my gosh, oh my gosh!" I screamed. "There's a man in Mrs. Thornton's casket!" I wanted to move but I couldn't. My legs were stiff and planted on the carpet. "Oh my gosh! Breathe, breathe. At times when I am afraid I will trust in Thee! Breathe, breathe."

"Carol Ann?"

"Oh! He's calling my name! Someone, help me!" I screamed in a high–pitched, piercing voice. Two massive hands grabbed my shoulders and turned my body around. "Aah!" I screamed again. The gargantuan hands belonged to Mr. Odell Shores.

"Good Lord, girl. What on earth are you doing in here?"

Tears flowed down my cheeks. "Mrs. Martin… made me… pin the cor…sage to the bod…y," I sobbed.

"She did *what*?"

"She made me…pin the corsage on…Mrs. Thornton…there." I pointed to the casket. "But there's a man in her casket!" More sobs.

"What on earth? Why, children aren't even allowed in the viewing rooms. She ought to know better." He replied. I put my hands over my face and sobbed some more.

Mrs. Martin prissed herself in Parlor room A and yelled, "What in the *hell* is going on in here? Oh, Odell, I thought you were out." She changed her tune rather quickly.

Mr. Odell shot a look at Mrs. Martin that would scare the devil himself. "Carol Ann, you go on back to Betty's. I'll take care of this," Mr. Odell said.

"But…what about…the man in Mrs. Thornton's ca…ca…casket?" I couldn't control my voice.

"What man?" Mrs. Martin asked.

"*That one!*" I screamed as I pointed to the open casket.

"You stuck the corsage on Mr. Derryberry? Can't you tell the difference between a man and a woman?"

"You said the room on the *right*!"

"Yes, and this is the room on the *left*!"

I pointed at the casket with my right hand. "*Right!*" I yelled.

"*Left!*" she yelled.

"Ladies, please. There is a grieving family down the hall. Carol Ann, I am sincerely sorry for what happened to you today. Please accept my apologies. You should not have been put in a position like that." His eyes drilled holes in Mrs. Martin. "Now then, why don't you run on over to Betty's. I'll call her and explain everything, all right?"

"Yes, sir." I wiped my face with his handkerchief. "Thank you."

I hoofed it out of Shores as fast as humanly possible. I sprinted all the way to Daddy's store and into the bathroom. I wretched until there was nothing left in my stomach.

"Carol Ann? It's Daddy. Are you sick?"

"Daddy?" The hysteria returned. "Daddy!" I opened the door. "You won't believe it. I had to…" I wretched some more. Daddy held my hair while I stuck my head in the porcelain bowl.

"You're okay, Carol Ann. Take a deep breath when you can." I exhaled and stood upright. The tears were back.

"Daddy, Mrs. Martin made me put a corsage on a dead person. It was awful." Daddy took me in his arms and stroked my hair.

"Okay, it's okay. Just take your time." He patted my back. "You're okay. Inhale…that's my girl…now exhale." My sobs subsided. The Lawson family was big on breathing.

"Now then," Daddy said, "come on in the office and tell me what happened."

We walked into the office he shared with Uncle Ed. My uncle came in and sat next to me. His cigar smoke was making me green around the gills.

"Ed, how about you finish that cigar later?" Daddy asked.

"Oh, sorry about that. Sure thang." He snubbed the end of the cigar in the ashtray I made for them at Vacation Bible School. Both men stared at me.

"Well, it's like this. Aunt Betty told me to take a corsage to Shores. It was for a lady named Mrs. Thornton." Daddy nodded in agreement. "And when I got inside, Mrs. Martin was filling in for everyone because they are all in Ft. Worth at a convention or something." The tears were making their way back to my eyeballs. "So, I told her that Aunt Betty said for me to deliver it before the family arrived, you know, for the viewing and all. That's when Mrs. Martin told me that *I* had to put the corsage on the corpse."

"*Blast* that woman!" Uncle Ed yelled.

"Ed, watch you language," Daddy said.

Uncle Ed looked me square in the eyeballs. "Did she make you do it? Did she make you pin a flower on a stiff?"

"Ed!" Daddy was raising his voice.

"Yes, sir, she did! And it wasn't Mrs. Thornton. Somehow a man got in her casket and I pinned the gardenia on him. A colored man! Oh, Daddy, it was awful; just awful!" Vomit made its way back up. Daddy grabbed a trash can. I heaved but nothing came up.

"Ed, I'm going take Carol Ann home now. I may or may not be back today." Daddy had the same tone in his voice that he used the night he grounded Nita Sue for sneaking out of the house and riding around town with a group of teenagers.

Uncle Ed stood up and pulled his pants over his beer belly. "I'm going over to that funeral parlor and I'm going to give that hussy and her boyfriend a piece of my mind." He grabbed his .22 off the gun rack and started for the door.

"Ed, you aren't going anywhere," Daddy said with resolve. "This is our affair, not yours. I'll handle Erma Martin and Odell Shores later." Daddy's veins stuck out on the right side of his neck. Maybe Uncle Ed would shoot her and I could see to it that she didn't get a corsage for *her* viewing. I'd show her…

"Not my affair? That flower shop is as much my affair as this here store. Wait 'til I give that street–walking woman a piece of my mind." Uncle Ed loaded his .22 rifle. "...making a child do her work...that woman's been a burr under my saddle long enough..."

"Ed!" Daddy interrupted, "what are you going to do? Shoot her? And Odell?"

A smile appeared on Uncle Ed's face. "As much as I'd like to shoot her sorry self and mount her next to Buck there," he pointed his rifle at Buck, the mounted twelve point, "no Dan, I ain't going to shoot anybody. But talking to her and Odell Shores with this here rifle in my hand will make a bigger impression than talking at them without one." Uncle Ed hitched his pants over his belly for the last time, bit the end off a new Roi-Tan, and made a beeline for the door.

"Ed, don't do something you'll regret, it's not worth it." But Uncle Ed was already out the door and halfway there.

We stood in the middle of the archery section of Daddy's store. I tried to close my mouth but it stayed open. *Did I do this? Was this my fault?* All I did was run to my daddy and tell him what that wretched woman made me do.

"Daddy, I'm sorry. I didn't mean for any of this to happen. I should've gone back to Aunt Betty's like Mr. Odell told me to." The tears returned. "I'm so sorry."

"Come here; sit down a minute." I sat on an old nail keg next to the binoculars. Daddy walked to the front of the store and flipped the OPEN sign to PLEASE CALL AGAIN. He turned off the lights and joined me on another nail keg.

"Carol Ann, do you remember how you felt the Sunday that Senator Nowlin came to town and spoke to our church?"

"Yes, sir. I guess so."

"Wait. Let me rephrase that. Do you remember how you felt when Brother Paul gave the invitation? How the Holy Ghost convicted you and you knew in your heart that you needed to be saved?"

"Yes sir," I replied. *How could I forget?*

"You see, honey, it's like this. Ed has never had an experience like that. He's not come to the point in his life where he recognizes the need for salvation. Do you understand?" Daddy suddenly looked very sad.

"You mean Uncle Ed's not saved?"

"Well, it's not for us to judge—only God can see into a man's heart—but by all outward signs? No, your uncle has not been saved."

"But how? I mean, he grew up in church just like you and Aunt Ada, right?"

"Yes, that's right. But you know that sitting in church doesn't make a man a Christian any more that sitting on this nail keg makes me a nail." Daddy leaned forward and took both my hands. "Honey, your mother and I have prayed for Ed's salvation for years. And we believe that one day he will see the light just like you did." He smiled and patted my hands.

Wow. So many things made sense now. His language. His driving. His prejudice. The *Playboy* magazines.

"Do you think he'll shoot Mrs. Martin and Mr. Odell?" Panic made its way back to my stomach.

Daddy chuckled. "No, he won't shoot anyone. He'll just wave his gun around and give those two a piece of his mind. I imagine he unloaded the barrel as soon as he walked out the door." We sat in silence. "Come on, honey. Let's get you home."

"Yes, sir."

Devil's juice: n. Sometimes used in reference to alcoholic beverages

I was still upset from the episode with the dead man. Daddy put me to bed and threatened Nita Sue within an inch of her life if she told anyone about the ordeal.

She agreed. She knew better than to disobey Daddy.

Every time I closed my eyes and tried to sleep, I saw that casket. I couldn't get it out of my head. When I thought about actually touching the dead man, vomit would rise in my throat. I still couldn't believe Mrs. Martin made me do it. And then to find out that Uncle Ed probably wasn't saved? How much more could a girl take?

Pops sat on the edge of my bed and tried to help me fall asleep by humming and rubbing my back. I was just about asleep when I heard Nita Sue scream from the kitchen "They're here! They're here!"

Pops jumped up and looked out the bedroom window. It was Aunt Vestal and Uncle Claude. Along with the other relatives who were coming to Lake View for the combination family reunion and baptism weekend, was our most colorful aunt and uncle, Vestal and Claude. They drove all the way from California for the weekend.

Aunt Vestal had been quite the beauty queen in her day. Long legs, auburn hair and the greenest eyes in Bowie County, she worked as a stand–in for some of the biggest movie stars in Hollywood. One day, or so the story goes, Aunt Vestal showed up with Uncle Claude's lunch pail and, out of the blue, got a job as an extra at the movie studio. Aunt Betty says she hobnobs with the stars.

Uncle Claude built movie sets for one of the movie studios and worked with the trade unions "out there" as he says. Everything is better out there. When they come home to Lake View for a visit all they can talk about are the stores out there, the trees out there, and the freeways out there. Apparently, everything was bigger and better out there when it came right down to it.

They pulled in the driveway towing a silver camper behind their Datsun. I knew it was a Datsun because I'd seen the commercials on television. People in Lake View favored American made automobiles—mainly pickup trucks. Only in the bigger cities like Tyler or Holly Springs did folks tool around in foreign automobiles. A man could get himself shot for driving a sissy, foreign–made compact car around here.

Not wanting to miss out on the excitement, I threw on my clothes and joined the family. Pops was more excited than anyone else. He hadn't seen Aunt Vestal in over a year, with them living on the west coast and all. And since Grandma died, Pops was happy to spend as much time as possible with his family.

Nothing prepared us for what stepped out of the beige Datsun. It was like a camera filming an event in slow motion. When the car door opened, the longest pair of legs I'd ever seen stepped onto our driveway. And they were as bare as a pair of legs could be, this side of naked. The platform shoes gave new meaning to the words high heel. And the top, it was another matter altogether. She was wearing a halter top—the kind you saw on beach movies—but it looked much better on her. This couldn't be the Aunt Vestal I remembered. This woman looked more like her daughter, but they didn't have a daughter.

Her thick auburn hair was cut in a stylish pageboy and had just enough tease in it to look natural—not like the hairdos that came from the Miss Mattie's House of Hair. People used to say that I resembled her because of my strawberry blonde hair. Wow. Double wow.

Pops was the first one to close his mouth long enough to say anything. "Well, it's about time you two got here. Come over here and give your daddy a hug!" Aunt Vestal gave Pops a big hug. Daddy and Uncle Claude shook hands like real men. (I wasn't sure how men greeted one another in California). Then Momma, Nita Sue and I hugged Aunt Vestal. She smelled of mystery and excitement.

"Is that a camper?" I asked Uncle Claude.

"Yep," he replied.

"Are y'all going camping?" I asked.

"Nope," he answered. I'd forgotten that Uncle Claude was a man of few words.

"So, why'd you bring it?" I asked.

"So we could stay in it when we got to Texas."

"Oh, but Senator Nowlin is letting all the family…" Momma cut me off.

"Y'all must be worn out from all that driving. Come on in and get some iced tea. I just brewed a fresh batch," Momma interjected.

Nita Sue walked around the Datsun, checking it out. Her hands were cupped against her face as she pressed them to the window to get a better view of the inside. We'd only seen them on TV.

"Check it out. How cool is this car?" she said.

I did the same. But it hurt my nose to press it against the hot glass, so I opened the door and plopped down in the driver's seat.

"Get out of their car, your moron. You can't just open the door and get in like that."

"Nita Sue, look. What's this?" I held up an empty can. It wasn't a Coke.

"Let me see. What the hell? It's beer, that's what. Mother and Daddy will have a hissy fit if they see beer cans ten feet from the house. Put it back where you found it and for Pete's sake, don't say anything about it to them or to Pops."

"But…" Someone was walking toward the car.

"Put it down!"

A familiar face closed in on the passenger's side. "Well, well, what do we have here?"

"Sorry about that," I stumbled over my words. "We were just looking at your Datsun. It's so cool."

She leaned down and stuck her head through the open window. "Listen, girls. What your mother doesn't know won't hurt her. Catch my drift?" Her privates were practically falling out of her halter top. "Hand me my cigarettes."

I handed over the cigarettes.

"Now, if you ladies could help me with a slight problem, I would appreciate it." She lit a Virginia Slim and blew smoke into the air like a movie star. "Are there any clubs around here?" Another drag.

I chirped up. "Oh, yes, ma'am. We have a lot of clubs here. There's the Garden Club, the Rotary Club, the…" Aunt Vestal laughed hysterically.

"No, doll. Clubs. You know? Where a person can get a drink and do a little dancing?"

Nita Sue answered for both of us. "Well, here in Lake View there's the Hay Loft. It's the club that's connected to the Lone Star Inn out on Highway 59. Holly Springs has two clubs, the Pines and the Silver Spur. Saturday night is ten cent drafts at the Silver Spur." I stared at Nita Sue in astonishment. How did she know about all these clubs? She dated the son of a Baptist preacher.

Aunt Vestal looked first at Nita Sue, then me. "Can you two girls keep a secret?" Another drag. "I'm not supposed to be partaking of the devil's juice if you know what I mean." Exhale. "So let's just keep this between us."

"Cool," Nita Sue said.

"Yeah. Cool," I said. We watched Aunt Vestal priss her way back to the house. She waved her hand in the air as she extinguished the cigarette butt with her shoe then disappeared through the sliding glass door.

Prom Queen: n. The honorary title awarded to a girl by the high school football team

"Girls? You out there? Supper's ready." Momma called us in from the Datsun. Nita Sue leaned over and reminded me not to say anything about our conversation with Aunt Vestal. I wasn't going to say a word. I'd had enough trauma for one day.

"Okay. Everyone gather around so we can say the blessing," Daddy instructed. "Waylon, would you lead us?" Pops thanked God for Aunt Vestal and Uncle Claude's safe trip, the food that was about to nourish our bodies, and asked forgiveness for our sins of commission and omission.

The door opened.

"Why shoot–a–monkey!" Aunt Betty exclaimed. She and Uncle Ed finally showed up, late as usual. "Vestal Cinaretta and Clifford Claude. Look at you, look at you!" Aunt Betty was hugging them like she hadn't seen them in twenty years. Now it was Uncle Ed's turn.

"Claude," Uncle Ed said.

"Ed," Uncle Claude answered.

"How's California? (Cal-i-forn-EYE-aye)" Uncle Ed asked.

"Good," Uncle Claude answered.

"Good," Uncle Ed said. He turned to me. "How ya feeling, Carol Ann?" Daddy cleared his throat with a don't–bring–up–that–casket–thing kind of sound. All eyes were on me.

"I'm fine. Just fine." I sat. "Could you pass the fried okra, please, Momma?"

"Sure, honey." She passed the okra.

"Vestal? You been in any movies lately? Seen any of them big stars?" Aunt Betty asked. Leave it to Aunt Betty to be the originator of a juicy Hollywood story or two. I don't think she learned a thing from the Atkinson scandal.

"I was a stand–in for a movie star since I saw you last." Gasps went around the table. "*Valley of the Dolls*. You guys heard of it?"

Aunt Betty grabbed her at her bosom. Uncle Ed's eyes lit up. So did Daddy's. Pops acted like he didn't hear it.

"How nice for you, Vestal. More tomatoes? I know y'all can't get tomatoes like this in California," Momma said. Real Texas ladies had a way of taking control of conversations like this one and getting them back on an acceptable track.

"Sure, Sis. I'd *love* some more tomatoes." Aunt Vestal's tongue licked the tines of her fork. I hope she didn't do that out in public. People would stare.

"What's it like being a stand–in?" Nita Sue asked. Momma shot her a look that could have killed a horse.

"It's okay. The movie stars don't say much to us peons, though. They say their lines and go back to their trailers. Occasionally an actor will talk to me. James Garner is probably the nicest one I've met." I thought Aunt Betty was going to fall over in her plate of fried chicken.

"James Garner? You actually met James Garner?" Momma's Hollywood antennae were up now. James Garner was a good old boy from Oklahoma who'd made it big in Hollywood but never forgot his Southern roots. Talking to Jim was acceptable in Momma's book.

"Yeah, he talked to me. I guess he picked up on my accent or something because he walked over to me and said 'Texas or Oklahoma, which one is it?'" "Wows" and "what do you knows" filled the kitchen.

"Is he as handsome up close as he is on the movie screen?" Aunt Betty asked.

"More so," Aunt Vestal said.

Licking his fingers Pops said, "Claude, tell us what you've been working on. From the looks of your tan, I'd say you've been building outdoors."

"Yep. Been building on the MGM lot. Had to create an entire western town in one week." We all stared at him waiting for more information. He didn't budge.

Momma said, "Claude, did you see Pop's scooter outside?"

"It's a motorcycle, Hazel Jean. Not a scooter," Pops corrected.

"I know, I know. It's just hard for me to get used to the idea of my father riding all over the country on a motorcycle."

"How long you had it, Pop?" Uncle Ed asked.

"Over a year, I reckon."

"How fast can she go?" Uncle Ed was shoving okra in his mouth.

"Oh, you know, the speed limit, of course," Pops answered as he cleared his throat.

"Uh huh," Aunt Vestal mumbled, "and I got some prime beach front property to sell you when you're ready to move to Arizona." This got a big laugh. I didn't get it. I didn't know Aunt Vestal owned anything in Arizona or why her statement was so funny.

Conversation slowed as everyone ate. The fried okra and tomatoes were just about gone. Everyone was sucking down their food except Aunt Vestal. Maybe you had to eat light to keep a figure like hers.

"Vestal, weren't you the homecoming queen your senior year?" Aunt Betty asked.

"Yes, why?" She methodically took a cigarette out of the pack and stuck it between her lips. "Mind if I smoke?"

Momma answered first. "Could you *wait*?" she asked in her sweetest voice with her head tilted slightly.

"Do I have a *choice*?" Aunt Vestal answered in her sweetest voice with her head tilted slightly.

Daddy quickly stood and announced, "Ice cream in ten minutes. Who'll help me with the freezer? I made a big batch of vanilla with fresh peaches. Nita Sue? Betty? Pop?"

I thought Momma and Aunt Vestal might get into a fistfight right there at the kitchen table over one, little Virginia Slim. Evidently, Daddy did too. He was doing his level best to distract everyone with his homemade ice cream.

Aunt Betty didn't catch on, which wasn't too unusual. She said, "Lordy, lordy, Vestal. I'd almost forgot about you being a past queen. They moved homecoming up this year and instead of it being the end of October, it's in the middle of September. I could just shoot them coaches. Shoot them deader than doornails. Anyway, every year, you know, they invite all the queens from years past to the game and the parade. I know the committee would be thrilled to have you participate in the activities. What do you think? Will you do it?"

Momma choked on her tomato. Without missing a beat, Uncle Ed slapped her on the back until she finally asked him to quit hitting her. Daddy disappeared to find his ice cream freezer. Pops was right behind him.

Nita Sue said, "Cool! I didn't know you were homecoming queen. How come no one ever told me you were a homecoming queen?" She looked at Momma like she had omitted part of our family lineage.

"There's a lot of things about me no one's ever told you."

"Excuse me," Momma said. She began clearing the table.

"Oh, quit fussing with the dishes and sit down, Hazel Jean. They aren't going anywhere," Aunt Betty chimed in. Momma sat.

"So, what do you say, Vestal? Will you do it? I'll make you the biggest double mum corsage this side of the Red River." She lowered her voice and leaned over the table as if she and Aunt Vestal were the only ones with ears. "I do all the flowers you know, and I'll see to it that yours is the gaudiest of all the other queens. Why, shoot–a–monkey! Them coaches may have done me a big favor. A blessing in disguise—that's what this is—a blessing in disguise!"

Uncle Ed leaned back in Momma's kitchen chair and belched.

"Ed, that's so gross. And at Hazel Jean's table." Aunt Betty had forgotten all about her blessings.

"Beg your pardon, ladies. But if I don't relieve some of that pressure, it builds up and before I know it, I got heartburn big enough to kill a steer and then some." He hit his chest with his fist. "My, my, you sure can cook, Hazel Jean."

"Daddy has some Rolaids, want me to get you some?" I asked.

"Is that the one that consumes forty–seven times its weight in excess acid?"

"Yes sir, that's the one."

"Better get me some, there, Carol Ann. This here's been a heartburn kind of day, if you know what I mean." I prayed he wouldn't bring up the casket incident.

"Yes, sir. Be right back." I got up from the table and started toward the bathroom. Momma stopped me before I could get there. "I'll get them, honey. I know right where they are. Why don't you go out and check on the ice cream?"

I hesitated and shrugged my shoulders. "Okay by me."

Daddy and Pops were inspecting the salt and ice levels in the freezer. Then Daddy said, "I know it does, but why does it *melt* the ice on the driveway? I can't keep enough rock salt on hand for the one or two ice storms we get around here."

Then Pops said, "I don't understand it either. I guess it's just one of those things we won't know until we get to the other side." Then they both nodded their heads in agreement. Aunt Vestal materialized out of thin air and lit another cigarette.

"They reinventing the wheel over there?" A steady stream of smoke curled its way upward and over the roof of the house.

"I don't know. I don't think so, though. They were talking about rock salt on driveways or something."

"God, I'd forgotten how dull this town is."

"Aunt Vestal, will you do me a favor?"

"Sure, kiddo. What is it?"

"Well, would you mind not using God's name like that? It makes me nervous sharing the same air with someone who refers to the Almighty that way. I've had about all the excitement I can stand for one day."

She threw her head back and laughed.

"Did I say something funny?"

"No, doll. I'm sorry, I'm not laughing at you. It's just the Bible Belt mentality around here, that's all. Out there, people don't care what you say or do, or who you do it with. People are free. Free to be whatever they want to be without being judged and talked about all the time."

"But we're free here, Aunt Vestal. I mean, I'm free to pick and choose what clubs I want to be in at school, and what clothes to wear, and what friends to hang out with."

"I'm glad you still see it that way. But one morning you'll wake up and realize that there's got to be more to life than riding on a homecoming float and knowing every stanza of *Amazing Grace*. Trust me, I know what I'm talking about."

"Ice cream's ready. Come and get it." Pops yelled.

Aunt Vestal mocked, "Did you hear that? The ice cream's ready. Stop the presses." I wasn't sure I wanted to look like her after all. Seemed to me California had been about as good for her as it was for Roxy's mom and that wasn't saying a whole lot.

***

Later that evening, Pops left for the Lone Star Inn on his motorcycle, and Aunt Betty and Uncle Ed went home. Nita Sue and I were getting ready for bed when we heard music coming from outside our bedroom window.

"Do you hear that?" I asked.

"Yeah. Who do you suppose is playing music that loud this time of night?"

"I don't know." I pulled the curtains back on the window as Nita Sue pushed it open. Rhythm and blues rode in on the thick air. "Wow! Would you look at that?" I said. Aunt Vestal and Uncle Claude had parked their trailer at the end of the driveway away from our house. Sandwiched in the pine thicket, we could see their tiny silver trailer from our window.

"Let's go out there and see what they're doing," Nita Sue suggested.

"No way. I'm not going out there. Besides, why do you care what they're doing?"

"Are you crazy? This is as close to California and *Cosmopolitan* as we'll ever get. I want to see what the inside of their trailer looks like, don't you?"

"Yeah, I guess so. But it's past our bedtime. Maybe we should wait until tomorrow and ask for a tour."

"You're still scared from that casket thing aren't you? Well, get over it, little sister. People die around here all the time. Let's try to live a little while we have the experts fifty yards away. Now come on."

She had a point.

We climbed out the bedroom window—the same one Nita Sue used to sneak out with Randy—and headed down the gravel driveway toward the trailer. As we got closer, we saw Chinese lanterns strung across an awning. The red and green lights cast an eerie glow against the silver. A portable radio played music.

"Let's go," I whispered to Nita Sue. "I don't think we should be down here. They might be out back in the woods or something."

"Look, their Datsun's gone. I bet they went to town to do some dancing and drinking. Come on, I just want to see the inside and then we'll leave."

"Oh, all right. But just a peek, then I'm going back. With or without you."

We stepped inside the tiny trailer. "Wow" was all I could say. I'd never seen anything like it. It had a little bed, a little kitchen, a little table and a little TV. It was like a playhouse, only real.

"Cool, check this out," Nita Sue said. "Real martini glasses. And tiny umbrellas just like the ones on the Dean Martin Show." She held up a glass and pretended to take a sip. "Check out the size of that television. I didn't know they made them that small." She was drooling over the television when I spotted all the liquor.

"I thought she wasn't supposed to drink the devil's juice, isn't that what she said?"

"Who cares? She and Uncle Claude have enough booze here to last them a long time."

"Momma and Daddy will die when I tell them there's a bar in their driveway," I said.

"You aren't telling them anything, little sister. You're going keep your pie hole shut. That's what you're going to do."

"But Nita Sue, you know Momma doesn't per..."

"Yes, I know Mother doesn't per*mit* alcoholic beverages in her home, but technically, this isn't her home, it's Aunt Vestal's. And it's none of our business what she does in the privacy of her own home." Nita Sue sounded more like Perry Mason every day.

"Well, Big Sister, if it's none of our business, then why are we in the middle of their trailer, huh?"

"Good point. Let's go. I've got a lot of thinking to do." We took one last look and hiked up the gravel driveway to the house. It was much easier climbing out the window than climbing back in.

"You've come a long way, baby. To get where you got to today. You've got your own cigarette now, baby. You'll come a long, long way."

Virginia Slims jingle

We awakened to the sounds of saws and hammers outside our bedroom window.

"What the hell is going on?" Nita Sue hollered.

I sat up in my bed to see the silhouette of someone through our curtains. "Who's out there?" I asked.

"I don't know who the hell it is, but I wish they would stop." Nita wasn't a happy camper; she was a firm believer in getting her beauty sleep.

"Rise and shine, girls." Daddy had entered our bedroom.

"Oh, good morning, Daddy," Nita Sue said in a sweet voice. "Who's making all that noise?"

"For your information, all that noise is your Uncle Claude," Daddy said as he walked to the window and pulled back the curtains. He pecked on the window and Uncle Claude waved.

We waved back.

Daddy was lifting the window when he noticed that it wasn't locked. "Have you girls opened your window in the last couple of days?" he asked.

"Uh, why do you ask?" I answered.

"Because it isn't locked and I just checked all the windows a few days ago." He turned and stared at Nita Sue. "Nita Sue, is there anything you would like to tell me?"

Nita Sue's face went white as a ghost's.

"You know what?" I said, "I opened it last night. I heard music and couldn't figure out where it was coming from. I guess I forgot to lock it back. Sorry, Daddy."

Daddy looked at me then at Nita Sue. "Is that right, Nita Sue?"

"Yes, sir. We heard music coming from outside and opened up the window to see what it was."

"So what was it?"

I answered, "It was Aunt Vestal's music coming from their trailer, that's all."

"You girls be sure you to lock the windows after you open them. It's not safe to sleep with the windows unlocked." His huge hands pushed the window up. "Morning, Claude."

"Dan."

"I was fixing to tell the girls the good news."

"That so?"

Daddy turned around and announced, "Girls, in just two short weeks you will be the proud owners of your very own bathroom. What do you think about that?"

Nita Sue and I jumped out of our beds and started screaming. "Really? Our very own bathroom?"

"Yes, your very own bathroom." About that time, Momma came in to see what all the commotion was about. Nita Sue and I hugged her neck, we hugged Daddy's neck, we hugged each other, and would have hugged Uncle Claude but he was on the wrong side of the window.

"What's going on in here?" Pops had arrived and heard all the hubbub.

"We're getting our very own bathroom!" I yelled. "Can you believe it, Pops?"

"Why, shoot–my–monkey!" he said. That got a lot of laughs.

"Who wants bacon and eggs?" Momma asked.

"What a silly question, Hazel Jean," Pops answered. "How about you let me fix breakfast for everyone?"

"Fine by me." It didn't take a lot of arm twisting for Momma to let someone else cook a meal or two. "Girls, we need to start thinking about what colors you want to use in your new bath."

Nita Sue and I were still reeling from the news that we would finally have our own bathroom. I'd be a rich girl if I had a nickel for every time I'd had to wait on someone else just so I could get into the bathroom. And hot water? I'd never take another cold shower again. BJ would be so happy for me.

After everyone had cleared out of our room, Nita Sue thanked me for lying for her. "I wasn't lying, I simply didn't tell the entire truth, that's all. I mean, we did hear music and we did open the window. Right?"

"Right."

"So, technically, we told the truth, don't you think?"

"Technically, no. Not at all." Uncle Claude's voice floated through the open window. We spun around and stared. Had Uncle Claude been standing there the whole time? Had he heard the conversation? And more importantly, had he spoken—I counted on my fingers—five words?

"Uh, sir?"

"By my calculations, you didn't tell the truth. You crawled out your bedroom window, walked down to our trailer, took a look around, then walked back to your window and crawled back in. You forgot to lock it—that's where you made your mistake, girls. Always finish what you start." I didn't know if I should thank him for the carpenter's wisdom he had just imparted or if I should apologize for being caught in his trailer.

So I said, "I'm sorry, uh, that is, we're sorry about snooping around in your trailer, Uncle Claude. Aren't we, Nita Sue?"

"Yes. Very sorry, Uncle Claude. Do you think you could find it in your heart to forgive us?"

"I forgave you last night." He pried a few nails loose while he talked.

"If you don't mind me asking," Nita began, "how did you know we were in your trailer?"

"Because I watched you walk in."

"Where were you? Your car was gone."

"Vestal drove to town to pick up a few things. I was in the woods."

"Oh," Nita Sue said with her head hung slightly. I wasn't sure if she was truly repentant or just sorry that she got caught. Either way, it had the intended effect on a childless man.

"Don't go worrying yourselves. I won't tell Dan or Hazel Jean, but you girls shouldn't be sneaking out at night like that. Your dad is right—keep your window locked. You can't believe some of the things that go on nowadays. Out there it gets pretty dangerous and I would hate to see anything happen to you girls." And just like that, he was gone. I shut the glass pane and made double dog sure I locked it.

"Do you think he'll tell on us?" Nita Sue asked.

"Well, he said he wouldn't. See there! I told you we shouldn't have gone. But did you listen to me? No, I'm just the little sister. No one ever listens to me."

"Quit your whining. Look at the bright side; you're the little sister who no one listens to, but with her own bathroom."

As always, she had a point.

YWCA: Young Women's Christian Association

By the time Nita Sue and I sat down at the kitchen table most of the food was gone. "Early bird gets the worm, ladies," Daddy said as he shoveled the last pancake on to Nita Sue's plate. From the looks of it, I'd have to go to Gus' Bait Shop for my breakfast.

"Is this all there is?" I asked.

"It's all that's left from the food that Pop cooked," Momma replied. "What took you two so long, anyway?" She sipped her orange juice.

"Oh, you know. Girl stuff."

"There's always cereal. Check the pantry. I think I have some puffed rice left." I walked to the pantry and sure enough there was puffed rice. Cardboard blown into small balls and sprinkled with dirt. Why couldn't we have Cap'n Crunch or Rice Krispies like every other normal family?

"Did you find it, honey?" Momma asked.

"Yes, ma'am. I think I'll just have a piece of toast or something."

"Here, let me make you some of my famous cheese toast for breakfast," Pops said. "What do you say?" He was already pulling the slab of cheddar cheese from the icebox. How could I refuse?

"Yes, sir. That sounds good." While Pops made my toast, everyone chatted about the new bathroom. Uncle Claude was going to do all the work. The foundation, the insulation, the painting—everything. Momma and Nita Sue were discussing which colors would work well with the carpeting in our room. Daddy and Uncle Claude were talking about the cost of lumber; well, at least Daddy was. Uncle Claude nodded occasionally. I was the only one who noticed Aunt Vestal when she walked into the room until her aroma filled all of the nostrils within ten feet of her.

"Morning all," she said as she opened the china cabinet and retrieved a cup and saucer. Pops stared for a moment at her but quickly resumed his composure long enough to fill her cup with coffee. I guess nothing shocked old preachers.

"Well, good morning to you, too, Merry Sunshine." He pecked her cheek with a kiss. Aunt Vestal chose that moment to stretch her arms above her head and yawn. Once again, her privates were almost visible. We sat silently and watched as she poured sugar and Creamora into her coffee cup. Momma broke the silence.

"Did you sleep well, Vestal?"

"You could say that," she answered. She stirred the coffee with a spoon.

I was still trying to figure out why she had slept in her clothes. Maybe she forgot her pajamas. "Aunt Vestal, you can borrow some of our pjs if you forgot yours. We have plenty."

She started laughing. There it was again—laughing at something I said.

"Thanks, kiddo. But I don't need your pajamas. I haven't actually been to bed yet."

"You haven't been to bed?" I asked. Then, someone interrupted me.

"Pops, the toast! The toast is burning." Everyone yelled at the same time. Smoke billowed out of the oven. Arms waved in the air. Daddy went for the window. Momma fanned the air with a dishtowel. Nita Sue was holding her nose and fanning her face with her other hand. Everyone seemed to be fanning something except Uncle Claude and Aunt Vestal. They were staring at each other.

"I'm sorry, Hazel Jean, I got distracted. Here, let me take this outside." Pops headed for the door with the burnt bread.

"Here, Pop," Momma said as she redirected him toward the kitchen sink, "I'm not so sure the birds will eat that." They began scraping the black gunk off the cookie sheet into the garbage grinder.

"So why did you stay up all night?" I asked Aunt Vestal.

"I met up with some of my old high school buddies and we had ourselves a mini class reunion." She lit a cigarette.

"Vestal, please don't smoke in here," Momma said as politely as she could.

"Hazel Jean, I don't think my cigarette smoke can do any more damage than burnt cheese toast." She kept right on puffing.

Nita Sue said, "So who did you see?"

She blew a smoke ring in the air. "I ran into Hank Jeeter and Bunnilynn at the Piggly Wiggly. God, I haven't seen them in ten or fifteen years. I bet Bunnilynn weighs two hundred pounds." Another smoke ring. "They thought we should call some of our old group, so we did. Within the hour, most of my running buddies were there."

"At the Piggly Wiggly?" I asked. Aunt Vestal let out a howl and turned to me. "No," she said as she lifted my chin and looked deep into my eyes, "not at the Piggly Wiggly."

Something about those green eyes bothered me.

"So, Aunt Vestal? Tell us what it was like being a homecoming queen," Nita Sue said.

"Sure. Why not? But can you get me an ashtray, Carol?" I glanced around the table. I guess I was Carol. I grabbed my favorite ashtray, Leonardo DaVinci. His face was glued to the bottom of a square glass ashtray with gold leaf on all four sides.

"Here you go. I made this one last year at Y–Teens." I was proud of my art work. Heck, I'd made a lot of ashtrays in my short life. Everyone seemed to like Mr. DaVinci best of all. I wasn't sure why—he wasn't handsome or anything. Momma displayed it on the coffee table even though she didn't let people smoke in her house.

Aunt Vestal flicked a couple of ashes in it then lit another Virginia Slim from the one she was snubbing out. "Y–Teens." She inhaled. "That still around? I'm surprised the Women Libbers haven't shut it down by now."

"Why would they do that? The YWCA is for women," I said.

"No it's not. Not really."

"Yes, ma'am it is. That's what it says on the door. The Young Women's Christian Association—YWCA."

She chuckled. "So, who runs it now?"

"Mrs. Nelson."

"LaWanda Nelson? God, I thought she'd be dead by now. The woman's got to be a hundred years old."

"I don't think so. She still drives her car and I see her grocery shopping and stuff. I don't think she's one hundred, do you Nita Sue?"

Nita Sue rolled her sleepy eyes at me. "It's just an expression, Carol Ann. So tell us about being the homecoming queen."

Aunt Vestal leaned her head against the back of the chair and closed her eyes. "It was incredible. The parade. The game. It's one of my better memories."

"What did your dress look like?" Nita Sue asked.

"Which one?"

"The one you wore when they announced you were the queen." Nita Sue had that dreamy, faraway look in her eyes.

"My dress? God, I haven't thought about that dress in years. Do you remember it, Hazel?"

Momma was scrubbing the cookie sheet with an SOS pad. "The purple one?"

Aunt Vestal let out a sigh, "The purple one."

"I remember it. Mom sewed nonstop on that formal."

"Grandma made it? What did it look like?" Nita Sue was practically drooling on the table.

"The bodice was a deep purple, the best velvet Murphy's had on hand." She balanced her cigarette on the ashtray. "It stopped right here," her hands lined up just below her bust line, "and purple chiffon flowed from there down to the floor. But the best part was the sleeves. Mom used the velvet to make cap sleeves that came to here," she pointed just above her elbow, "and then chiffon from there to the wrist. I felt like a real queen that day." Smoke swirled up from Leonardo's head toward the light fixture.

"Cool," Nita Sue said.

"Yeah. Cool," I said.

"What about the parade? What did you wear?"

Aunt Vestal started laughing. "I wore a brown suit with a hat. Mom made me wear it. She thought it looked classy but it looked like a big cow pie."

"It was lovely, Vestal. You looked like Joan Crawford in that suit," Momma said.

"I remember that suit," Pops said. "It nearly put me in the poor house."

Nita Sue couldn't sit still. "So who took you to the dance? Uncle Claude?"

The room became deathly silent. Mom stopped drying the cookie sheet and looked at Pops. Daddy looked at the floor. It seemed that time had stopped for a moment.

"James Robert Cunningham. Jim Bob, that's who took me to the dance."

"It's time to go, Vestal." Uncle Claude had, once again, said five words.

Aunt Vestal picked up her pack of cigarettes and lighter and exited the same way she entered.

"When you're weary, feeling small. When tears are in your eyes, I will dry them all."
Simon and Garfunkel

"What the hell was that all about?" Nita Sue whispered as we cleaned up the kitchen.

"I don't know, but Jim Bob whatever his last name is, must have done something bad."

"What makes you think that? Maybe Aunt Vestal did something bad."

"I don't know, Nita Sue. Did you notice how quiet it got? I mean, even Momma stopped talking when she said 'Jim Bob'. Wonder if he was an axe murderer or something?"

"Right, dipstick. An axe murderer."

I dried another plate.

"He wasn't an axe murderer. He was a very nice young man."

Oops.

Momma was standing behind us. "You girls come sit down for a minute. I want to talk to both of you." I poked Nita Sue in the ribs and mouthed the words, "You and your cussing."

"What I am about to tell you girls is very serious, and I want both of you to sit here and listen." Momma never sat us down for a talk unless it was about someone dying. We hadn't even had our talk about the birds and the bees yet.

"I'm sure you've probably wondered why Vestal is a *little* different from the rest of our family." A little different? That was an understatement. "The truth of the matter is that your Aunt Vestal had something very tragic happen to her when she was in high school. Did you notice how quiet it got when Jim Bob's name was mentioned?" How could we not notice? "You see, Vestal was named homecoming queen her senior year. But what you don't know is that she was expecting a baby at that time."

"How could she be expecting a baby if she wasn't married?" I asked. Momma and Nita Sue exchanged looks.

"I tell you what, Carol Ann. We'll have our birds and bees talk very soon." She rubbed her thumb across my cheek and smiled. "All right?"

"Yes, ma'am." I was ready to get back to the good stuff.

"When we were growing up in Pine Ridge, all the smaller schools fed into one big high school. It was completely different than it is now. Back then we didn't have the prison to employ so many people in this area like we do today. And while Lake View and Pine Ridge seem small to you now, they were even smaller then." Momma flattened both hands on the table. "Your Aunt Vestal got mixed–up with the wrong crowd. She spent a lot of her time with kids that Mom and Pop didn't know. And as much as they tried to control her, Vestal was a stubborn, hardheaded, teenage girl. The more our parents clamped down, the more rebellious she became.

"One day Vestal came home and announced that she and Jim Bob were getting married."

"What did Pops do?" Nita Sue asked.

"He set her straight. He and Mom told Vestal that she was only seventeen and that she needed to wait for the right time and the right boy. Besides, she had to finish high school."

"What did Aunt Vestal do?" I asked.

"After she screamed at them for a while she broke down and admitted to them that she was pregnant." Momma's eyes filled with tears. "It was the only time I ever saw my father cry; until Mom died."

"Poor Pops," Nita Sue said. "I can't believe this."

"Then what?" I asked.

"Well, Pop went looking for this Jim Bob boy and found him. Had he not been a Christian, I think Pop would have beaten him to a pulp. But Pop did the right thing. He talked with this boy and his parents and together they decided that the best thing for Vestal and Jim Bob would be for Vestal to go away and have the baby. That way she could give it up for adoption and move back home and no one would be the wiser." Momma wiped her tears with the bottom of her apron. Nita Sue and I just sat there. I didn't know what to say.

"You can imagine how well that went over with Vestal. She really loved this boy and evidently he loved her too. So, sometime during the homecoming dance, Vestal and Jim Bob snuck out. They'd made plans to elope."

"Did they elope?" Nita Sue asked.

"No, honey, they didn't make it that far. On their way out of town, Jim Bob and Vestal got into a car wreck. It killed him and almost killed Vestal." Momma began to cry. My throat tightened and I thought I might start crying, too. Nita Sue was glued to her chair, her eyes as wide as saucers.

"What about the…the baby?" I whispered.

"She lost the baby that night."

"Oh."

Momma regained her composure and continued, "After Vestal got out of the hospital she went into a deep depression. She wouldn't come out of her room. She wouldn't eat. Mom and Pop didn't know what to do. So they took her to a hospital where she could get help."

"Did it help?"

"At first. But when Vestal came home from that hospital she was different. The light had gone out in her eyes. She started drinking and staying out all night. It got so bad that Pop was spending most of his time bailing her out of the county jail or driving her home from some bar." Momma blew her nose and continued, "Vestal wanted to move away, someplace where she wouldn't be reminded of Jim Bob and the baby all the time. She needed to go where people didn't know her. A place where she could start over. So she moved to California and lived with our aunt while she finished high school out there."

"Wow. Is that why she lives in California?" I asked.

"Yes, honey. That's why she lives in California."

"Did she stay out there, or did she come back home?" Nita Sue asked.

"She stayed there. The wreck happened during homecoming of her senior year, so I guess it was probably around October. By the time May rolled around she had finished high school out there and made new friends so she stayed."

"May's a good month," I said.

"Why's that?"

"Because it's my birthday."

"Yes, it is, sweet girl." Momma studied the smeared mascara on her apron.

"Does Uncle Claude know all this? I mean about the baby and all?" Nita Sue asked.

"Yes, he knows. And you know what? He loves your Aunt Vestal in spite of her past." This brought a smile to her face. "Claude loves her with all his heart and accepts her just the way she is. That's one of the reasons we all love him so much—because of the way he loves Vestal. Not many men would marry a woman with that kind of history, girls."

I mumbled, "Just like the woman at the well."

"Do what?" Momma said.

"I was thinking that it's just like the woman at the well. You know when Jesus was…"

"She knows the story, Carol Ann," Nita Sue interrupted. Momma shot her a look.

"Go on, honey. What about the woman at the well?"

"I was just thinking. Jesus knew the woman had a bunch of husbands but he loved her anyway. He just told her not to sin anymore. Is that the way it is with Uncle Claude?" Momma smiled and cupped her hand to the side of my face.

"Yes, that's exactly how it is with Claude. Your Uncle Claude is a good man and he puts up with a lot from Vestal. But he married her and he'll stay with her through thick and thin. I think coming back here may not have been such a good idea after all. This place holds a lot of bad memories for Vestal."

"Is that why she didn't come home when Grandma got sick?" Nita Sue asked Momma.

"Yes, honey. The two of them never reconciled after Vestal moved to California. It just about killed Pop." The tears were back.

"Does Aunt Betty know about all this?" Nita Sue asked.

"No. She and everyone else in town thought that Vestal moved to California to get over Jim Bob's death. Doc Pennings was the only person outside our two families who knew she was pregnant. And he's passed on." Momma wiped her eyes and smoothed her hair. "Look at me, girls."

We looked.

"Sin affects *everyone*—not just the person committing it. Do you understand what I'm telling you?" We both nodded. "Vestal's rebellion resulted in a young man losing his life, a family losing their son, and my family never being the same. I can't emphasize this enough. Sin affects everyone. Never forget that."

"Yes, Momma," I said.

"Yes, ma'am," Nita Sue answered.

"Now, I want both of you to get yourselves cleaned up and ready for the day. We have a lot of work to do with everyone coming in town and all. And Nita Sue?"

"Ma'am?"

"Take one slip from the grounding jar for your potty mouth."

"Yes, ma'am."

Consequence: n. (kän-sə-kwens) something produced by a cause or necessarily following from a set of conditions

Nita Sue was busy scrubbing the baseboards in the kitchen and den. That'd make her stop swearing—actually it wouldn't. She'd just whisper those words from now on.

I plopped down on my bed and replayed the conversation. Who would have thought that Aunt Vestal had been through so much? And poor Pops and Grandma. I couldn't imagine how much their hearts must have hurt. First Uncle Ed, now Aunt Vestal. How could these things happen in a family like ours? After all, Uncle Ed grew up in the same house as Daddy, and Aunt Vestal grew up with a preacher for a father.

I closed my eyes and asked God to help me understand these things. What if I made bad choices? Or Nita Sue? I asked God to show me what I could do to avoid the same mistakes. A verse that I had memorized in Training Union popped into my head: Proverbs 3:5-6, *Trust in the Lord thy God with all thine heart and lean not unto thine own understanding. In all thy ways, acknowledge Him and He shall direct thy paths.*

I knelt beside my bed and asked God to please help me acknowledge Him in everything. I asked him to please help me and Nita Sue make good choices and to direct us in the right path. I also asked Him to please save Uncle Ed and to help Aunt Vestal get better. Then I thanked Him for giving me the kind of parents who loved me enough to take me to church and teach me the Bible. I was still praying when a jackhammer nearly scared me out of my skin. Uncle Claude was back. I closed by asking God to bless Uncle Claude.

Angry: adj. (an-grē) to have a hissy fit with a tail on it

Momma stood in the bathroom fixing her face. Mascara was smudged around her eyes and her nose was red. She hummed a Frank Sinatra song.

"Momma, can I ask you a question?" The jackhammer was back.

"Do what, honey?"

"Can I ask you a question?" She poked her head around the corner as she spread powder on her face.

"Sure, honey. What is it?"

"What happens to babies when they die? I mean, I know they go to heaven and all, but are they babies when they get there, or are they all grown up? Or do they grow up in heaven?"

"Hmm," she continued to pat powder along her jaw line, then stopped. The color drained from her face.

"To tell you the truth, Carol Ann, I've never thought about it before. Isn't that something? I honestly don't know. But I know who will. Why don't you ask Pop when he comes back this afternoon?"

"Okay, I will." Wow. Momma didn't know the answer to a Bible question. That had to be a first in our family. She and Daddy could answer most questions put to them, even when Nita Sue said things like 'show me where it says that in the Bible' when she got into trouble.

"I got it!" Nita Sue hollered as she ran toward the ringing phone. Several yes ma'ams later and we learned that Aunt Ada and Uncle Elmer had arrived. They were settled comfortably in their room at the Lone Star Inn, according to Aunt Ada.

"Well, that about does it. I think all the relatives who are coming are here," Momma said. "Let's see now, that's Ada and Elmer, Vestal and Claude, Betty and Ed, your father and me, Pop and you two girls. Have I left anyone out?" Momma was half–talking to herself and half–talking to us.

"What about Uncle Jerry and Aunt RoyceAnn? Aren't they coming?" I asked.

"No, Jerry couldn't get off work this weekend. They won't be here."

Great. Now I'd be forced to visit with Aunt Ada. But, hey, at least she wouldn't be sleeping in my bed and worrying that I might use her Merle Norman make–up. I guess there really is something to be thankful for at all times.

"Okay, girls. Let's finish this food. I don't want to be rushed when everyone shows up for lunch."

"Where's Pops?" Nita Sue asked.

"I think he and Vestal were going for a ride on his scooter. Vestal said she needed some fresh air." Nita Sue looked at me with raised eyebrows.

"It's a mo–tor–cy–cle Mother, not a scooter," Nita corrected. Momma couldn't bring herself to calling the two–wheeled vehicle a motorcycle.

As usual, I got potato salad duty. I sat in the middle of the den floor and watched a Bonanza rerun. Hoss was beating the tar out of some bad guy. I still didn't understand how all three of Ben Cartwright's sons could look so different. It didn't matter. Little Joe was my favorite, even though Hoss was a native Texan.

"Carol Ann, you finished with the potatoes?" Momma asked.

"I'm peeling the last one now. Can I please go ride my bike when I finish with this one?"

"Sure," Momma answered from the kitchen, "but don't stay gone long. Everyone will be here in two hours. Okay, honey?"

"Okay, Momma." Hot dog! This hadn't been one of my better weekends with the casket episode and all, so I was ready to get out of the house for a while. I wanted to leave before Aunt Ada and Aunt Betty blew in. I love Aunt Betty to death, but when those two got together it was like Miss Mattie's House of Hair times ten. Nita Sue said if they had a talk–off they would both drop dead because neither one would shut up first.

I rode over to B.J.'s house to see if she wanted to go down to Potter's Creek. She was at ballet lessons. Her little brother volunteered to go in her place but I politely declined. McDeaver's was always a good place to kill time. I liked looking at the make–up and the magazines. Maybe I would go pay Mrs. Breeland a little visit and see what color her hair was today.

I pedaled to the square taking in the sights and sounds. Murphy's Five and Dime was hopping today, but I didn't have any money so there was no use going there. I didn't like to shop at the Five and Dime if I couldn't buy what I wanted. At McDeaver's I could look at the magazines for free.

"Hello, Carol Ann," yelled Mr. Woodard. He was perched in front of his barbershop, The Lion's Mane.

"Hi there!" I yelled back. I hit the brakes on my bike and coasted.

"Looking forward to tomorrow."

"Me, too."

"Be sure your feet stay down." He planted his feet on the concrete sidewalk as he rocked forward then backward in his weathered rocking chair.

"Yes, sir, I will."

Everyone remembered Nita Sue's baptism and figured I'd do the same thing. I guess they assumed it was a family trait or something—feet flying in the air and splashing the choir. But with my new socks, I wasn't worried.

The bells clanged as I opened the door to the drugstore.

"Afternoon, Carol Ann," Mr. McDeaver said from behind the pharmacist's counter. "How can I help you today?"

"I'm just browsing. You mind if I look at the magazines?"

"Don't mind a bit. Mrs. Breeland's in the back. She'll be there in a minute." He went back to filling prescriptions. "Good luck tomorrow. We're awful proud for you."

"Yes, sir. Thank you."

I enjoyed looking through the crossword puzzle magazines, but there wasn't much use in spending my valuable break time reading them because they were too hard for me to work. So I snooped around to see what else was available on the shelves. *Cosmopolitan* was toward the back of the rack, but I knew better than to look at it. Momma would know about it before I made it home. Mr. McDeaver had been known to call parents if he saw their children looking at adult magazines like *Cosmopolitan* or *True Detective*.

Seventeen was a possibility. We weren't allowed to buy it but I didn't think it was bad or anything. After all, it was written for teenage girls. I pulled it from the shelf and parked myself on the bench beside the men's shoe creams and bunion bandages and began flipping pages. Maybelline was selling blue eyeliner. The headline read: *Guaranteed to help you get the boy of your dreams*.

I turned the page and saw a girl about Nita Sue's age in white go–go boots and a short skirt. Her hair was so short that it made Daddy's look long. I didn't know any girls in Texas with hair that short. There wasn't enough to curl with rollers. What respectable girl wanted hair like that?

I was reading the horoscopes column when I heard the all–too–familiar voice of Mrs. Erma Martin. My stomach churned. She was planted a few aisles over talking to Mrs. Breeland, whose hair was a bit darker and poofed a bit higher than usual. I could see a good two inches of it above the LectraShave and Old Spice bottles. I kept reading and scooched over on the bench hoping no one would notice me. No way was I going to eavesdrop on those two. Mrs. Martin might take a notion to order me out of the store and into the funeral parlor. Besides, I wanted to read what Libra had in common with Taurus.

"Sally?" Mr. McDeaver hollered, "You have a call on line two. I'll sign for the delivery in the back."

"Thanks. I'll get it over here," she answered and walked to the harvest gold phone on the make–up counter.

"And give Miss Lawson there a Coca–Cola on the house. She's being baptized tomorrow morning." I lowered the *Seventeen* and smiled. Two heads peered around the men's aisle. Mrs. Martin glared while Mrs. Breeland gave me her big, toothy smile. Aunt Betty said that Mrs. Breeland was so bucktooth she could eat corn on the cob through a picket fence. I think Aunt Betty may have been right.

I lifted the magazine back to eye level hoping that neither woman would notice that I was in the same room with them. I was wrong.

"Being baptized, huh?" I heard from the other side of *Seventeen*. I was afraid to move. Mrs. Martin just might try to scratch my eyeballs out with those nails of hers.

"Yes, ma'am."

She yanked the magazine out of my hands. "Well, I hope you swim better than you pin on corsages." *Seventeen* dropped to the floor and landed with a thud. "And tell that uncle of yours he doesn't scare anyone with his pitiful gun. Especially me." The store's only copy of *Seventeen* was twisting back and forth beneath the three inch heel of Mrs. Martin's cheap shoe. The model's crumpled face lay on the floor as the guilty party exited the drugstore. I decided to skip the Coke all together and leave before I caused more damage to Mr. McDeaver's magazine inventory.

"Here you go," Mrs. Breeland said.

"Thank you."

"What on earth?" She stared at the magazine on the floor. "Did you do this?" She picked up *Seventeen*.

"No, ma'am, I promise," I answered. And then, I even crossed my heart and hoped to die and added the "stick a needle in my eye" part for good measure.

Mrs. Breeland glanced at my dirty Keds and back at the magazine then back down at my dirty Keds.

"Erma Louise stepped on it, didn't she?" Her fake eyelashes were in rare form today. "Didn't she?"

"Yes, ma'am," I whispered.

I was afraid Mrs. Breeland might stroke out then and there if her fake eyelashes didn't slow down. "Imagine a growed woman acting out like that. She ought to be ashamed of herself."

What could I say? Mrs. Martin didn't like our family and, evidently, the feeling was mutual but, I didn't know why.

"Do you want me to pay for it?"

"No, hon. You didn't ruin it. Erma Louise did. I'll just put it on her account." She ripped off the cover and presented the mauled magazine to me. "Here, hon. You take this magazine and this Coca–Cola and…would you like a moon pie? I know you have a soft spot for those."

"No, ma'am. But thanks just the same. I better be getting home. We have a lot of family coming in for the weekend, you know." As much as I wanted to stay and chat it up with Mrs. Breeland, I decided I better leave. I thanked Mr. McDeaver for the free Coke and nodded at the other customers who wished me well with my baptism. I was almost out the door when Lurleene grabbed my arm.

"Here. I want you to wear this tomorrow morning? It'll keep your hair in place?" Lurleene ended her sentences like they were all well–worded questions. It was unnerving. She gave me a lime green, plastic headband lined with gigantic teeth. "I drew a four leaf clover on the inside for luck? I know you Baptists don't believe in luck and all, but a good luck charm should help you to-morrow?"

"Thank you, Lurleene," I said, "I really like it, a whole lot." I flipped it over and stared at the good luck charm. Momma would die before she let me wear a lime green headband in the baptistery.

"I knew you would? It matches your eyes and brings out the red in your hair? And remember, don't let your feet come up, you don't want to pull a Nita Sue?" She grinned. "And don't worry about that Martin woman, you know? She's had it in for Ed as long as I can remember? Ever since he shot her favorite dog?"

"Uncle Ed shot her dog?"

"You didn't know that?"

"No, when did that happen?" I had no idea.

"Last year, I think? Her dogs kept getting in Ed and Betty's trash, you know? At the house?"

"Uh huh."

"So, your Uncle Ed told Erma Louise that if her blasted dog got in his trash again he was going to shoot it?" Lurleen certainly knew a lot about our family's history.

"So, Uncle Ed just shot her dog?"

"Well," Lurleen looked around for any eavesdroppers, "he *said* the dog ran out in front of his pickup, but when Erma Louise found him he had a bullet in his belly and tire tracks on his body?"

"Wow, that doesn't sound like Uncle Ed. I mean, he waves his guns around and stuff but I've never heard Daddy say anything about him shooting her dog. Are you sure about this?"

"Uh huh?"

"But she's always shopping at Aunt Betty's. Calls her 'her favorite florist' and stuff."

"That's because your Aunt Betty apologized for your Uncle Ed and made a casket spray for the dog's funeral, you know?"

"They had a funeral for the dog?"

Lurleen leaned in a bit, "Don't you be telling this, okay? But, yes, they had a funeral, all right? Odell Shores used a child's coffin and he and Erma Louise had a little service for Brutus? Then, he buried the dog out on his farm, you know, the big one on Highway 59? You ever been there?"

"Uh, no. I don't think so." This was getting weirder by the minute.

"Girl, where've you been? Odell and Orten have themselves a pet cemetery out on their farm—I can't remember the name of it? But Sally told me that when Erma Louise sent the funeral and burial bill to your Uncle Ed that he sent it back full of buckshot?"

"*That* sounds like Uncle Ed."

"Anyway, all of that doesn't mean a thing today, you know? You're getting baptized tomorrow, girl!"

I left Lurleene and started home. Uncle Ed ran over Mrs. Martin's dog then shot it? How could I not know that? I'd learned my lesson about gossip. There was no way I was getting involved in Mrs. Martin's business—ever.

I placed the headband and magazine in my bicycle basket, putting the magazine on top of the headband so no one would see it. I rode past Miss Mattie's House of Hair and noticed that Miss Mattie had added another piece of yard art to her tiny lawn: a pink flamingo.

Evidently, Aunt Betty had seen it too, because it had a miniature cowbell necklace glued to it.

Miss Mattie's House of Hair was hopping today. Christian ladies had their hair set and their nails manicured on Saturday so they would look good for Sunday church services. Momma had her hair set yesterday so it would look extra nice for the family reunion weekend.

Miss Mattie's beauty shop gave me the creeps. She'd decorated it with a Hawaiian jungle theme a few years ago when it was called THE ALOHA. But when she changed the name to Miss Mattie's House of Hair she didn't remove the jungle décor; she just painted all the Hawaiian flowers a disgusting hot pink and the foliage a bright green. She paid Mrs. Frazier, the owner of Dee and Dot's, to sew new draperies out of a bamboo print that looked more like a can of rotten shoe string potatoes than jungle prints.

Even though her decorating skills had a lot to be desired, she and her girls sure were good at what they did. I could always tell which ladies at our church were Miss Mattie's regulars and those who weren't. Plus, Miss Mattie styled hair for all the dead white ladies at the funeral parlor.

Dark clouds threatened rain. I hoped it wouldn't rain because all the relatives would be crammed inside our tiny house. And with

Uncle Elmer and Aunt Vestal smoking like a couple of chimneys, it could get mighty stuffy.

"Carol Ann," I heard. "Carol Ann, over here." Daddy was waving me over to the post office.

"Coming," I answered as pea gravel spun beneath my back tire. He was finishing up a conversation with Mr. Knight, our postman, as I skid to a halt.

"I'll see you, Sam. Hope Elaine feels better. Call me if we can do anything." Daddy shook Mr. Knight's hand and turned toward me. "Well, there's my favorite redhead," he said.

I rolled my eyes.

"I know, I know. You're my only redhead. But what a pretty one, indeed," he replied and mussed my hair. "Your momma just called and she needs you to buy some Charmin and take it on over to the house. She didn't realize she was using the last roll when she did her hair last night." He handed me a five dollar bill. "Ride on over to the Piggly Wiggly and then head home, alright?"

"All righty," I answered.

"And I'll be expecting change from that purchase."

"Yes, sir." I started to ask Daddy when Uncle Ed had run over and shot Mrs. Martin's dog, but decided better. I had enough on my mind.

"Later, alligator," Daddy said.

"Afterwhile crocodile."

Both Momma and Aunt Betty wrapped their hair in toilet paper at bedtime. I didn't understand how this procedure helped a hair-do, but they both swore by it. Momma sure looked silly propped up in bed with Charmin wrapped around her head like a turban. But I guess if I paid someone to set and style my hair every Saturday I would do whatever it took to keep it looking good until the next Saturday, too.

So much for my hour of carefree bike riding.

"Please, don't squeeze the Charmin."
Mr. Whipple

"I'm home," I hollered, "with a whole bunch of Charmin for a whole lot of kinfolk." The sliding glass door hesitated as I closed it. I froze when I saw Aunt Ada propped up on the couch filing away on her nails.

"Hello, Carol Ann," she said without looking up.

"Oh, hi Aunt Ada. How are you?" I mumbled.

"Fine, just fine," she sighed. "I understand you're being baptized tomorrow, is that right?"

"Yes, ma'am."

She raised her head and analyzed me from the top of my head to the soles of my Keds. "If you died tonight would you go to heaven?"

"Ma'am?"

Obviously put out with me, she repeated, "If you died tonight, would you go to heaven or wouldn't you?" That gross mole between her nose and upper lip moved up and down during the interrogation.

"Yes, ma'am?"

"Well, is that your answer or a question?"

"Yes, ma'am, I'm going to heaven." Who did she think she was, Billy Graham?

"That's good to know, John 3:16." Aunt Ada ended a lot of her sentences with Scripture references. "Now, please tell me you plan on doing something with your stringy hair before you step foot in the baptistery." As the word "baptistery" came out of her mouth, Nita Sue walked behind the couch on her way to the kitchen and made an awful face as she passed by. I started laughing.

"Did I say something funny?" She came up off that couch like a cat does when it stretches its back and then each leg. Come to think of it, she reminded me of a cat. A black cat. A mean, black cat with sharp claws.

"Oh, no ma'am. I was thinking of how silly I must look with all this toilet tissue in my sack." She ambled over and looked inside the Piggly Wiggly bag.

"Charmin? Hmph," she said. Then I heard her say, under her breath, "Hazel Jean must think money grows on my brother's trees." She closed the sack and resumed her fingernail filing. "I buy the off brand, myself. It's much less expensive."

"Charmin *is* more expensive, Ada, but I try to buy the best for company." Momma appeared out of nowhere and walked over to check the grocery sack. "Thank you, honey. I appreciate you running errands for me at the last minute." She kissed me on the cheek. "Ada, would like some more tea?"

"Yes, I would. But don't fill it so full this time, Hazel Jean. I don't like to be wasteful." Her beady, cat eyes stared at Momma. "Do you have any more of those mint Girl Scout cookies? Elmer D. ate my entire box."

"I probably do, let me check the freezer. Carol Ann, why don't you restock the bathroom for me and then come in the kitchen. Nita Sue needs help with the Spam Salad."

"Yes, ma'am." I'd do anything to get out of talking to that woman. I went to the bathroom and flung open the door.

"DON'T YOU KNOCK?" I heard as I opened the door. Uncle Elmer was sitting on the commode looking at one of Daddy's hunting catalogs while he smoked his cigar. Stench filled my nostrils.

"Sorry." I had to put my hand over my mouth to keep from gagging. Our bathroom would never be the same. I ran to the kitchen and saw that Nita Sue and Momma were huddled by the washing machine giggling.

"What's so funny?"

"Did you just open the door on Elmer?" Momma asked.

I grinned. "Yes, ma'am." Nita Sue grabbed my Girl Scout uniform that was hanging over the washer and laughed into it so Aunt Ada wouldn't hear her.

"I'm so sorry, honey. I forgot he was in there when I sent you in with the toilet tissue." Momma was trying to hold back her laughter but wasn't having much luck.

"He's been in there for over an hour. Couldn't he do his business at the motel?" Nita Sue whispered. "What's taking him so long?"

Momma shook her head and regained her composure. "Let's get this Spam salad finished before the others arrive."

Legalism: n. (lē–gə–li–zəm) strict, literal, or excessive conformity to the law or to a strict or religious moral code

I hoped this reunion turned out better than past reunions. Aunt Ada and Aunt Betty usually ended up in a theological argument over something the apostle Paul had said in the New Testament. Aunt Betty would resort to name calling and Aunt Ada would get her feelings hurt, then Daddy or Uncle Ed would have to jump in and referee. Uncle Elmer ignored them.

Aunt Ada was the self–proclaimed Bible scholar and know–it–all in the Lawson family. When she wasn't criticizing her preacher, she was forever spouting off at Nita Sue and me about what she would do if she were our mother and what Momma should do differently. She liked to think that Jesus himself had left her in charge of pointing out everybody's shortcomings. Just yesterday, Momma reminded Nita Sue and me that we were to ignore her critical spirit and pray for her. 'It's hard to dislike someone when you pray for them on a regular basis' she had said.

Personally, I didn't think it was possible for me to like Aunt Ada with her self–righteous attitude and all. Especially after I witnessed her stealing Momma's camellias and gardenias and stashing them in her handbag. If someone else had done that, she would have called them a thief. But in her mind, she was simply helping herself to her brother's flowers.

I sat in a lawn chair and watched my family. Momma and Aunt Vestal were sitting in the wicker porch swing that we'd given Momma for Mother's Day. Daddy and I hung it from the huge magnolia tree in our back yard. The limb bounced up, then down, then up again with each push of their feet. Aunt Vestal looked a lot better than she did this morning. For one thing, she was wearing more clothes and all her privates were covered.

When they were side–by–side laughing together like that, you'd never know Aunt Vestal was unhappy. I thought about how beautiful she was—even more beautiful than Momma. I mean, Momma was pretty, but Aunt Vestal was drop–dead gorgeous. How sad to be that beautiful and unhappy. Their laughter glided through the air with the same ease as the back and forth movement of the old swing. As I watched them, I wondered why people turned out the way they did. Would Nita Sue and I end up like them or would we be happy with families of our own?

Aunt Betty and Aunt Ada were inspecting our vegetable garden. Evidently, Aunt Ada didn't leave her tomatoes on the vine as long as Momma did. And according to Aunt Ada, the fried okra we ate for supper would have been better if Daddy had used different compost. Both aunts preferred a true compost to the store bought brand.

Horseshoes clinked and whoopees rang out across the backyard; Uncle Elmer had scored a ringer. He and Uncle Ed played against Daddy and Pops while Uncle Claude refereed the game—a job that required five words or less. The winning team had bragger's rights until the next family reunion.

My thoughts were broken as Aunt Betty made yet another trip home to answer nature's call. Aunt Betty spent a lot of her day driving back and forth between our house and hers. She had a thing about using other people's bathrooms—she just wouldn't do it. She and Uncle Ed couldn't take vacations because of it. Momma called it a phobia, whatever that was. And Daddy threatened Nita Sue and me with death if we ever told anyone about it. Nita Sue remarked that folks probably knew already since Aunt Betty was forever saying, 'Excuse me, ladies, but nature calls,' and speeding off in her car. Once, Sheriff Whitehall followed her into her house to give her a ticket for speeding through a downtown crosswalk. The whole time she was yelling, "Nature calls! Nature calls! Excuse me, Sheriff! Nature calls!" I didn't mind Daddy's threat of death because I knew that I'd never tell anyone about her phobia; it was too embarrassing.

Aunt Ada saddled up next to me in a green and white aluminum lawn chair. "Elmer D. loves those horseshoes." Whiffs of Tigress perfume drifted by me with each wave of her funeral fan.

"Yes, ma'am."

"I suppose all men have one hobby or another."

"Yes, ma'am."

Her fanning stopped. "Cat got your tongue?" She stared at me like I'd committed some horrible sin that only she could forgive.

"Uh, no ma'am."

"Well, for the love of Pete, say something, child. Don't just sit there like a bump on a log." She resumed her fanning.

"Yes, ma'am." I paused. A long pause. A very, very, long pause. "So, how is Louisiana?"

"Louisiana? Hmph. It don't hold a candle to Texas. This here's God's country."

"So…you don't like Louisiana?" I asked.

"Not particularly." She fanned some more.

"Why don't you move?"

She didn't miss a beat. "Because the wife doesn't always get what she wants. And good Christian wives submit to their husbands. Ephesians 5:22." Those catlike eyes stared into a place that only she could see. The fanning continued.

"Yes, ma'am."

"Your parents still letting you listen to that rock and roll music?" Faster fanning.

"Yes, ma'am."

"Hmph. If you were my daughter, you wouldn't be listening to it."

"Yes, ma'am."

"Do you go to Training Union?"

"Oh, yes ma'am. Every Sunday night." That should have pleased her.

"And Bible drills? You do those, I hope?"

"Yes, ma'am. I'm pretty good at those," I said triumphantly. I'd like to see her find something wrong with that.

"What book comes before Jonah?"

"Do what?"

"What book comes before Jonah?"

The lawn chair stuck to my legs. Sweat poured down my sides. "Uh, well, let's see now." I had to think for a minute. I knew the answer, but she made me nervous.

"Well, either you know it or you don't." Left. Right. Left. Right. She fanned away.

"Oh, I know it. I just have to think for a second. Obadiah. That's it. Obadiah comes before and Micah comes after."

The fanning stopped and she almost smiled."You need to be quicker about it."

I think she forgot that I was sitting next to her because she didn't say another word. Just fanned. Back and forth. Back and forth. Her eyes stared into space.

"Who needs a refill?" Momma hollered as she and Aunt Vestal carried two pitchers of iced tea to the picnic table. Nita Sue followed with a bowl of ice.

"Where have you been?" I asked my obviously irritated sister.

"None of your beeswax." Typical Nita Sue. Happy when she got her way, and mad at the world when she didn't.

"Do y'all know that Yankees don't serve iced tea in the wintertime?" Uncle Ed asked this as though he were the expert on all things Yankee. The picnic table buzzed as my family contemplated this earth–shattering revelation.

"Why not?" asked Momma. She poured the tea while Nita Sue replenished the ice.

"Well, according to old man Peters," Uncle Ed lowered his voice to a whisper, "he's a traveling salesman you know," he raised it again, "he was in Maine or Maryland or one of them "M" states and ordered iced tea with his meal. The waitress told him that it was out of season."

"You don't say" and "what on earth" bounced off the iced tea pitchers like an echo.

"So, old man Peters said he looked at the waitress and says, 'what do mean it's out of season? You gotta shoot it up here or something'?" Everyone laughed.

"Yankees." Aunt Ada said, "You can't live with them, and you can't shoot them."

"That doesn't sound very Christian if you ask me," Aunt Vestal said.

Aunt Ada stopped her fanning and glared at Aunt Vestal. I stepped over by Momma in case they got into a fight or something. "No one's asking you, now are they, Vestal Cinaretta?"

"Hey, I got an idea!" said Pops. "How 'bout we take a trip into Holly Springs? They got a brand new Baskin Robbins ice cream parlor over there with thirty–one flavors of ice cream. How about it?" Pops was the best at changing the subject at just the right time. Maybe they taught that in the Ft. Worth seminary.

"Pop, we still have homemade ice cream from last night," Momma said.

"I know that, Hazel Jean. But let's live a little. We can have homemade ice cream any day of the week and twice on Sundays—we're talking big time Baskin Robbins!"

Uncle Ed chimed in. "We can take my Caddy." His wrinkled forehead moved up and down when he spoke of his Cadillac.

"I say we do it! Let's live it up! Come on, Carol Ann. Ride on my motorcycle?"

"Oh no, Pop. No way are you driving that thing to Holly Springs with my baby on board," Momma said.

"Please Momma? Please? We'll be careful, won't we Pops?" I begged.

"Carol Ann? What did your mother say?" Daddy looked at me over the top of his black rimmed glasses.

"Yes, sir. But can I ride with you, Daddy?" No way was I getting in that orange death trap with Uncle Ed behind the wheel. If the rest of them wanted to, fine but not me.

Pops continued, "First of all let's see how many of us are going. Okay now, raise your hand if you want to go." Ever so slowly, hands went up in the air. First Pops, then mine, then Uncle Elmer and Aunt Ada. Uncle Ed was a given. "Hazel Jean, wouldn't you like a double dip of Rocky Road in a pink cup? With a pink spoon?"

Momma started laughing. "Okay, Pop. I'm in. But only if Vestal agrees to ride along, too."

"Oh, what the hell?" Aunt Vestal's arms went up—and some of her tube top slid down. Aunt Ada yelled at Aunt Vestal to cover herself. Everyone else acted like they didn't see it.

Pops continued, "Dan? Claude? You fellas game?"

Daddy answered first. "Nope. I'm fixing to go check on the store and help close up."

"Believe I'll stay right here," Uncle Claude answered. I counted his sentence on my fingers.

"Okay. We got Ed, Hazel Jean, Vestal, Ada, Elmer, Carol Ann and me. That's seven."

"Wait a minute," Momma interrupted. "I can't go if the top's down, it'll ruin my hair."

Aunt Vestal rolled her eyes.

"Here. I got an extra rain bonnet." Aunt Ada dug through her purse and produced something the size of a money clip. She unfolded it about twenty times and handed it to Momma.

"Thank you, Ada. But I think I'll pass."

"Suit yourself," she answered and launched into refolding.

Momma hollered for Nita Sue to come outside. "I bet Nita Sue would enjoy a trip to Baskin Robbins." Nita Sue strolled over to the Caddy and pronounced that she, too, would like a sample of the thirty–one flavors.

"Can we get seven in your car, Ed?" Pops asked.

"Does a wild bear spit in the woods? Carol Ann may have to sit on someone's lap but she don't mind. Do you, Carol Ann?" Six pairs of eyes stared at me.

What could I say? "No, sir. I don't mind. I don't mind at all."

Secret: strong enough for a man but made for a woman

Seven people piled in Uncle Ed's burnt orange Caddy. Uncle Ed, Aunt Vestal, and Pops in front; Uncle Elmer, Aunt Ada, Nita Sue and me in back. The family–filled Caddy pulled out of the driveway. Uncle Ed lit a Roi–Tan and before he could close his Zippo lighter, Aunt Ada was complaining about his cigar smoke.

"My car. My cigar, big sister." Uncle Ed laughed and lit his cigar, anyway. We zoomed off to Baskin Robbins anticipating thirty–one flavors of heaven in a cone.

Uncle Ed honked his horn and *Texas Fight* blared through the streets of downtown Lake View. People around here were used to it and most of them waved to us when we went around the square. Mr. Woodard tipped his hat as we drove by the Lion's Mane. Mrs. Frazier smiled from the window of Dee & Dot's. She was draping a scarf over a mannequin's shoulder.

Owners were locking up their stores this time of day. Most closed around three or four o'clock so they could enjoy Saturday evening and Sundays with their families before they had to start the process all over again on Monday morning. Little girls jumped rope while they waited for their mothers outside of Miss Mattie's House of Hair. I spotted Sheriffs No.1 and No. 2 walking out of the dry cleaners with Beulah. She was jawing at them about something.

"Think Betty would like some ice cream?" Pops asked as we passed Betty's Bloomers.

"We'll bring her something. You know how she is about using other people's johns." Nita Sue and I looked at each other. We'd been threatened with death if we said anything about her phobia.

"Elmer D., you're squashing me. Can't you move over some?" Aunt Ada said.

"If your butt wasn't so big, maybe you'd have a little more room."

Ignoring his remark, Aunt Ada turned her rain–bonnet–covered head to me. "Sit on your sister's lap, Carol Ann. I'm not riding to Holly Springs like a sardine in a can."

I looked at Nita Sue. She wasn't thrilled, but let me sit on her lap.

Uncle Ed put the pedal to the metal and off we went. Aunt Vestal put her hands up in the air each time we went downhill. I thought it looked like fun so I did it, too.

"WHAT'S THAT SMELL?" Aunt Ada yelled over the sound of the wind.

"SMELLS LIKE B.O.," Uncle Elmer shouted.

"Maybe it's your upper lip," Nita Sue said to no one in particular.

"WHAT'D YOU SAY?" Aunt Ada yelled. The wind was doing a number on her rain bonnet.

Nita Sue leaned to their side of the car. "I SAID, 'DON'T WANT TO LOSE YOUR GRIP'," and pointed to Aunt Ada's cheap, white vinyl handbag. She nodded in complete agreement and clutched it tighter. I vowed to never forget my deodorant again.

The wind whipped harder as Uncle Ed sped up. Then the unthinkable happened—someone passed us.

"Did you see that? That idiot just passed me and I was doing seventy! Who does he think he is, passing me like that? Is he trying to run me off the blasted road?" The other car faded into the horizon. I felt the car accelerate.

Nita Sue's hair was plastered against the back of the seat while mine blew all over the place. Sitting in someone's lap in an open convertible doing seventy miles per hour was not my idea of fun, especially with Uncle Ed behind the wheel. Uncle Ed wasn't going to let this guy get away with passing him. No one passed Ed Lawson and lived to tell about it. I held my breath, shut my eyes and began reciting Psalm 23. Brother Paul read that psalm at funerals so I figured it might be appropriate to recite it now.

Around verse two Uncle Ed was side–by–side with the other car. Aunt Vestal was shouting and clapping at him to "Go faster, Ed! Go faster!" Pops found the seat belt and pulled it tight. From my spot in the backseat, I saw the driver tip his hat to Aunt Vestal and return his hand to the steering wheel. Uncle Ed's knuckles were white from gripping the wheel so hard. With a cigar clenched between his teeth, he pressed on. Uncle Elmer must have been impressed because he kept saying something about the engine.

By verse four, we had taken our rightful place in front of the other car.

"Teach him to pass me," Uncle Ed hollered.

"Woohoo!" Aunt Vestal yelled, clapping her hands overhead like she was at a rock concert or something. "Leave him in the dust, Ed. Leave him in the dust!"

"Sail on Silver Girl, sail on by. Your time has come to shine."

Simon and Garfunkel

By the time we pulled into Baskin Robbins, I felt like someone had shot me and left me for dead. My legs were limp and I couldn't hear very well. If there weren't bugs in my hair it would be a miracle but Nita Sue wasn't the least bit phased. She walked in to Baskin Robbins like she owned the place.

The air inside the ice cream parlor was freezing. Two refrigerated cases housed thirty–one flavors of ice cream. I'd never seen so much ice cream in one place in my life.

"What's your pleasure, kiddo?" Aunt Vestal asked.

"I don't know." I looked at the pink and brown sign. "Hey, look. The sign up there says *One Flavor for each Day of the Month*. You could eat here for a whole month and never eat the same flavor twice. I'll never make up my mind. What are you getting?"

"Daiquiri Ice."

"What's that?"

"It's a drink from south of the border." She licked her lips.

"Would I like it?"

"Let's find out." She motioned for the boy to come over and help us.

"Let me have a taste of your daiquiri ice, amigo."

"Sure thing, ma'am." A good looking teenage boy gave me a tiny, pink spoon topped with pale green ice cream.

"What do you think, Carol?" Aunt Vestal asked.

"It's okay. Not very sweet, though. I think I'll get something else."

"Give me two scoops on a cone," she said. I slid down the glass freezer trying to decide what to order. Pink Bubble Gum looked good but so did Mississippi Mud. I bumped into Nita Sue who was flirting with a different teenage boy behind the counter. "…oh, I don't know, what do *you* think I should have, Tommy?" she said.

"I'll have one scoop of vanilla in a cup," Aunt Ada said.

"Vanilla? We're at Baskin Robbins, Ada. Get something you can't get at home, woman." Uncle Elmer obviously disapproved of her selection.

"I happen to like vanilla, Elmer."

"At least get two scoops then. Hell, we drove all the way from Lake View." Aunt Ada was trying to calculate the cost of two scoops as opposed to one scoop on her fingers.

"She'll take two scoops of vanilla," Pops interrupted. "My treat, Ada. Get as many scoops as your heart desires."

"It just seems so, I don't know, sinful, Waylon," she said.

Pops laughed and patted her on the back. "Even the best of us need to indulge ever now and again. That's a fact."

Aunt Ada actually blushed. Pops had that effect on people.

"Oh, all right. Give me two scoops of vanilla in a cup then," she said.

Aunt Vestal leaned over my shoulder and whispered, "If there's a hell, that woman is in charge of it. Mark my words." I stared into the glass case hoping no one else had heard her.

"I'll have two scoops of Here Comes the Fudge and Mississippi Mud on a cone, cowboy." Uncle Ed tugged at his belt. No wonder his pants never fit.

"Give me one scoop of rum raisin and one of rocky road," Uncle Elmer said.

"Elmer D, you are not eating anything with the word rum in it. Romans 14:21."

"Don't tell me what I can and can't eat, Ada."

She wouldn't let it go. "Excuse me son, but is there alcohol in that raisin ice cream?"

"Gee, I don't know ma'am. I can get the manager if you want."

Uncle Elmer spoke louder. "Give me what I ordered. Don't pay attention to her." Then he told Aunt Ada to eat her ice cream and to shut her yap. She did.

"And he's going to be her sidekick." Aunt Vestal was whispering in my ear again. I scooted toward Pops.

"Whatcha having, Nita Sue?" Pops asked.

"I'll have two scoops of Luna Cheesecake in a cup." She batted her eyes at Tommy. "If it's good enough for the astronauts, it's good enough for me." More blinking and hair twirling. Tommy scooped.

"How about you, Carol Ann? What's your pleasure?"

"I'll have two scoops of Pink Bubblegum on a cone, please." The other teenager filled my cone.

"Give me two scoops of Baseball Nut, young fella, and two scoops of rocky road in a container with a lid." Pops tapped the counter with his hands. "You should join the birthday club, Carol Ann. Lookee here," he pointed to the pink and brown polka dot sign. "It says you get a free scoop of ice cream on your birthday."

I took the post card and stuck it in my pocket. I couldn't eat an ice cream cone and write at the same time. I'd fill it out when I got home.

"Ed? What would Betty like?"

"Get her two scoops of their Pistachio Almond," Uncle Ed answered.

Tommy asked, "Will there be anything else, sir?" Pops paid the bill while the rest of us licked our way into paradise.

*"Now troubles are many, they're as deep as a well.
I can swear there ain't no heaven but I pray there ain't
no hell."*
Blood, Sweat and Tears

Aunt Betty was swinging with Momma when we returned from Baskin Robbins with two semi–melted cartons of ice cream. Momma said not to worry, that it would refreeze just fine. Aunt Betty kept yelling "shoot–a–monkey" when she learned we had gotten her Pistachio Almond. I wanted to go to my room, sit on my bed and listen to Bobby Sherman, but Aunt Vestal had other plans.

"Carol? Come on down to my trailer. I've got something for you." Her lips wrapped around another cigarette.

"Really? For me?"

"Yes, for you."

"Let me wash my hands first. They're all sticky from the ice cream."

"Okay, kiddo. Take your time. I'm not going anywhere."

I washed my hands in the bathroom and tried to erase the image of Uncle Elmer from earlier. The mirror revealed one massive tangle of hair. Daddy would have to work long and hard tonight on this mess.

Uncle Claude was finishing up his carpentry for the day and whistled an old country western song I recognized from the radio. I tapped on the window and waved. He nodded. Nothing more. Nothing less. Just nodded.

Walking down the driveway, I thought about the afternoon and how much fun it had been in spite of Aunt Ada and Uncle Elmer. And to think that there was an ice cream parlor with a flavor for each day of the month this close to home.

"In here, Carol." Aunt Vestal was pouring a clear liquid into a martini glass. It looked like one of the glasses on the Dean Martin Show. She pulled an olive jar from the tiny refrigerator and skewered three olives with a fancy toothpick. "Ever tasted one of these, kiddo?"

"Oh, no ma'am. Mommy would snatch me baldheaded."

She laughed. "You're probably right. She and old Dan aren't much on drinking, are they?"

"No ma'am."

She stirred the martini with her fancy toothpick.

"Would it be rude of me to ask your age? I'm eleven, you know."

"I know exactly how old you are. How old do you think I am?"

"I don't know. Momma's thirty–four so I guess you're…thirty, thirty–one?"

"Twenty–nine. And, drop the yes ma'am and the no ma'am, okay?"

"Okay." She looked just like Rita Hayworth or Joan Crawford with that martini glass in her hand. Her nail color matched her lipstick.

"Sit down," she said.

I sat.

"So you're getting dunked tomorrow."

"Yes ma'…" I hesitated, "Yes. Yes, I'm getting baptized tomorrow."

"Never did that myself. But you probably know that already." She held her cigarette and martini glass in one hand and wiped the corners of her mouth with a cocktail napkin.

"You've never been baptized?"

"Nope. Never saw much need for it."

"Wow. I just assumed that you had, I mean, with Pops being a preacher and all."

"Well, you assumed wrong, kiddo." She sipped some more of the devil's juice.

"Would it be disrespectful if I asked you why?"

She laughed, "No, not at all. I never saw the need for it. Religion and I don't get along."

"Oh," I said.

"Religious people are some of the meanest people alive."

"But you want to go to heaven don't you? I mean, you don't want to wind up down there, do you?" I pointed toward hell.

"You mean where Ada and Elmer will be in charge?" She snickered. "Like the song says *I swear there ain't no heaven and I pray there ain't no hell.*"

She took a long drag then blew smoke into the air. "All the do–gooders in this town, the so–called Christians? They'd just as soon stab you in the back as look at you. Don't forget, I grew up around here and witnessed these Christians firsthand. If they're the ones occupying heaven, well, I guess I'll just have to pass. Besides, I don't really believe in heaven or hell." Another puff. "Personally, I think it's a load of crap. There. I said it."

I didn't know what to say to her. Anyone who didn't believe in hell was probably headed straight for it. I'd heard more sermons preached on hell than heaven for that matter. I knew I sure didn't want to wind up down there.

Aunt Vestal said, "Bet you never heard anyone say that before."

"Uh, no. But what about God and Jesus? You believe in them, don't you?"

She downed the rest of her martini and poured herself another. But this time, she speared a tiny onion with the same toothpick she used on the olives. "See, that's the trouble with all you Bible beaters. You only like people who are carbon copies of yourselves. And you don't accept people who believe anything different. Ever heard of Buddhism?"

"No."

"Hinduism?"

"No."

"See? You've never even heard of other religions, have you? Heaven forbid that a person around here might have an original thought." She lit up again. "There are millions of people all around the world who think differently than ninety–eight percent of the people occupying the pews of First Baptist Church in Lake View, Texas. Take my word for it.

"Besides, anyone who has the guts to believe in some*thing* or some*one* other than Jesus isn't thought of very highly around here. Take Ada, for example. Do you think she has any love in her heart for someone like me who doesn't buy into her religious crap?"

I shrugged an "I don't know."

"Sure you do." She fanned the smoke away from my face. Funny how smoke always migrated toward the people who wanted to smell it the least. "Why that viper only loves the other Bible bangers who think just like her."

"What's a viper?"

"It's a snake."

"Oh." This actually brought a smile to my face. A vision of Aunt Ada's face on a snake's scaly body popped into my head.

"See? You don't really like her either, do you?"

"But Momma says we ought to pray for her, not spend our time thinking about how mean she is."

"That sounds like her. Trust me, when you finally leave this Godforsaken town, you'll change your tune. Just watch. You'll change your tune in a hurry. I sure did."

I thought about Roxy and her family being atheists. I wondered if they taught atheism in California or something.

"What's going through that pretty little head of yours?" she asked.

"I was just thinking about people who call themselves atheists. Do you know any?"

She laughed. "Carol, I know more atheists than Christians. Let me tell you something. Christianity isn't the biggest religion in this world. Only here in the South.

"Out there, people don't put you down for believing something different from them. Can you imagine an atheist trying to live in this town?"

Actually, yes. I could. "So if atheists don't believe in God or Jesus, who do they think created everything?"

"There's lots of scientific evidence to prove that no one created anything. It just happened."

I thought about that for a minute and decided it was probably the dumbest thing I'd ever heard. I didn't care how smart the people in California were, I knew who made everything and no one was going to change my mind.

"Did you say you had something you wanted to give me?"

She answered, "I almost forgot, wait right here." She pulled a small train case from the back of the trailer and opened it. "I know it's here, somewhere. Here, hold this for me." She set the train case in my lap. I noticed several necklaces and a faded pink pouch in the bottom. The pouch was embroidered with Aunt Vestal's initials.

"Here, kiddo."

"What is it?"

"Open it up and see for yourself." Inside a black, velvet box was the most beautiful cameo ring I'd ever seen.

"Wow, this is for me?"

"Yep, kiddo. That is for you."

"Aunt Vestal, this is the most beautiful thing I've ever seen. Why are you giving it to me?"

"I...I..." Tears welled in her eyes. She turned around and began mixing her third martini. "I need a drink."

Once she composed herself she answered, "That belonged to my mother. Since I will never have a daughter, I want you to have it. Your mother has the matching necklace and plans to give it to Nita Sue on her sixteenth birthday. And since I'll probably never come back to this hellhole, I thought you might like to have it now."

"Wow, I don't know what to say, Aunt Vestal. Thank you." I reached over to hug her neck.

"Well, you deserve it. You're a pretty good kid, even if you do look like me." She took a long sip of her drink.

"I can't wait to have my picture taken with you during the half-time show!"

"Me, too, baby girl." She grinned. "Now, you head on back to the house and help your momma with supper. I'm not terribly fond of fried fish, myself."

"Thank you, Aunt Vestal. This is the best gift I ever got."

Faith: n. (fāth) firm belief in something for which there is no proof

On Saturday night, it didn't rain a drop. The clouds disappeared and the stars shone brightly. Everyone was in the backyard helping with the fish fry except Nita Sue. She found my Baskin Robbins birthday card and was writing a letter to Tommy. What a drip. She had been so busy with her new love that she didn't pay any attention to the cameo ring Aunt Vestal had given me. Momma teared up when I showed it to her. She said not to mention the necklace to Nita Sue because she had, indeed, planned on giving it to her on her sixteenth birthday.

Pops was sitting on an old quilt humming *Deep in the Heart of Texas* when I plopped down beside him.

"That was one of your grandmother's favorite songs. Did you know that?" I shook my head. "She used to sing it when we went camping. I remember lying on our sleeping bags and looking up at the stars." He plucked a piece of grass then stretched out on the quilt. "She'd be so proud of you." He stuck one end of the grass between his lips. "We prayed for you before you were even born."

"Really?"

"That's a fact."

"Wow."

"Yes, ma'am. We ended every day on our knees, asking the Lord to save our family members. From your momma's generation on down. Yep, she would be one, proud grandmother today." He blinked. I guess he thought I wouldn't notice the moisture in his eyes.

"Pops, wasn't it sweet of Aunt Vestal to give me this ring?" I couldn't take my eyes off of it. The ivory silhouette and gold band was so dainty. I felt special just to have it on my finger.

"Yes, it was. I gave your grandmother that ring and necklace on our thirtieth wedding anniversary. She was one happy lady."

"Pops, I wish people didn't have to die."

"Oh, but they don't. That's the beauty of being born–again. Just like that," he snapped his fingers, "you breathe your last breath on earth and the next second you're in the arms of Jesus."

"Yes sir, I know that. It's just that, well, I mean, I wish I could have known Grandma while she was alive. You know? Spent time with her and stuff. You know what I mean, don't you?"

Pops took my hand in his. "Yes, ma'am, I know exactly what you mean because I wish it, too. But think about this, Carol Ann. In John 14:3, Jesus says that He is going to prepare a place for us and that He will come again and take us unto Himself; so that where He is, we can be there also. Do you realize that your grandmother is there, right this minute, in the special home that Jesus prepared for her? And one day you and I will go there, too? We'll have eternity to get to know one another."

"I guess I never really thought about it that way. Can I ask you a question, Pops?"

"Sure can."

"I was asking Momma about babies and about what happens to them when they die. I know they go to heaven but do they go as babies? Or are they already grown up when they get there?"

Pops thought about this before he spoke. "Well, the apostle Paul tells us flesh and blood does not appear in heaven. We know then that babies won't be the same as they are when they were on this earth. Just like you and I won't be the same flesh and blood that we were on this earth. Does that answer your question?"

"I guess so."

"Carol Ann, I think the most important thing to remember about heaven is that we won't be so concerned with ourselves anymore. We will be consumed with worshipping Jesus. It's going to be a glorious time."

"Pops? Mind if I ask you another question?" I didn't want to wear him out; he was retired after all.

"You can ask me anything."

"Well, I know people who say there's no such thing as hell. And if heaven is real, and it's full of people who are mean and hateful, then they'd rather not go there. I know hell is real and I sure don't want to go there, but what do you say to someone who says they don't believe in heaven or hell?"

"That's a hard one, Carol Ann. Some folks think they must touch or see things in order for them to be real. I tell people you can't see love, but you know it's real. For that matter, you can't see germs, but you know they're real every time you get sick.

"That's where faith comes in. I can't see God or Jesus, but I know they're both real because I have faith. The Hebrew word for faith in relation to an invisible God means "conviction based upon hearing." He looked at me and said, "Sounds like a sermon, doesn't it?"

I laughed. "Sort of."

Pops reached over and hugged me. "Carol Ann, I could go on, and on, and on about how Jesus himself spoke of hell more than anyone else in the New Testament. But the truth is, all of us have an emptiness in our hearts; all of us. Some of us try to fill it with drugs, alcohol, money—you name it. But those of us who fill it with the love of Jesus have faith. Pure and simple. As for hateful people being in heaven, I hope they are there because heaven isn't for perfect people, it's for people who realize they're hateful and need the blood of Jesus to cover their sins. Like the bumper sticker says *I'm not perfect, just forgiven*."

"Brother Paul hasn't preached much about that."

"Or…could it be that you weren't listening?"

"Maybe," I said.

"Now that you're a Christian, you'll be surprised at how hungry you get for God's word and how much you'll love it. And that's a very good thing, Carol Ann. Don't ever run away from it. And if I ever hear of you being hateful, I'll come back here and yank a knot in your tail, hear me?"

I put my head on Pops shoulder.

"I love you, Pops."

"And me, you."

Party Line: n. (pär tē līn) single circuit used for two or more telephone users

My thoughts about faith were interrupted when I heard Daddy yell, "Telephone, Carol Ann."

"Coming," I answered. "Hello?"

"C.A.?" I heard on the other end.

"Oh, hi Roxy. What's up?"

"Je suis tres fatigue," she answered.

"Huh?"

"I said that I am very tired."

"Can you talk a little louder? We have a lot of people at our house right now and I can barely hear you." There was a pause on the other end of the phone.

"I SAID THAT I AM TRES TIRED."

"Why are you so tired?"

"I spent the day in Tyler shopping with mon mater."

"Cool! Did you get some new clothes?" Roxy was known for her cool clothes.

"Oui."

I answered, "Tres bien." I'd learned a word or two of French, myself.

"We drove to Tyler in hopes of finding a natural, health food store."

"Did they have one?" I asked.

"Oui. But it was rather backward. Louis found what he'd been looking for so I guess it was worth the trip. I got something for you, mon ami."

"Really?" This was great. Roxy bought something for me. "What is it? What did you buy?"

"It's a surprise. I'll give it to you tomorrow. Will you be home in the morning?"

"No, I'll be at church. I'm being baptized, remember? I told you about that." Someone laughed. "What's so funny?" I asked.

"What?"

"Are you laughing at me, Roxy?"

"I didn't laugh," she answered. There it was again.

"Is someone listening in? If you are, would you please hang up?"

"Keep your feet down, Carol Ann. You don't want to do what that sister of yours did." Click. Mrs. Taylor was listening in on our party line again.

"Sorry about that. Mrs. Taylor likes to listen in sometimes. Where was I?" I asked Roxy.

"You said that you were being baptized tomorrow."

"Oh yeah. Hey! Why don't you and your family come? I know that you're," I lowered my voice to a whisper, "atheists and all, but why don't you come anyway? BJ and her family are coming."

"Perhaps. It depends on Mother—if her stars are lined up and all. Ca va?"

"Okay," I said. "I hope her moons are in the seventh house or wherever they're supposed to be because it really would be cool to have my two best friends there."

"Bon soir," she said.

"Bon soir." Roxanne Wojowitz had to be the most amazing person, ever.

***

All the relatives had left for the Lone Star Inn except Uncle Claude and Aunt Vestal who were dancing in front of their trailer. Nita Sue and I watched them from what was left of our bedroom window. Earlier that night, Uncle Elmer thought he should give Uncle Claude a little manly advice on framing and knocked a hole in the window. Uncle Claude patched it with visquine and duct tape. Momma didn't want him to take out the broken window until he was ready to replace it with another one. I think she was afraid Nita Sue might run off to Baskin Robbins searching for Tommy.

"How romantic is that?" Nita Sue held her arms in the air like she was dancing with someone. Her body swayed to the music.

"Do you think she's happy?" I asked.

"I don't know. What's not to be happy about?"

"You know, with Uncle Claude and that business with the boy who died and the baby?"

"That happened so long ago, I bet she doesn't even think about it anymore. Just look at them." Uncle Claude dipped Aunt Vestal, and she laughed like she didn't have a care in the world. The Chinese lanterns fluttered in the slight breeze.

"What are they listening to?" I asked.

"The Ray Coniff Singers. Nauseating if you ask me." Nita Sue glided across our bedroom.

"Well, it's not Bobby Sherman, but they must like it."

"Bobby Sherman? He's so bubblegum. You need to move up in the music world, little sister. Which reminds me, have you seen my new Beatles album? I can't find it."

"No. Where did you put it last?"

"In one of your Jackson 5 jackets."

"You mean the one I loaned to BJ?"

"Carol Ann, why did you give it to her? I have a Rolling Stones in there, too." Her slow dancing had stopped and her tune had changed.

"Well, how was I supposed to know you hid it in there? Why can't you use your own jackets for once?"

"If we didn't live in a house with such fuddy duddy parents, I might. But Daddy would snatch my arm off and beat me with a bloody stump if he caught me with those. Margaret had to buy them for me at Murphy's. I can't buy anything there without Nettie Mc-Carty calling Mother and telling her what I look at, much less what I buy."

Nita Sue was right about that. The store owners in our small town took their jobs seriously when it came to selling merchandise to kids.

"I know. I'll talk to BJ tomorrow, okay? She's coming to see me get baptized. I'll ask her about it then."

Momma and Daddy came in to tell us goodnight. "You nervous, Carol Ann?" Daddy asked as he sat down on the edge of my twin bed.

"No sir, not really. Pops gave me those socks with the rubber soles. So, I guess not."

Daddy leaned over and kissed me on the forehead. "You'll be fine. With or without socks. Good night, sweetie."

"Good night, Daddy."

Momma tucked Nita Sue in bed. "Good night, Carol Ann. Sweet dreams." Momma blew me a kiss and turned out the lights.

"Raindrops keep fallin' on my head and just like the guy whose feet are too big for his bed, nothing seems to fit. Those raindrops keep fallin' on my head they keep fallin'."

BJ Thomas

We arrived at FBC Lake View thirty minutes earlier than usual. I had to get my hairbrush and dry underclothes to the baptistery changing room before Sunday School. Momma was trying to get Aunt Ada and Uncle Elmer settled in the LOA (Love One Another) Sunday School Class before they upset somebody.

Deacon Wilder was waiting for me. "Just leave your things there, Miss Lawson. I'll keep an eye on them," he said.

"Yes, sir," I replied. "Thank you." I double checked my Piggly Wiggly sack: bathing suit, underwear, knee socks, training bra, hairbrush, Secret, lime green headband, and pink socks. Yep. I was ready for the immersion waters today.

"Excuse me, miss. You seen Brother Paul Mitchell anywheres?" A grungy looking man in a maintenance uniform was opening and closing doors as fast as greased lightning. He even opened the one marked:

Baptistery Restroom Only
Everyone else use the one off the choir room, please.
That means you!

"No, sir."

"Who's in charge 'round here when you can't find the preacher?" he asked.

"Deacon Wilder is right over…" I looked around, but he was gone. "I guess Brother Eddie Earl. He's the music director."

"Where 'bouts would I find him, miss?"

"He's usually in the church office making last minute changes to the choir folders and stuff."

"Huh. We got us a king–sized problem with the baptistery pool today and I figure we ought to get her fixed before some poor sap gets in it."

WHAT? Was I that poor sap?

"What's wrong with it?" My voice was about two decibels higher than that used in church settings.

"Well," he said while adjusting his *I Love Jesus* ball cap, "I do all the maintenance work on this church and the Methodist church down the street. You know the one with them real perty stained glass winders?"

"Yeah, I know it. What's wrong with the baptistery?"

"Well, I was over here yesterday, and I was a fillin' her up—for the second time I might add—with the garden hose when all of a sudden I seen me what looked to be another rat. But now, don't quote me on that."

"A RAT?" I screamed.

"Well, it pert near looked like a rat to me. But now I seen lots of varmints wandering around in churches. Polecats, 'possums, armadillers. I even seen me a skunk in the Holiness Tabernacle Apostolic Church outside town. You know the one with the big old bell that rings every…"

"A RAT?" This was awful. I couldn't get baptized with a rat.

"Well now, don't go quoting me on that. Like I said, it coulda been a baby 'possum or …"

"A RAT?"

"You gotta 'member now, varmints come in here to get outta this heat. He probly just heard the water running and decided to take hisself a little swim that's all. Shucks, I don't blame him. It's been hotter than blue blazes. Did you see what the Pentacostal church put up on their sign last week?" Mr. Maintenance Man fanned both hands out in the air like he was lighting up a neon sign. "It said 'HELL'S HOTTER!!!'. Ain't that the cleverest thang you ever saw? I laughed until I dropped at that one. Them Pentacostal folks, they…"

"I CAN'T GET BAPTIZED WITH A RAT!"

"Heckfire, miss, I wouldn't worry. That rat's probably gone by now anyways."

I relaxed a little. "Really? You think?"

"It's the snake I'm worried 'bout."

"SNAKE? A SNAKE!"

"You know the old sayin' *Where there's a rat, there's a snake.* My grandpappy used to say all kinds of…"

About that time, Brother Paul came around the corner. "Hester Lee? You looking for me?"

"Oh, Brother Paul!" I screamed. "There's a rat, a snake, a…" I was screaming at our preacher.

"Slow down, child." Brother Paul put his hands on my shoulders. "Now what's all the excitement about, here?"

Mr. Hester Lee or Dee or whatever the maintenance man's name was said, "I thought I seen me another rat in the baptismal pool yesterday and I came to…"

Brother Paul cut him off. "Hester Lee, would you excuse us please? I need a minute with Miss Carol Ann. And please remove your ball cap, you're in the house of the Lord."

Hester Lee removed his cap rather quickly.

"Carol Ann, there are no rats or snakes in the baptistery. Hester Lee saw one of Miss Arleva's guinea pigs, that's all. She brings two or three of them up to the church every Friday morning to show the staff the latest costumes she's sewn for them. I was giving a tour of the sanctuary to our new members who happen to have small children and when Miss Arleva learned that there were little children up here, she came on up to show off her guinea pigs and one of them got loose.

"By the time I rounded up Hester Lee to aid in the search, the poor little thing had fallen into the water and was swimming ninety–to–nothing. Evidently, the children thought it was some kind of rat—which, technically, it is I suppose—but that's neither here nor there. I caught it climbing out of the baptistery by way of the garden hose and returned it safely to Miss Arleva."

He patted my hand. "So, there's no rat and certainly no snake. I had Hester Lee drain the water, clean the baptistery and refill it Saturday. Even I, your fearless pastor, wouldn't get near the waters if I thought there was a chance I might be sharing them with a snake."

What a relief. "Thank you, Brother Paul. I've been so worried about my feet coming up and splashing the choir that I never had time to worry about rats or snakes." He gave me a sideways preacher's hug.

"The only thing that could possibly go wrong today is that I wouldn't get to meet all of your aunts and uncles. What a blessing to have so many relatives at your baptism."

If he only knew.

Holy Spirit: n. the third person of the Christian trinity

"Praise God from whom all blessings flow.
Praise Him all creatures here below.
Praise Him above ye heavenly hosts.
Praise Father, Son, and Ho-ly Ghost. Amen."

Brother EdEarl swiveled around and faced the congregation. Looked like his toupee would be intact today.

"Before we sing the next hymn, I would like to take a minute to thank the Berean Ladies Class for sewing the new tablecloths for the hand bell table. This will be the first year that our Baptist Belles Hand Bell Choir has had matching robes and tablecloths. So, thank you, Bereans.

"I also have one change in the bulletin today. While God's word is most holy and accurate, the printed hymn number is not." He got quite a few chuckles with that one. "The correct hymn number is 131, not 331. So, if you would please turn in your hymnals to hymn No. 131. That's one, three, one. We'll sing the first, second and last stanzas."

Brother EdEarl nodded at Mrs. Herron. She pounded the first chord of *There is a Name I Love to Hear*. I giggled to myself as I thought about how many times Nita Sue had leaned over and whispered, 'Play Ball' before Mrs. Herron's preludes and offertories. What our organist lacked in talent she made up for in loudness.

As the congregation sang about the worth of Jesus' name, Brother Paul and I walked toward the baptistery. He looked more like a duck hunter in his waders than a preacher. Deacon Wilder stood beside me at the top of the north baptistery steps and ordered me to wait until he gave me the thumbs up. Brother Paul had walked around to the south entrance and was wading into the waters.

From the top step of the baptistery I could see way out into the congregation. My family took up two whole pews. Momma and Pops weren't holding hymnals—I guess they knew all three stanzas by heart. Pops was probably smiling the biggest of all the relatives. Aunt Betty was fanning herself; her hot flashes must have started up already. Uncle Ed tapped his fingers to the beat of the hymn on the back of the pew. No singing for him. He was tone deaf just like Daddy.

When they got to the chorus, Pops actually lifted his arms up in the air like he was going up for a rebound.

> *"Oh, how I love Je-sus,*
> *Oh, how I love Je-sus,*
> *Oh, how I love Je-sus,*
> *Be-cause He first loved me."*

I'd never seen anyone do hand motions during the worship service. Sometimes in Vacation Bible School we'd do sign language to the songs but not at the 11:00 worship service. Party lines would buzz about him for a week. Aunt Ada didn't smile one time while she sang the hymn. Uncle Elmer didn't bother singing at all.

BJ and her family were on the row behind my family and they looked just as happy as always. Mrs. Dodge was wearing her best hat and pearls. She was known for her extensive hat collection. I leaned over as far as I could, looking for Roxy, but I didn't see her. I guess her mother's stars weren't lined up.

As soon as the congregation finished the hymn, Deacon Wilder leaned over and whispered, "You're up." Motioning for me to walk down the steps, I walked into the baptistery pool that, as of yesterday, had been a swimming hole for one of Miss Roberts' guinea pigs.

Easing into the water, I was happy that my rubber soled socks were working just like Pops said they would. Brother Paul smiled at me and whispered, "You ready?"

"Yes sir," I whispered back.

"Good morning," Brother Paul said to the church.

"Good morning," the congregation answered rather weakly.

"I said, 'Good Morning'."

"Good morning," they answered again, rather loudly, that time.

"Folks, it is a good day to be in the house of the Lord." Amens bounced around the sanctuary. My feet stuck to the baptistery floor.

"The twenty–eighth chapter of Matthew instructs believers to: 'Go ye therefore and teach all nations, baptizing them in the name of the Father, and of the Son, and of the Holy Ghost: Teaching them to observe all things whatsoever I have commanded you: and lo, I am with you alway, even unto the end of the world'." At our church, the congregation said the Great Commission along with Brother Paul whenever someone was baptized.

"This morning, it is my privilege to bring before you, Miss Carol Ann Lawson. Carol Ann has given her heart to Jesus, folks. Amen?"

"Amen!" I heard a swoosh and saw that Mrs. Taylor had opened a red umbrella right below us in the choir loft. The nerve of that party line eavesdropper!

"Carol Ann, have you accepted Jesus Christ as your personal Lord and Savior?"

I answered, "I have." I turned sideways to the congregation and looked up at Deacon Wilder who was picking his molars with a toothpick but still found time to smile and wave at me. Brother Paul put the handkerchief over my nose and raised his right hand in the air. I held on to his hand real tight.

"In obedience to the command of our Lord and Master, and upon your profession of faith, I baptize you my sister, Carol Ann Lawson." Leaning my body backwards, Brother Paul gently pushed; then pulled me under. I remembered to bend my knees and my feet stayed down. "Buried with Christ in baptism, raised to walk in the newness of life." I heard lots of amens. Exiting the waters, I noticed one person sitting alone in the balcony.

It was Uncle Claude.

By the time I got out of my wet robe, Momma was waiting for me outside the baptistery restroom. "I am so proud of you, Carol Ann." She hugged me so tight, I coughed.

"Sorry, honey."

"That's okay. My feet stayed down, Momma. Just like Pops said they would."

"Of course they did, sweet girl." She kissed me on the head and helped me comb out my hair. I was glad to get out of the wet baptism gown. The heater was broken in the baptistery and the water was rather cold.

We walked around the outside of the church so we could enter through the front doors and slip into our pew without causing a disturbance. Standing in the foyer, I remembered that I had spotted Uncle Claude in the balcony. Before Momma could open the door to the sanctuary, I pulled her aside and told her about Uncle Claude. The two ushers who were waiting with collection plates in their hands stared at us. Maybe it was my wet hair dripping all over the carpet or the sight of my pink swimsuit sticking out of the Piggly Wiggly sack. Whichever, Momma told them that we needed to check on something in the balcony and for them to go on ahead.

We peeked through one of the three square windows in the balcony door. What I saw that morning would change how I viewed my favorite aunt and uncle forever. Huddled together in the corner of the balcony were Aunt Vestal and Uncle Claude. Aunt Vestal sobbed uncontrollably, yet quietly. Rocking back and forth like a mother with her baby, Uncle Claude consoled Aunt Vestal with tender words and small kisses. The harder she cried, the more he soothed.

Her head was buried deep in Uncle Claude's chest and her arms rested on his shoulders.

Momma gently pulled me away from the tiny windows that had allowed us to act as intruders into her sister's private moment. Instead, we parked ourselves on the top step of the balcony stairs. Momma tried to speak, but each time she moved her lips they quivered so hard she was forced to close them again. I didn't know what to say. It was obvious to me that Aunt Vestal and Uncle Claude had every intention of attending my baptism because they were both dressed in their Sunday clothes. Why they chose the balcony over sitting with the rest of the family was a mystery.

Why was Aunt Vestal crying? Was she upset about something that was said during the baptism? Had I done something to make her cry?

Momma's deep breath indicated that it was time for us to leave this painfully intimate scene. She patted my hand and smiled a sad smile. Taking a tissue from her pocket, she wiped her tears and stood.

We walked down the steps, past the ushers, through the double doors and sat down next to Daddy. We were just in time to hear Mrs. Grimes sing today's solo, *Sweet, Sweet Spirit*.

About the time Mrs. Grimes grabbed hold of the podium with both hands, Brother EdEarl jumped up from his chair and practically pushed her out of the way. He said, "Before Miss Ruby sings the next song, I feel the need to point out something. The chorus of this particular song is written: *sweet Holy Spirit, sweet heavenly dove, stay right here with us, filling us with your love.*

"Now as good Baptists, we know that the Holy Ghost never leaves us once we get saved. There's been some discussion on whether or not we should even sing a song that was written by a member of another denomination who believes that the Holy Ghost can come and go. But…"

"FOR THE LOVE OF PETE, SING THE SONG ALREADY!" a man screamed. What? I couldn't believe somebody actually yelled at Brother EdEarl during the worship service. I looked down our pew, along with fellow worshippers, to see who it was. It was Uncle Ed.

I was so embarrassed I didn't know what to do. Of all the days to pick a bone with Brother EdEarl, Uncle Ed chose today, my baptism Sunday.

Clearly, Brother EdEarl didn't know what to do, either. He stood at the podium staring at the congregation with his mouth open. It was bizarre, to say the least. I looked at Daddy and saw those two veins popping out on the side of his neck—the same ones that popped out whenever he got upset—usually at Nita Sue or me. I didn't move an inch. I knew when to sit still and keep my mouth shut and this was definitely one of those times.

"Ed Lawson," Aunt Betty whispered loudly, "keep your voice down."

"I WILL NOT KEEP MY VOICE DOWN," Uncle Ed hollered. Then he shot up out of the pew and addressed Brother EdEarl. "Would you please quit talking us to death every week? For the love of God, let the woman sing her song!"

"ED." Daddy said through clenched teeth. "Sit. Down. Now." Uncle Ed sat down.

Brother EdEarl was escorted to his chair by Brother Paul.

Mrs. Herron struck the organ and Mrs. Grimes began singing *Sweet, Sweet Spirit*. She didn't miss a beat. After all, she had accused her husband of adultery from that very podium on a Sunday night.

I could feel the heat radiate from Daddy's body. He was one angry man, and I was glad that I wasn't going to be on the receiving end of his wrath. If God really did smite people, I had a feeling that Uncle Ed might be the one who was smited. Or smote. Or whatever. Today, I was glad to be sitting next to Dan, not Ed, Lawson.

Yankee: n. (yān kē) a native or inhabitant of the northern United States

Instead of the customary Sunday pot roast dinner at our house, we drove to the Coffee Cup restaurant in Holly Springs. The Lion's Den couldn't hold that many Lawsons and McClanahans at one table, so Daddy insisted that we celebrate the last day of our reunion there.

As we pulled into the parking lot, I read their new slogan out loud, "Our Great Food Will Never Leave You."

A golden, billboard sized, coffee pot poured thousands of sparkling, black bits of coffee into a billboard sized, golden coffee cup. No matter which way you looked at that big Coffee Cup sign, the black coffee sparkled. The liquor store down the street had the same sparkling, silver pieces—only it poured out of a champagne bottle into a champagne glass. Nita Sue would poke me in the ribs and act like a drunk any time we passed it.

The Coffee Cup was famous for its Sunday buffet with every kind of meat and vegetable known to man. They served exotic dishes like salmon croquettes with tartar sauce. Their pies had meringues so tall they looked like Miss Mattie had made them. Eating there was definitely a treat for Nita Sue and me.

The Coffee Cup had a bubblegum machine filled with pink bubblegum and another machine filled with cheap jewelry—plastic rings, necklaces and bracelets. At the end of a meal, the manager always gave Nita Sue and me tokens for one of the machines. Last time we ate there, I got a peace sign necklace on the first try.

A hostess in a gold uniform wearing a coffee cup necklace and matching earrings seated us at a long table. Daddy had called on Saturday and reserved it.

I made a beeline for Momma and Daddy. There was no way was I sitting by Uncle Elmer and Aunt Ada. Not today. I'd had enough of them to last me a while.

Uncle Ed and Daddy must have called for a truce back at the church because they were talking up a storm like nothing had happened. I gathered that when you were old, you could tell your siblings off in public and still make peace with them later.

Everyone was seated at the long table except for Aunt Vestal and Uncle Claude. We didn't see them after the service, and Momma told me not to say a word about the balcony scene to anyone.

"Afternoon, y'all. My name's Neva Jo and I'll be your waitress today. All these on one ticket?" she asked Daddy.

"Matter of fact they are," responded Uncle Claude as he and Aunt Vestal materialized when Neva Jo the waitress showed up to take our drink order. I counted the words in his sentence in my head. Five…

"Mighty proud for you, girl," Uncle Claude whispered in my ear as he and Aunt Vestal walked to the other end of the table. Thank you's went up one side of the table and down the other as everyone acknowledged Uncle Claude's generosity.

"Well, then," Daddy said as he rubbed his hands together, "I believe I'll have a sweet tea."

"Me, too," said Momma.

"Coke for me, please," I said.

"Tab, please" answered Nita Sue—like she even knew what Tab tasted like.

"What's on tap?" Aunt Vestal asked.

"We don't serve alcohol on Sunday, ma'am," Neva Jo replied. Aunt Vestal lit a cigarette, pondered her choices and said, "Well, bring me an RC Cola then." Aunt Ada made a remark under her breath. Uncle Elmer told her to pipe down.

"I'll have coffee, please ma'am," Uncle Claude said.

"Ditto," said Uncle Elmer, obviously pleased with himself.

"I'm sorry, sir. We don't have that," Neva Jo answered in between gum smacks.

"What?"

"We don't have Ditto, sir." Uncle Elmer rolled his eyes. "I'll have a cup of coffee."

"May I please have a sweet tea?" Aunt Ada asked like she was the queen of England.

"I'll have me one of them RC Colas," Uncle Ed announced.

"Good choice, Ed," Aunt Vestal said as she tapped her Virginia Slim in the gold ashtray.

"I didn't know you could get Tab here. Bring me a Tab on ice, honey." Aunt Betty was downright giddy.

"Sweet tea for me," Pops answered.

Neva Jo said, "Okay, let's see here." She pointed her pen at Daddy and went around the table. "We got us one sweet tea, sweet tea, Coke, Tab, RC Cola, coffee, coffee, sweet tea, RC Cola, Tab and sweet tea?" Everyone nodded in agreement.

Uncle Ed said, "Well, now, that's some good order taking there, Miss Neva Jo."

Neva Jo smiled at Uncle Ed and said, "This ain't my first rodeo, cowboy." She was flirting with him right there in front of God and Aunt Betty, but Aunt Betty was too busy studying the plastic flower arrangement on the table to catch on.

"Well butter my butt and call me a biscuit," Aunt Vestal said under her breath. Nita Sue and I giggled to ourselves.

"Y'all all getting the buffet today?" Everyone nodded.

Then, Aunt Ada spoke up. "Not me. I believe I'll have the Chef Salad Surprise with Thousand Island dressing on the side. On the side, you know what that means?"

Neva Jo stopped writing on her little pad and looked up. "Yessum, I got it."

Pops spoke. "I'd like to offer up the blessing before we head over to the buffet line." We bowed our heads—even Neva Jo. Pops thanked God for the good food we were about to eat, the hands that had prepared it and safe travel for all who were headed home. I said my own little prayer and asked God to please send Aunt Ada and Uncle Elmer packing. I guess He heard me because Uncle Elmer started talking about the prison accounts he had to call on tomorrow.

I practically ran for the buffet. Daddy filled his plate with roast beef, mashed potatoes and gravy, and two or three different vegetables. Momma and Pops commented that they liked the Coffee Cup's vegetables because they put sugar in them just like Grandma did. I grabbed a salmon croquette before they disappeared.

Today, the Coffee Cup proudly displayed red Jell–O salad with floating cherries. Upon closer inspection, I could see some other kind of fruit suspended in the red gelatin but couldn't tell what kind it was. I didn't care. Getting Jell–O salad was a real treat. I grabbed one and put it on my tray. Nita Sue got a yellow one with marshmallows.

The dessert table offered the everyday desserts that cafeterias and restaurants around here served: pineapple upside down cake, German chocolate cake, Texas sheet cake and the usual assortment of homemade puddings. But the Coffee Cup was famous for its homemade pies. Aunt Betty said the Coffee Cup was the only restaurant she knew of that actually served six slices of pie instead of the standard eight slices. She was telling this to a complete stranger standing at the dessert table.

There was one piece of chocolate cream pie left. Momma made us eat everything on our plates before we could choose a dessert. I was afraid someone else would take it before I finished my salmon croquette and Jell–O. Uncle Claude must have seen the panicked look on my face because he snatched it up, gave me a wink and smiled. I smiled back.

The reunion kinfolk were enjoying a pleasant Sunday lunch until Neva Jo delivered Aunt Ada's Chef Salad Surprise. "Here you go ma'am. One Chef Salad Surprise with Thousand on the side." Neva Jo placed Aunt Ada's salad bowl in front of her.

"I told you to put the Thousand Island on the side, didn't I?" Aunt Ada said. Neva Jo looked at Aunt Ada, then the salad and said, "I did, ma'am. It's on the side." Eleven sets of eyes stared at a hefty white bowl with a circle of Thousand Island dressing carefully positioned on the lip of the salad bowl.

"That is not on the side," Aunt Ada said. "This is on the side." She scooped the dressing off the bowl with a spoon and slung it onto Uncle Elmer's empty coffee saucer. "On the side means in a separate dish. See? Now it's on the side."

Neva Jo stood there smacking her gum and staring at the salad. "You a Yankee or something?" she asked. Aunt Vestal spewed her RC Cola all over the table. Pretty soon everyone was giggling into their napkins or their hands, including me.

"No. I most certainly AM NOT a Yankee. For your information, I am a member of the Daughters of the Civil War *and* the Joseph Duncan Confederacy Club, thank you very much."

"Them the ones that wear the hoods over their heads?" Neva Jo asked. Aunt Vestal spewed again. She was looking more like a volcano than a movie actress stand–in.

Aunt Betty chimed in. "You mean the Ku Klux Klan? Land sakes, no. They don't allow women in their club. Everyone knows that."

Pops sprang into action. "Excuse me, Neva Jo is it?"

"Yes, sir."

"The chef salad looks delicious, and I thank you for taking a special order especially since the rest of us chose the buffet. Do you think I might have a little refill on my sweet tea, please?"

"Me, too," said Daddy.

"Me, three. I'll take another Coke," I said. Heck, if everyone else was having seconds and Uncle Claude was paying for it, why not? I mean, I was the woman of the hour, right?

"I think you've had enough Coke for one day, honey," Momma said. "Bring her a glass of ice water, please." Neva Jo seemed happy to be on refill duty.

Nita Sue whispered, "Nice going, buffalo breath." I booted her as hard as I could underneath the table.

"Wrong leg," Aunt Vestal said.

"Oops, sorry."

Aunt Ada started up again. "The nerve of that woman. Thinking I'm a Yankee. Colonel Joseph Duncan just rolled over in his grave. That's what he did. Just rolled over in his grave." Aunt Ada was miffed.

"Well, big sister, you can put your boots in the oven but that don't make them biscuits," Uncle Ed said to her.

"And what exactly is that supposed to mean?" She was slinging Thousand Island dressing on her salad like there was no tomorrow.

"It means exactly what it means. You can say you're a "southern daughter whatever" all night and all day but it don't make it so."

"You want to see my lineage papers, Ed?"

"No, sister, I don't. I couldn't care less who you're related to on either side of the Mason–Dixon Line."

"For your information, Ed, you are just as much related to them as me and Daniel." Aunt Ada deposited the last of the Thousand Island dressing on her Chef Salad Surprise.

"Ada, what's the point of getting your dressing on the side if you put it all on your salad anyway?" Aunt Vestal was picking a fight of the Goliath proportion. Aunt Ada glared.

"For your information, Vestal Cinaretta, I like it on the side because they typically give you more salad dressing if you ask for it ON THE SIDE THAN IF YOU JUST LET THEM PUT IT ON TOP OF THE SALAD!"

"You know you just added about four hundred calories to that salad, don't you, Ada?" Aunt Vestal asked.

Oh, this was great. We were going to have a cat fight right here in the middle of the Coffee Cup on my baptism Sunday.

"Careful, Ada. Colonel Duncan might be listening," Uncle Ed said.

"Oh, hush up, Ed." She shoved a forkful of salad in her mouth. Uncle Ed elbowed her and grinned. Uncle Elmer continued to eat his frog legs and ignored all of them.

Aunt Vestal reached across the table and speared a tomato wedge coated in Thousand Island and declared, "A moment on the lips…forever on the hips," and popped it in her mouth. Uncle Ed elbowed Aunt Ada again. She laughed. I mean, she actually laughed. The Lord does work in mysterious ways. Maybe we wouldn't have a cat fight after all.

"Pass this to Carol Ann." Uncle Claude handed my piece of chocolate cream pie to Aunt Vestal, who gave it to Nita Sue, who eventually gave it to me. She held on to it a little too long, like she was going to do something to it. I mouthed the word "incense" to her and she set it down.

"Thank you." I dug into that pie like flies on honey.

The adults drank their coffee and ate their desserts. The manager came over to our table and thanked us all for dining at the Coffee Cup. As always, she awarded two tokens to Nita Sue and me for the vending machines. An ERA NOW button was pinned above her nametag. Her name was Gloria.

"You a feminist?" Aunt Betty asked.

"Yes, I am," answered Gloria. Gloria must have been a hardcore feminist because she wasn't wearing a brassiere.

"Well, isn't that cute, honey?" Aunt Betty said. I don't think Aunt Betty's response was the one Gloria was expecting. She mumbled something to herself and walked off. Nita Sue and I excused ourselves and hoofed it to the front, straight for the vending machines.

I was trying to decide if I wanted to go for the cheap, plastic jewelry or bubblegum. I went for the sure thing. Bubblegum.

"You girls need to use the restroom before we start home?" Momma asked.

"Mo–ther." Nita Sue looked around to see if any cute boys had overheard her mother tell her to use the crapper. Momma shook her head and walked to the car.

"Hells Bells," Nita Sue said when her token jammed. "What's up with this machine?"

"You have to twist it a little harder," someone said. That someone turned out to be a football player for the Holly Springs Hawks, according to his jersey. Nita Sue practically slobbered on the poor guy as he twisted the knob until a plastic container shaped like an acorn plopped through a silver door. "Here you go," he said and handed her a black spider ring.

"Thank you. I'm Nita Sue Lawson," she said with her head tilted ever so slightly. I thought I might puke right then and there.

"Ricky Hilman. Nice to meet you. You live around here?"

"Sort of. We live in Lake View." Her eyelashes fluttered.

"Oh," Ricky Hilman answered.

Aunt Ada rounded the corner by the cigarette machine. "Nita Sue, did you use the bathroom yet?" Nita Sue's face turned bright red. Ricky Hilman looked down.

"Here. You're going need this. They're out." Aunt Ada handed Nita Sue a purse packet of Kleenex tissues.

Needless to say, Nita Sue was rather quiet on the ride home. It took everything I had not to laugh or make some catty remark. While I detested Aunt Ada and her self–righteous, Confederate–loving, Bible–beating self, I was pretty sure she didn't know what she was doing when she offered Nita Sue toilet paper in front of a good looking boy.

When we got home, Nita Sue went straight to our room and shut the door. I decided to leave her alone for a long time. Maybe until bedtime, or perhaps, eternity.

"Put your hand in the hand of the man who stilled the water. Put your hand in the hand of the man who calmed the sea. Take a look at yourself and you can look at others. By puttin' your hand in the hand of the man from Galilee."

Ocean

Momma and Daddy were busy reading the Sunday paper when I asked Momma if I could talk to her about something. "Sure, honey. What is it?" She folded the Living section of the newspaper and laid it on her lap.

"Well, it's just that, uh," I looked over at Daddy reading the sports section and then back at Momma.

"Would you like to go outside and sit in the swing, honey?"

"Yes, ma'am." Most of the girl talk that transpired in the Lawson household took place in the porch swing beneath the big magnolia.

"Is something the matter?" Momma asked.

"Momma, I can't stop thinking about what we saw today. You know, in the balcony?"

"Yes, honey, I know." Momma fiddled with a piece of pine straw as her feet pushed the swing backward and then forward.

"Carol Ann, I don't know what to tell you mainly because I don't know what to think myself. I know Vestal and Claude wanted to be at your baptism. And I know they came to Sunday dinner and laughed and acted like nothing happened, but I don't know why Vestal was crying. Perhaps being back in church sparked a deep hurt or a regret. I simply don't know. But what I do know is this; God brought Vestal and Claude here for a reason. And it wasn't simply to build a bathroom."

She looked at me and smiled. "There is no doubt in my mind that the Lord is up to something where Vestal is concerned."

"But *how* do you know that, Momma? I mean, look at the way she drinks and smokes and talks. Sometimes it scares me just to be breathing the same air as her. Yesterday, she told me that she doesn't believe in heaven or in hell. *And* that she really doesn't believe in God or Jesus either. And that if really hateful people like Aunt Ada are in heaven, then she'd rather not be there. So how can you say "you know" that God is up to something? That's what I don't get. It looks to me like she doesn't care about church or Jesus or anything else for that matter."

"I understand that, honey. But what you have to realize is that God's ways aren't our ways—He sees eternity—not just last week, or today, or twenty–five years from now. He sees the big picture. And you have to remember something else. A lot of people have been praying for Vestal for many years. The Lord sends the Holy Ghost to convict people at the right time."

"But how do you *know* that?" I asked.

"I know that because God's word tells me that."

"*Where* does it say that?"

Momma stopped the swing and put her arm around my shoulders. "In Romans, I think; it's in chapter one or maybe chapter two, we can check when we go inside. But it says something like this: God has revealed the truth to us—*all* of us. From the time He created the world, people have seen the sky and the earth and all of the things He made—the visible qualities of God. Those are the things we can see and touch. We can see God's invisible qualities, too. His divine power. His eternal nature. I heard a preacher say one time that it takes more faith to not believe in God than to believe in God. I think Aunt Vestal has had so much pain in her life that she can't get past it long enough to see God."

She continued. "So, remember that when pain comes, and believe me it will, you can do one of two things. You can try to dull the pain with drugs, alcohol or false teachings or you can give it over to the Lord and let Him handle it. Aunt Vestal is simply not there yet."

"But Momma, that's the part that doesn't make sense to me. I mean, she grew up in church just like you. How did she turn out this way?"

"Honey, the answer is the same. You make a choice. Do I receive Christ and let the Holy Ghost dwell in me and handle my problems for me? Or do I continue to try and fix things my way? It really does boil down to that."

"Pops said the same thing. Only he used a lot of big words and stuff."

"Did he throw in some Hebrew or Greek?" Momma asked.

"How did you know?"

Momma laughed. "He always does that when someone asks him a thought–provoking question about Scripture."

"I thought Aunt Vestal seemed happy at the Coffee Cup, didn't you?"

"Yes, I did." The swing creaked as our feet pushed off the grass.

"I mean, she was kidding around with Aunt Ada about the salad, you know? And she even got her to laugh."

"I know."

"Momma, do you think Aunt Ada is happy?"

She bit her lip. "That's a good question. What do you think?"

"I think Aunt Vestal is right about her being mean, you know? And the way she quotes Scripture all the time? Why does she do that?"

"That's the big question. Remember what we're supposed to do for Ada?"

"I know, I know. Pray for her, right?"

"That's right."

"Oh, look Carol Ann. The lightning bugs are out."

We sat in the swing for a long time, not saying anything, just swinging. My head in Momma's lap and her fingers combing my hair. After a while, Momma leaned over and said, "You ready for school tomorrow?"

"Yes and no. I'm ready to see B.J. and Roxy."

"What about homework? Do you have any for tomorrow?"

"Yes, ma'am, but I've already done it."

"Well then, what do you say we go inside and watch *The Wonderful World of Disney*?" I bolted out of the swing. "You mean no church tonight?"

"Nope. Not tonight."

"Oh, thank you!" I hugged her neck and ran for the house. I was going to see Tinker Bell tonight!

"Hey, well, I'm the friendly stranger in the black sedan, won't you hop inside my car?"
The Ides of March

Homecoming week was finally here and I was helping with the French Club float.

According to BJ, building the float was the best part of homecoming. I wouldn't know—the only part of homecoming I knew about was the slave labor part that took place at my aunt's flower shop.

The Ashfords generously volunteered their barn that year. Theirs was the biggest in the county and the only one large enough to house a fifty foot trailer. Madame Philbert had a brilliant idea that was sure to take first place in the homecoming parade. Somehow, they were going to take a Volkswagen Beetle and turn it into a larger–than–life Lake View lion. I didn't know how that would happen, but I was fixing to find out.

"Hey," BJ said.

"Hi there," I answered.

"You ready to work?"

"I guess so." I lowered my voice so no one else would hear me. "I'm more excited about hanging out with the cheerleaders than anything."

We both giggled. "What's that VW Beetle doing up on the trailer? Oh my gosh, you mean we're turning her *car* into a lion?"

"Oui. We're turning her Volkswagen beetle into a lion." Roxy had appeared out of thin air. Tonight she was wearing a skin tight smock over a pair of bell bottom jeans. Her black, silky hair looked perfect as always.

"How are we going to do that?"

"Oh, it's the coolest thing ever," volunteered BJ. "You cover the car in newspaper, then chicken wire, then you stuff the chicken wire with napkins and spray paint it to look like a lion. It's really not that hard."

Silly me.

Madame Philbert began yelling instructions to the French Club. "Okay people, listen here. We're fixing to start on the float. I want all the girls up there working with newspaper. I don't want y'all cutting chicken wire. Boys, y'all get with Monsieur Ashford over there and he'll instruct you on what to do with the chicken wire.

"Now, I don't have to tell y'all how dangerous chicken wire can be. You can put your eye out in no time. So, listen up, people, and follow his instructions. Everyone is to stay inside this barn and I mean everyone. If I catch any of y'all sneaking off, it'll be trouble. Big trouble."

I couldn't figure out why anyone would sneak off when there was so much work to be done. But BJ told Roxy and me that last year some of the kids went out back to smoke and got caught.

"Belinda Jean, you and your friends get on the trailer and start taping newspaper to the car, please. I'll be over there." Mrs. Dodge was posted at the barn door to discourage any hankie pankie, according to BJ.

I taped newspaper to the Volkswagen Beetle until my hands were numb. The car may have looked small, but it wasn't, especially when you had to cover it with newspaper. Mr. Ashford was rubbing his bald head with one hand and pointing at the car with the other. I don't think the teenage boys understood what he wanted them to do.

"Did you see No. 10 over there?" Roxy whispered.

BJ and I looked around for the number ten—we didn't see one.

"The football player No. 10, mon amis." She rolled her eyes at us.

"You mean Jake Miller? What about him?" I said.

"Don't you think he's sexy?" Roxy said.

"Roxanne, don't talk like that. You'll get us in trouble."

"What? For saying sexy?"

"Yes, for saying sexy."

"You guys are so square sometimes."

"I'd rather be square here, than at home doing homework or housework, that's for sure," I said.

"Okay, people. Listen up, now. You girls by the car? Y'all get off and let Mr. Ashford bring the chicken wire up."

Mr. Ashford and a group of boys carried the wire frame up to the car and began molding it around the Beetle. Mr. Ashford accidentally cut his hand and said a word that was definitely not in our family's vocabulary. Roxanne piped in with a few questionable French words herself.

"Here, start stuffing." BJ handed me a stack of dinner napkins. I unfolded one napkin, grabbed the center and began stuffing every octagon between here and Ft. Worth.

"This is harder than it looks," I said. "How many are we supposed to put in each hole?"

"As many as it takes," BJ said. Within an hour, the front half of Madame Philbert's Volkswagen was beginning to take shape.

"Hey, this is pretty cool," I said. "When do they paint it?"

"When every single hole is stuffed and ready. Mom usually does the detail work. Did you see the lion's mane? Mom and Dad made a huge mane from the plaster that Dad uses when he sets arms and legs in casts. It looks pretty good."

We hopped off the trailer in search of the lion's mane. BJ was sure it was outside the barn somewhere. "Mom, where did you put the mane? I want to show it to Carol Ann and Roxy."

"It's in sections. Over by the car, I think." Mrs. Dodge was taking her role as gatekeeper seriously. She stepped aside so we could pass. We walked over to the other end of the barn where all the cars were parked.

"Do you smell something?" BJ asked.

"Yeah, it smells like smoke." I could identify cigarette smoke with my eyes closed. We'd had enough of it at our house to last a lifetime. Sure enough, three teenagers had snuck around Mrs. Dodge (I wasn't sure how) and were puffing away behind some farm equipment. We walked a little closer looking for the mane. I heard a girl giggle, then a boy laugh, then another giggle. Before we could stop ourselves we landed on top of a cheerleader and two boys. The boys were smoking like a couple of chimneys. One who was none other than Randy Mitchell.

"Oh my gosh!" I hollered.

"Oh my gosh!" BJ hollered.

"Quelle barbe!" Roxy hollered.

Suddenly, all three stood up and started making excuses for why they were hiding behind a rusty piece of farm machinery. Before I could ask Randy Mitchell anything else, he sprayed some Binaca on his tongue and practically ran inside the barn.

"Isn't that the boy your sister…"

"Yep."

"The preacher's…"

"Yep, that too."

"Wow."

"Double wow."

***

BJ, Roxy and I piled in the back of the Dodge's station wagon. Roxy was the first to be dropped off.

"We enjoyed your baptism service, Carol Ann," said Mrs. Dodge.

"Thank you. It was nice of y'all to come."

"Is your family still here?"

I answered with relief. "Only my Uncle Claude and Aunt Vestal. He's building the new bathroom on our house."

"How nice. I know you and your sister will enjoy that."

"Yes, ma'am."

BJ whispered, "Is your aunt riding in the parade?"

I whispered back, "I don't know. I hope so—if she's not drinking." Mrs. Dodge's eyes appeared in the rearview mirror. I smiled.

"Well, here we are," Mrs. Dodge said as she turned the car onto our street. "What's that?" Chinese lanterns glowed through the pine trees. Aunt Vestal sat in a lawn chair wearing a pair of *short* shorts and a bikini top. She raised her martini glass in a mock salute as we passed.

"That…is my aunt."

"Oh, how nice." Mrs. Dodge smiled and waved back at Aunt Vestal. BJ elbowed me and I shrugged. What else could I do? I thanked Mrs. Dodge for the ride and walked into the house.

Clearly, the cleaning fairies had not been at work in our house. Momma had been busy helping Aunt Betty during the day and saving the household duties for the Lawson women to tackle at night. I was quite surprised that Momma and Daddy had allowed me to help out with the homecoming float at all. I guess they figured homecoming only came once a year and household dust was there all the time.

Momma stood at the kitchen table folding a load of laundry while Daddy worked on some papers from his store. The adding machine clicked away.

"Hi, honey. Did you have a good time tonight?" Momma asked.

"Yes, ma'am. It was tres bien mon mater." They laughed. "Where's Nita Sue?"

Momma answered first. "She's talking to someone on the phone about the girl who was crowned queen. Do we know the girl who got it?"

"Kind of. She was new last year or the year before last. She's the one whose grandmother came in the shop and got so ugly with Aunt Betty. Remember? The one from Oklahoma?"

Momma stopped folding clothes. "I don't think Betty knows that. At least she didn't today when we were making corsages."

"Is there a problem?" Daddy quit pulling the handle on the adding machine.

"Oh no," Momma answered. "It's just that Betty had a little run-in with the lady—that's all. It didn't amount to much. Betty blamed it on a hot flash."

Daddy made a face. "You gals sure get away with a lot because of those hot flashes, don't you?"

Momma threw a towel over his head and said "Men!"

Daddy pulled Momma to him and tickled her.

Personally, I couldn't care less about the homecoming flowers. I'd done all the work required of me. Besides, tomorrow I'd be riding on the back of the French Club float with my two best friends.

If our new bathroom were finished, I'd take a shower and roll my hair. But since it wasn't, I'd have to settle for one in the old bathroom. Uncle Claude's timetable was about as reliable as the facts that came from Miss Mattie's House of Hair. His "this won't take any time job" had turned into a long, drawn out job. It, by the way, had put quite a damper in my newfound social life. I mean, how was I supposed to work on my new look spending only fifteen minutes a day in front of the bathroom mirror?

Uncle Claude blamed it on the lack of supplies here in east Texas, the lack of supply stores here in east Texas, as well as almost anything he could think of. Nita Sue was convinced that Uncle Claude really didn't want to go back to California, that instead he really liked the slow pace of Lake View. I told her she was crazy.

Why would anyone choose Lake View over California? Nita Sue claimed to have a sixth sense about these things. I knew her sixth sense alright—it was the stethoscope and I wasn't about to get caught with that thing again. I may have been young, but I wasn't stupid.

"Hey, little sister, did the French Club finish their float?"

"Yeah, mostly. It'll be ready in time for the parade. Looks pretty good, too." I stood a little straighter when I spoke of the Le François Club float. "What about the Spanish Club? Is it finished?"

"It's as finished as it's ever going be. Someone should shoot Mrs. Simms and put everyone out of their misery. She's making us all wear sombreros just to throw candy. Randy's not happy about it, that's for sure. He's mad as hell. After all, he *is* the vice–president of the Spanish Club, you know."

"So, he's in the Spanish Club, not the French Club?"

"Yeah, why?"

"No reason, I just wondered." No way was I getting in the middle of Nita Sue's soap opera life. "Too bad Aunt Vestal's not riding in the parade. I thought she would since they're still here, didn't you?"

"She *is* riding in the parade, you moron."

I was tired of being called a moron by my only sister. "Quit calling me a moron. I'm sick of it." I stood with my hands on my hips staring down at my older sibling. "You know what? You treat the dog better than you treat me—your own flesh and blood." I was getting madder by the minute. "And you know something else? Christians aren't hateful to each other, Nita Sue. And they don't cuss like you do, either. So there! Take that!"

Deliberate clapping followed my little speech. "Well done, little sister. You've finally learned to stick up for yourself." She smiled that no–good smile of hers.

I felt empowered, so I continued. "Spill the beans, Nita Sue. When did Aunt Vestal decide to ride in the parade and more importantly—what is she wearing?"

"How should I know? You ask her what she's wearing. All I know is that today after school, I had to go to the flower shop with an updated list of homecoming stuff before the pep rally, and Aunt Betty and Mother were finishing her corsage for the parade tomorrow." Nita Sue licked her finger before she turned the page of her most recent issue of *Cosmopolitan*.

"I can't believe Momma didn't tell me." I thought about this for a minute. "You don't think she'll be drinking do you?"

Nita Sue didn't miss a beat. "Of course not. She may like the juice, but she's not going to embarrass herself or our family. I'd bet the farm on it."

"You don't have a farm."

"I know. I just like the way it sounds."

"Is she riding on a float or in a convertible?"

"Mother said she's riding in a convertible. All the old queens are."

"Convertible? As in, Uncle Ed's convertible?"

"Bingo."

Great. I could see it now: Uncle Ed and Aunt Vestal leading the pack in his burnt orange caddy. Her drunk and him puffing away on his cigar.

"I'm going to bed."

"Goodnight, little sister."

"No matter what we get out of this, I know I know we'll never forget. Smoke on the water and fire in the sky. Smoke on the water..."

Deep Purple

School let out at 1:30 on Friday. Someone told me once, that in Texas, if schools kept kids in class until 1:30, they could count it as a full day and still get money from the government. Sounded kind of fishy to me, but what did I know? What did I care? That day, I would ride on a high school float in the homecoming parade.

"C.A.! Wait up!" Roxy hurried toward me in the funkiest getup I'd ever seen. "What do you think? I got it at the thrift shop in Holly Springs."

Not knowing exactly what to say, I said, "What are you supposed to be?"

"A French person," she said in disgust. Roxy had stopped using the word "man" and replaced it with "person" on all gender–related words.

"Oh, sure. I see it now." Pinned at a slight angle, the black velvet beret looked perfect on her, but she would look good wearing a Piggly Wiggly sack as opposed to me. Here I stood, in a pair of crisply ironed jeans and a Lake View Lions T-shirt. I tried to explain to Momma that people in civilized countries didn't iron blue jeans. *That was the purpose of blue jeans.* You could take them out the dryer and put them on your legs without lifting the iron or a can of spray starch. But, no…if a Lawson was wearing it, it was ironed stiff.

"Hey, there's BJ," Roxy said.

"Oh my gosh! Have y'all seen the queens? I bet there's twenty-five of them." BJ was completely out of breath.

"No, I just got here," I said. "Did you see my aunt?"

"Is she in your Uncle Ed's car?"

"Yes."

"I didn't see it, but I heard it. It's here somewhere."

I offered a silent prayer. *Lord, please don't let them embarrass our family. Please, please, please.*

BJ continued, "Surely she wouldn't be riding around now. It'd ruin her hair."

"Very true, mon ami. Let's find our float. I'm ready to wave at some cute boys," Roxy said as she adjusted her beret. If I didn't know better, I'd say some Kleenex tissues had found their way into Roxy's brassiere.

Homecoming to us was like the Macy's Thanksgiving Day Parade to New York, only on a smaller scale. Families lined the street. Some wore Lake View Lions T-shirts, but most dressed in school colors. Children sat at their parents' feet waiting for candy to be thrown their way. Vendors sold cotton candy, popcorn, hot dogs and funnel cakes.

The smell of funnel cakes filled the air and made my mouth water. I could shut my eyes and practically taste the fried doughy goodness topped with powdered sugar. If Mr. Haney's funnel cake machine cooperated, we were guaranteed to eat funnel cakes at least twice a year at the homecoming and rodeo parades. The joke was the same every year: "What's fifteen feet long and has four teeth? The funnel cake line in Lone Tree." I'm sure the Lone Tree people said the same thing about us, but I thought it was funny.

The Shriners drove their tiny cars and VFW members handed out American flags to anyone who would take one. The Boy Scouts and Girl Scouts marched in the parade just like everyone else despite not having a thing in the world to do with homecoming.

The high school band members tuned their instruments while the drill team practiced their high kicks and the cheerleaders fluffed their pompoms. The majorettes threw their batons in the air and caught them with ease. I couldn't see the horses, but I knew they were there because horse trailers lined the parking lot of the Methodist church.

Mrs. Knight summoned the three of us to the French Club float. The high school principal, Mr. Hankins, called for each group to line up according to their assigned number. We were No. 17.

Miss Gibbons yelled at the Allied Youth Club to quit littering the parking lot with gum wrappers, to pay attention and, "for the love of Pete, to stop eating the candy because it didn't grow on trees for crying out loud."

Texas Fight blared and Mr. Hankins made a snide remark about Uncle Ed. Miss Gibbons whispered something to him and he looked at me. He mouthed the word "sorry" as another car wheeled into the line. I smiled.I was used to it. Uncle Ed was in a league of his own.

The line of parade entrants grew longer as more groups arrived. I'd never seen so many convertibles in all my life. They had to be from other towns because only three people in Lake View owned convertibles and Uncle Ed was one of them.

Out of the corner of my eye, I saw the Morgue Mobile easing into the parade line. *Surely Mr. Shores isn't driving the hearse in the parade.* But lo and behold, Ms. Erma Martin was perched on the roof of the hearse wearing a mini skirt, a frilly blouse and flowers in her hair. Where did she think she was, San Francisco?

The parade line was so long that I couldn't see the end of it. As Mrs. Dodge instructed us (for the third time) to gently toss the candy, a voice boomed over the loud speaker, "Testing. One, two, three. Testing. One, two, three," and Mr. Caster, the Superintendent of Schools, gave the opening prayer. Applause followed and the parade began.

"I can't believe a school official just prayed in public," Roxy said with disgust.

"Why not?" I asked.

"Church and state, mon ami. That would *never* happen in California," she answered.

I had no idea what she was talking about, and didn't particularly care. Nothing could spoil today for me.

Our float was the best by far. The only other float that was half as good as ours was the FCA (Fellowship of Christian Athletes) float. The football team had constructed a miniature football field from green, artificial turf borrowed from Shores Funeral Parlor. Two vertical goalposts stood at either end. The football players wore their uniforms and threw miniature footballs to the crowd. The slogan on the footballs read: *What you miss by being a Christian—HELL.*

A cloud of carbon monoxide enveloped our trailer. We were moving now! The band played *Smoke on the Water* and our heads bobbed to the beat. Mary Grace Gifford had been instructed to leave both feet firmly planted on the floor of the float. Her daddy was the Church of Christ preacher and dancing for them was a sin. She swayed a little, but never lifted a foot.

The pep squad kicked into gear with hand motions. Their gloves flipped from the orange side to the white side with every beat the band produced. Pompoms shook left to right as the cheerleaders led the Lions on to victory.

It didn't take long for the horses to kick into gear. The drill teamed dodged horse poop with the grace that only Kilgore Rangerette wannabes could.

"Okay, start throwing the candy," Mrs. Dodge yelled.

I reached into my Piggly Wiggly sack and tossed candy like my very life depended on it. Roxy shouted French to the crowd. BJ waved and smiled.

"Did you see that?" BJ asked.

"What?"

"That little kid."

"Which one?" I asked.

"The one who just picked a sucker out of horse poop." We yelled "gross" at the same time and watched as his mother swatted his behind and clenched his hand until he finally dropped the sucker.

I felt something hit my shirt. Then my leg. Lamar Webb was hurling candy back at the floats.

As we rounded the first corner on the square my hand froze inside my Piggly Wiggly sack. I tried to speak, but couldn't. Balanced on the back of Uncle Ed's burnt orange Caddy was the most beautiful creature I'd ever seen. Aunt Vestal waved to the crowd with all the grace of a movie star. She'd chosen the light bulb changing wave. I knew this because she had demonstrated the different waves that beauty queens used while riding in parades and on runways.

Elegance didn't even begin to describe Aunt Vestal. Tears filled my eyes and pride swelled in my heart as I watched her and Uncle Ed travel along the parade route with the other homecoming queens.

"Holy cow. Is that your aunt?" BJ asked.

"Yes," I answered proudly. "That is my aunt."

"Wow, you really DO look like her."

Roxy chimed in. "Quelle barbe."

I had no idea what Roxy said and I didn't care. I wished time could stop and Aunt Vestal could be frozen in the moment forever.

"What a beautiful woman," I said to no one in particular.

**

The parade route ended back at the Methodist church. I could hear men calming their horses as they tried to maneuver them into their horse trailers. Teenagers were jumping off of the floats as fast as they could. The homecoming court was being introduced to the community of Lake View on the steps of the county courthouse. BJ, Roxy and I ran from the parking lot to the courthouse as fast as our freshly shaven legs would take us.

Mr. Caster began by thanking everyone for coming out and supporting the Lake View Lions. We were, after all, home to the Class AA state football champions of '67, '68, and '69. And dadgummit, we would be the state champs again this year! The band struck a chord and the drill team kicked up their heels and did a little dance number right there on the courthouse lawn. Everyone cheered. He then talked about the football game, and reminded everyone that kickoff was at 7:00 pm. He repeated the fact that outside food and drinks were strictly forbidden inside the stadium because, after all, that was how the booster club made their money.

The theme song from Hawaii Five-O filled the air as the football team and coaches sprinted to the makeshift stage.

"Wow, look at those orange pants. I didn't know you could buy orange polyester pants for men," BJ said.

"They must special order them for the coaches and players. I've never seen pants like that," I said.

"And look how they hug in all the right places," Roxy said.

"Roxy!"

"What? I just said out loud what you guys were thinking."

Two thick–necked football players spoke to the crowd. Apparently, we were going to stomp the Lone Tree Lobos and make them sorry for stepping foot into Lion territory. The Lion was the king of the jungle, and the king of the jungle didn't take no lip from a scrawny, gray wolf. Cheers went up as the football players walked back to their folding chairs.

Mr. Hankins asked the homecoming court and their escorts to come forward. Six couples walked to the temporary stage. A huge football made from chicken wire and orange napkins provided the backdrop for the homecoming court. I hoped the chickens in Lake View didn't get loose this weekend because Strong's Lawn and Garden had a sign in their window informing the general public that they were sold plum out of chicken wire and orange spray paint. But, more could be expected by Wednesday.

The homecoming maids were stunning in their black velvet skirts and jackets. Mrs. Frazier had outdone herself again this year. Their blouses were sewn from the finest orange satin that Murphy's offered. The queen's blouse was silver—a tradition from years past—to match her tiara.

As I watched them wave to the crowd, I thought of the thrill that must go with the honor. How cool it would be to hear your name called over the loud speaker. *Let's give a round of applause for Miss Carol Ann Lawson, Lake View's Homecoming Queen.*

"Carol Ann?" BJ elbowed me back to reality. "Look. It's your aunt."

A sudden calm came over the crowd. Mr. Hankins said a few words about her life out in California. Aunt Vestal nodded with the grace of a Miss Texas. I beamed with pride.

"She looks just like a movie star," Roxy said.

We watched as Aunt Vestal exited the stage.

Mr. Caster took the microphone and announced the winners of the parade. "Third place goes to the 4–H Club." Yeehaws erupted.

"Second place goes to the Fellowship of Christian Athletes." Football players grunted.

"And first place goes to…" he glared at the drummer who clearly missed his cue, "the French Club!" A few cheers rippled through the crowd. The three of us cheered and jumped up and down. The crowd was obviously tired and ready to go home.

Madame Philbert ran toward Mr. Caster and took the trophy. She practically pushed him down trying to get to the microphone. "I'd like to thank Madame Dodge for her continued support of the French Club. Also, Mr. and Mrs. Ashford for letting us build our float in their barn and to Strong's Lawn and Garden for donating a portion of the chicken wire and spray paint. Thank you one and all. Merci beaucoup. Merci!"

Mr. Caster regained control of the microphone one last time. Tapping the end of the microphone as if she had broken it, he concluded the assembly with the singing of the school alma mater. "Please rise and remove your hats." The band played the familiar tune as everyone, young and old, sang the Lake View school song:

"Hail to thee, O Lake View High.
We stand proud of you today.
As comrades come and comrades go
Our love for you remains.
The memories that wrap our hearts
In colors orange and white,
We vow to love forevermore
O Lake View, our delight."

"That's the dumbest song I've ever heard," Roxy said.

"I love that song," I answered. "What's dumb about it?"

She made a face. "...as comrades come and comrades go? What is this, Mother Russia?" We continued walking toward Betty's Bloomers. I hadn't given much thought to the school song. I just sang it.

"Are we sitting together tonight?" BJ asked.

"I think so," I answered. "We can't sit in the student section though. Momma and Daddy won't let me. Too many high school boys."

"What? That's the idea. Sitting with the high school boys," Roxy said.

BJ and I looked at each other. "Roxy," BJ said, "we're not even in junior high yet. What makes you think we can hang out with high school kids? My mother would kill me if she caught me near that group of boys. The only reason I got to help on the float was because she was the chaperone."

"Same here," I said.

We got in the funnel cake line. I dug out the quarter Momma had given me for the day's festivities. When it was our turn to order, my mouth was watering something fierce.

"Hello, ladies. What will it be?" Mr. Haney's VFW hat was coated in a thin film of powdered sugar.

"One funnel cake, please." I answered.

"Cotton candy for me, please." BJ answered.

Roxy said nothing.

"One funnel cake coming up." Mr. Haney drained the deep-fried dessert on a paper sack and dusted it with powdered sugar. "That will be 25 cents, Miss Carol Ann."

"Thanks, Mr. Haney."

"And one cotton candy for Miss Belinda Jean." We stood on our tiptoes watching as the pink sugar spun around the paper cone until it was plumped up with sugary goodness. "That will be 10 cents."

"Don't you want something, Roxy?" I asked.

"No. Mother says sugar is bad for you." And then she unleashed what was undoubtedly a string of bad words in French.

Betty's Bloomers came into view. "Well, I guess I'll see y'all tonight. I have to work the front desk this afternoon." I licked my fingers trying to get the last bit of sweetness. "Lots of corsages to be picked up, you know."

"Okay, bye." BJ said as she pinched another strand of cotton candy and stuck it in her mouth.

"See you tonight," Roxy said.

"When you're down and out, when you're on the street, when evening falls so hard, I will comfort you."
Simon and Garfunkel

"Get in here, Carol Ann." Aunt Betty hollered as I walked in the side door. "Lordy, Lordy there's still a heap of work to do. I'm so busy I couldn't enjoy watching Vestal ride in the parade."

Aunt Betty adjusted her brassiere strap. "How did you girls like that double mum on Vestal? She did our family proud. Yes sir, she did our family proud," she said.

When her boobies were secured, she remembered the task at hand and got stirred up all over again. I felt sorry for the rose she was clutching in her hand. She'd stripped its thorns about three times.

"But first, I need you to take that crate of empty Coke bottles over to the Piggly Wiggly for a deposit and some new Cokes. And don't start telling me you can't carry it because it's too heavy. Lord knows I already know it. Luther's going to help you. LUTHER! Get out here, son."

Luther emerged from the cooler.

"You and Carol Ann get this crate of empties over to the Piggly Wiggly. Lord knows I can't work in a stressful environment without a Coca-Cola." She wiped her upper lip with a hankie then fanned her bosom.

I protested. "Why can't Nita Sue go with Luther? I went last time. Besides, she's bigger and stronger than me."

"Don't start up with me today. I got enough to think about without having to listen to you and your sister squabble over whose turn it is to go to the store."

I looked at Nita Sue. She smiled her no–good smile.

"Yes, ma'am," I said. "Come on Luther. Let's get this over with."

I enjoyed a tall bottle of the Real Thing as much as the next person but I wanted to get out of there as soon as possible so I could begin transforming my hair for tonight's game. Now that our new bathroom was near completion, I had more time to concentrate in front of the mirror.

"Sorry about that," Luther said.

"About what?" I asked.

"Having to walk with me." Luther's shoulders slumped as his left arm held up his end of the crate.

"I wasn't upset about walking with you. I was mad because it was Nita Sue's turn." My end of the crate hung lower than his.

"You're a nice girl, Carol Ann, much nicer than your sister." He kicked a rock over the curb and down the parade route.

"Oh. Uh, thanks. I think."

"Nita Sue's so stuck-up she won't even talk to me at school."

"I'm sorry, Luther. She does that sometimes, but I wouldn't take it personally."

I readjusted my grip. The 4H Club members were removing trash from the parade route. Evidently, the good people of Lake View were quite messy. I took note of that fact and filed it away for next year's Litter Bug contest. "Can I ask you something?"

"Sure."

"Why do you work at Aunt Betty's? I mean, wouldn't you rather be playing football or bagging groceries after school or something?" We stopped at the corner and waited for a car to pass.

"I don't have a choice. Since my daddy's accident we need the money and your Aunt Betty gave me a job. All the other jobs were taken."

"What happened to your daddy?" I asked.

"He got drunk and had a wreck. Broke his arm and messed up his back pretty bad. He has to stay in bed for a couple more months before he can go back to work. That's if he can stay sober long enough."

"Luther, I'm really sorry. I didn't know."

"That's all right. Most people think he ran off again. I don't tell them any different."

When we reached the automatic door of Piggly Wiggly, Luther said, "I'll do this. You can wait outside if you want. Want a Moon Pie or Snowball?" His discolored teeth screamed for a good brushing.

"No thanks. I'm fine." I sat down next to the ice machine pondering what Luther had just confided in me. All this time I thought he was just a pimple–faced kid working at my aunt's flower shop. I couldn't imagine my daddy getting drunk all the time and my family having to depend on me or Nita Sue for money. We'd starve to death.

I decided right then and there to put Luther's name on my prayer list and pray for him every night. My list continued to grow.

"You ready?" he asked.

"Yeah, I guess so." I grabbed the crate and moaned as I hiked it waist high. "A lot heavier when it's full, huh?"

"Yeah," he answered.

"Luther? You going to the homecoming dance?"

"Nah."

"You're going to the game, though, aren't you?"

"Yeah, with Miss Betty. We're taking the flowers to the game for halftime."

"Think we'll win?"

"I hope so. Miss Betty's hard to be around when we lose."

***

Texas Fight played over and over and over with all the foot traffic. When Aunt Betty went to the storeroom, Nita Sue and I unplugged the door chimes. A person could only take so much.

"Nita Sue?" I whispered. "Did you know about Luther's dad?"

"What about him?" She continued tying ribbon around the corsage boxes.

"He got drunk and had a car wreck. That's why Luther works here."

"Get real, little sister. Luther works here because he's a loser." Miniature cowbells clanged each time she moved a corsage box.

"No, seriously. He told me when we walked to the store. He said his dad got drunk and had a wreck and now he has to work here to help pay the bills." She stopped tying and thought about what I said.

"Really? He told you that and you believed him?"

"Well, yeah, I believed him. I mean, who would lie about something like that? And he also called you stuck–up and said that you won't speak to him at school. Is that true? Are you that mean to people?"

Nita Sue's eyes narrowed and her left eyebrow hiked up. "First of all, it's none of your business what I do at school. Didn't you learn anything about gossiping? And second—I can't be seen talking to Luther or any other loser who happens to have a locker close to mine. Those are junior high rules, not mine. You just worry about Bobby Sherman and David Cassidy and leave the junior high stuff to me."

"You're mean, Nita Sue."

"I'm not mean, just popular." Our voices grew louder.

"You're mean."

"Am not."

"Are too."

"Am not."

"Are too."

Aunt Betty stormed through the curtain. "What in the Sam Hill is going on out here? You two quit arguing and start working. I'm not paying you to stand around here and bicker. Lord, I'll be glad when this day is over. I bet my blood pressure is sky high."

"May I help you?" I asked the woman who had snuck in the front door unannounced by the Texas fight song. I resumed my position as salesperson (I, too, was substituting "person" whenever I could) and took my rightful place behind the cash register.

"Yes, I'm here to pick up my son's homecoming corsage."

"Your name?"

"English. Beth English."

"Yes, ma'am. I'll be right back."

I bypassed Aunt Betty and her high blood pressure and grabbed the box from the cooler. *They must be rich. His date's corsage has enough cowbells for Borden's herd.*

I rang up the sale and waited for the next customer. Nita Sue was nowhere to be found. Aunt Betty was in the back jawing at poor Luther about something. I was so ready to get out of there.

Five o'clock finally came. I gladly locked the front door, plugged in the fight song and flipped the OPEN sign to PLEASE CALL AGAIN. I had to get home and work on my hair.

"I locked everything up, Aunt Betty. You want me to put the cash in the box?"

Aunt Betty kept the cash bag in a purple sanitary napkin box. She had a theory about burglars being too embarrassed to search a lady's sanitary napkin supply. I was glad Roxy had enlightened me on what they were. All that time I thought they were something only florists used.

"Shoot–a–monkey! Is it 5:00? Lordy, this day's never going to end. No, bring me the money, Carol Ann, I'm fixing to take it over to Ed's store and lock it in the safe. I don't have time to make a deposit today, and I don't want this much cash laying around."

"Can I go on home, then?" I looked around for my sister. "Where's Nita Sue?"

"She left half an hour ago." Aunt Betty bent over so Luther wouldn't hear her. "She's having her monthly visitor," she whispered. "Her cramps were so bad she had to go home and get under the heating pad."

Heating pad my foot.

"So, can I go home, too?"

"Yes, yes. Go on home. Luther and me will get thangs packed up for the ballgame."

Once again, I, the dependable Lawson girl, clocked out, grabbed a cold bottle of the Real Thing and ran out the back door.

"I hear her voice in the morning hour she calls me. Radio reminds me of my home far away. And drivin' down the road I get a feelin' that I should have been home yesterday. Yesterday."

John Denver

Things were winding down around the square as the 4–H Club cleaned the streets. The good people of Lake View were at home gathering up seat cushions, binoculars and megaphones. There wouldn't be a single car left on the square by 7:00. There were a few parked in front of Miss Mattie's House of Hair, but only because the richer families in town could afford Miss Mattie's full beauty treatment. During homecoming and prom season, wealthy girls were treated to a complete set and style, a manicure and facial.

GO LIONS, BEAT LOBOS signs hung in every store window on the square. The Lion's Laundromat spelled L–I–O–N–S with painted soap bubbles. Only the Piggly Wiggly would be open for business tonight and the only people shopping tonight were too old or too lazy to go to football games.

Daddy's store was closed, but Uncle Ed's convertible was parked out in front so I peeked inside the window. My hair caught on a splintered piece of window frame as I watched Uncle Ed simultaneously sweep the floor and chew on the end of a cigar. Merle Haggard blared through the portable radio. I got down on all fours and crawled beneath the windows praying he wouldn't see me.

I thought about Luther as I walked home that eventful Friday. It was true what Momma said about never knowing what went on in other people's homes. I'd always assumed that every other family around here was just like ours but I had been as wrong as rain.

In my short life, I'd never seen a six pack of beer or a bottle of wine until I went to Roxanne Wojowitz's house. I'd seen empty Schlitz and Pabst Blue Ribbon cans on the side of the road, but I'd never seen anyone actually drink alcohol until Roxy and Aunt

Vestal came to town. Roxy's home life was as different from mine as nighttime was from day. Aunt Vestal's daily life went without saying.

How different would my life be if I had to work at Betty's Bloomers to help pay the family's bills? To miss out on all the after school stuff? To not have a choice in the matter?

I dwelled on how lucky I was to have parents who lived what they preached. My daddy would die before he'd drink alcohol. And, in spite of what Nita Sue said, that was a good thing. I felt sorry for Luther and his family, and I vowed to never be mean to him again.

So much had happened since the two Californians had landed in Lake View. I got saved, I'd been baptized and I learned secrets about my family that, quite honestly, I wished I didn't know. I'd discovered that it was a whole lot better not knowing so many grown–up things. It made me sad to think about Aunt Vestal's life before Uncle Claude and all the pain she had caused Pops and Grandma. I had learned a lot about Uncle Ed, too, and it broke my heart to think that I might not see him when I got to heaven.

I thought Momma's talk about the birds and the bees would be the greatest revelation of my life, but I was wrong. As it turned out, family secrets would be the greatest revelation to this Texas girl and those secrets were something I could live without.

All in all, I was lucky and I knew it. I thanked God, once again, for all His blessings and vowed to always ask for help when I was unsure of things. I didn't understand His ways, but Momma had explained to me that she didn't either—none of us could.

That Sunday night in the porch swing, I had decided, right then and there, to be nice to everyone I met because you never knew what other people were going through. Especially behind closed doors. We all smiled and answered "fine" when asked how we were, but the truth was that we all hid behind masks of politeness and good manners. I wondered how different things might be if we shared our problems with one another. I mean, wasn't that what *bearing one another's burdens* meant?

Perhaps we all looked the same on Sunday mornings with our Sunday clothes and Sunday smiles, but the truth was that each and every person had their own set of problems, and God was the only one who knew what they were. And God was the only one with the answers.

As I continued walking toward home, I thought of Aunt Vestal and how excited she must be about tonight. I couldn't wait to tell her how beautiful she looked during the parade and how my friends thought that I looked like her. I couldn't wait to pop in her tiny trailer and see what outfit she was wearing to the game for the halftime show.

The air smelled differently than it had this morning. Someone was burning leaves and the sky had darkened. I closed my eyes and thought of hayrides, school carnivals and Halloween. Homecoming weekend marked the beginning of autumn in Lake View and autumn was my favorite time of the year. Momma said it was because of Halloween candy, but I knew it was because the summer heat fizzled and the humidity dropped to a hair–friendly level.

A car passed by, and I heard Neil Diamond singing about Cherry. I joined in and hummed Mr. Diamond's song the rest of the way home. I was in the middle of the second verse when I reached our house. I couldn't believe my eyes.

Aunt Vestal's trailer was gone.

No lawn chairs.

No Chinese lanterns.

Just gravel and weeds.

The sliding glass door stuck as I tried to open it.

"Where's the trailer?" I yelled. "Where's Aunt Vestal and Uncle Claude?" My voice got louder with every word.

"Slow down, Carol Ann." Momma stirred something on the stove. She left the wooden spoon in the pot and turned to me. "They're gone, honey."

"Gone where?" I screamed.

"Home, honey. They've gone back to California."

"They can't be gone. She's supposed to be on the field at halftime tonight with the other queens wearing her gaudy, double mum corsage!"

Tears spilled from my eyes and ran down my cheeks. She couldn't just leave me like that. Not today. People would see her on the field and tell me how much I looked like her. That's how I had planned it in my head.

Momma bent down and wiped my tears with her apron. I stopped crying.

"It was time, Carol Ann." She led me to the kitchen table where we had talked so many times before and pulled out a chair. "Here, honey, sit down for a minute.

"Claude and Vestal never intended to stay in Lake View. Remember? They came home for a family reunion and stayed long enough to finish a bathroom."

"But Uncle Claude hasn't finished the bathroom, Momma. There's still a lot of work to do. The…"

"It's finished. Go look for yourself."

I walked to the back of the house and, sure enough, it was finished. It was the most beautiful bathroom I'd ever seen.

"Vestal asked me to give you this." It was a sealed manila envelope with my name on it.

"What is it?" I asked.

"Open it and see for yourself." She kissed the top of my head and returned to the kitchen. I could hear her pulling dishes out of the china cabinet for supper.

I opened the envelope and read as I walked outside to the swing.

Dear Carol,

By the time you read this letter, I'll be halfway across Texas. I hope you can find it in your heart to forgive me for leaving without saying goodbye. But it was time, kiddo. I overstayed my welcome.

I made it through today without a drink, but there was no way I could walk out on that field like I did so many years ago without at least two martinis. (ha ha) Embarrassing my family is the last thing in the world I want to do. I've done that enough already.

You're a sweet girl, Carol, and you have the heart of a lion (no pun intended). I cried when I saw you get baptized. It was something I should have done when I was your age, but too much water has gone under that bridge.

Listen to what your momma tells you—she's usually right. You're lucky to have her and she's lucky to have you and your sister. Don't forget me. I'll never forget you.

You are with me always.

I love you, kiddo,
Aunt Vestal

I sat in the swing for a long time, reading her letter again and again. The smell of burning leaves had drifted to our backyard. I looked to the end of the driveway for the silver trailer that had become so familiar to me when I noticed Momma watching me through the sliding glass door.

As I returned the letter to the envelope, I felt something inside and shook out an embroidered, pink pouch. I loosened the faded ribbon and pulled out a tiny, beaded bracelet with the letters B, A, B, Y, G, I, R, L. Why would Aunt Vestal give me a plastic, BABY GIRL bracelet? As I twirled the letters between my fingers, my mind raced—searching for answers. Forgotten conversations replayed in my head and I connected the dots.

I couldn't breathe.

A swell of nausea rose from my stomach.

"Oh my…"

"Carol Ann," Momma interrupted, "I'm so sorry, honey. Come inside. We need to talk."

THE END

From the Author

Carol Ann Lawson is an imaginary character I created while grieving my mother's death in 2002. When I recounted stories from my childhood, friends encouraged me to write them down before I forgot them. How anyone could forget pinning a corsage on a corpse is beyond me, but I took their advice and this book was born.

I did not grow up in a small town. My hometown's population was 50,000 when I lived there in the 60s and the 70s. We relished homecoming parades, hayrides and football like most southerners. It was a simpler time—not necessarily better—but different than today. There wasn't the need to know and be known. We ate dinner as a family at the kitchen table whether it was fried Spam or steak. We rode our bikes until dusk (without helmets and kneepads) and read Nancy Drew books because there were only three TV channels to watch, and that was if the antenna wasn't blowing. (If you don't understand, ask your parents or grandparents)

We spent Sundays and Wednesdays at church and for that I am eternally grateful to my parents. I know most of the old hymns from memory and a whole lot of Scripture. And even if I haven't always lived like I believed it, one thing is certain: Jesus loves me and has never left me.

10032450R00141

Made in the USA
San Bernardino, CA
03 April 2014